THE BONES OF THE DEAD

DCI Will Blake Thriller Book 3

J. E. Mayhew

Obolus Books

ISBN-13:978-1-9998407-6-1

Cover design by: Meg Cowley

For Linda, my partner in crime.

Although the story is set on the Wirral, the names of some establishments and roads have been fictionalised to protect the unloved and godless... but you can have fun guessing...

JON MAYHEW

Drive your cart and your plow over the bones of the dead.

WILLIAM BLAKE - PROVERBS OF HELL

CHAPTER 1

Trevor Long had known for some time that his life would come to an end in this way sooner or later. He had been surprisingly calm about it at first but now his heart thumped pulsing the blood around his head and body. The cemetery lay shrouded in darkness, but he could see the outline of gravestones and statues where the streetlights penetrated the trees and bushes dotted around the burial ground. The light bounced off the stone, slick with rain, giving the place an eerie, haunted feeling.

Even the constant hiss of the rain added to his sense of isolation. Nobody would be out here tonight unless they truly needed to be. It was September, the end of summer. People would be sitting in their warm, mundane homes now, watching crap on TV. He had achieved so much more than they ever would; he'd seen things and been to places they probably couldn't even imagine. And yet it had come to this.

He saw the axe, glinting and held his breath as it fell.

The blood stain spread across the front of his green jacket, and Trevor stared in horror. So much blood! He hadn't thought it would be so

1

bad. He gave a short laugh of disbelief. It was suddenly so cold. The air felt frigid and the trees and gravestones around him looked icy blue.

The others just stood there, grinning while his life blood seeped into his coat and puddled across the gravestone.

This wasn't funny anymore. He wanted to get away, to run but his legs wouldn't move; they were stone, buried deep into the burial ground. The earth sucked at his ankles, pulling him down and down to the bones of the dead and black oblivion.

CHAPTER 2

If there was a creepier setting for a murder than Flaybrick Hill cemetery, then DCI Will Blake didn't want to know. It was one of the old Victorian graveyards built when the economy was booming and the town of Birkenhead expanding, rapidly filling its old churchyards with the dead. It reminded Blake of a miniature Highgate; family mausoleums crouched beside marble angels while row upon row of stern headstones bore witness to the passing of generations of well-to-do families. At one end was an imposing gateway and at the other the truncated, gothic spire of the ruined chapel loomed over the graves.

Malachy O'Hare, CSI Manager stood in his brilliant white coveralls, looking for all the world like some kind of celestial spirit. Until you got close to him; then you realised he was just a grumpy Irishman. The whole cemetery had been cordoned off and an inner cordon extended around the white tent that had been set up under the shade of a huge yew tree.

Blake suited up and signed in. "What do you want me to see?" he said to Malachy, who stood waiting patiently.

The smell hit him before his eyes adjusted to the dim light: blood, metallic and earthy. The gloom in the tent made the scene even more strange. A light green coat hung on a tilted gravestone tomb, and it was drenched in blood. More blood had pooled at the base of the gravestone, staining the dirty white gravel. It was everywhere. Blake wondered if he'd ever seen so much blood. An axe handle poked up; the blade half buried in the ruddy stones. Next to it, a wallet lay on the ground and a single black boot.

"That's a lot of blood, Malachy," Blake said. "How much?"

Malachy shrugged and Blake instantly regretted asking the question. He hated people shrugging; it seemed like an admission of defeat. "Dunno," the Irishman said. "With the rain we had last night, some might have been washed away. A good job we're in the shade of this tree. Whoever it was lost a whole lot of blood, I'd say. It's very strange."

"But no body to be found?"

Malachy shook his head. "We've got a few positive footprints but none for this boot."

"Who reported it?"

"Funny one really," Mallachy said, stroking his chin. "Keanu Reeves was coming back from a wild night out in Birkenhead, couldn't believe his eyes. Nearly fell off his unicycle"

4

Blake grinned. "A dog walker then? What kind of dog?"

"A blood hound," Mallachy said, waggling his eyebrows.

Blake shook his head and groaned "You suspicious?"

"Of the dog?"

"Of all this, soft lad," Blake said, pointing to the blood and the coat.

"You know how it is, Blake. We find blood and even body parts lying around on a regular basis. Especially after a big Saturday night. Drinkers bleed a lot. Monday morning? Less so. But if someone has lost this much blood, then I'd be very concerned for their welfare."

Blake looked at the wallet. "Any names?"

"There's a library card belonging to a Trevor Long. And a label in the coat too. Same name."

"Like a kid's name tag?" Blake said, squinting at the coat. "That's a big coat for a child."

"Unless it belongs to a vulnerable adult, Will."

Blake nodded. "Worth checking local hospitals or seeing if anyone has been reported missing last night. Having said that, Long could just as easily be the assailant, assuming something violent has gone on here."

Mallachy gave Blake an incredulous look. "All

this blood doesn't say, 'violent' to you?"

Blake frowned at the scene before him. "Yes but... I don't know. Does it look a bit... arranged, to you?"

Mallachy gave another infuriating shrug. "Dunno. What d'you mean?"

"I mean, if you were going to create a picture or one of those art installations entitled 'Murder Scene' it might look a bit like this. The way the axe is stuck in the centre of the grave, the boot to one side. The items look placed, rather than dropped."

"You think it's a murderous Banksy, cutting people's throats and leaving a few artefacts tastefully organised for the public? Either way, that's a mighty amount of blood."

"It could be pig's blood or red dye..."

"That's not red dye, Will. It could be animal, I'll grant you that. We'll get it tested as a matter of urgency. If it is human, then somebody was in trouble here last night."

Blake nodded. If that was the case, then time was of the essence.

*****

DI Kath Cryer watched the shadows move around inside the tent. Although several crime scene investigators were working outside and a couple of uniformed officers stood by the outer cordon, Kath suddenly felt alone. She pulled at her wrist splint. A cold breeze blew across the cemetery, making her shiver. After hospitals, graveyards were her least favourite place. She knew some people found Flaybrick Hill fascinating, with its history and atmosphere but she never liked the idea of all those dead people just a few feet beneath the surface. She'd go for cremation when the time came. Right now, she just felt like going back to bed. Her legs ached and she was dying for the loo.

A movement in the corner of her vision made her turn. Not far away, a shape stooped over a distinctive gravestone shaped like an anchor. Kath frowned. Whoever it was didn't have uniform on, so she assumed it was a member of the public. As Kath drew nearer, the figure straightened up and she saw it was an old woman.

She wore a dark blue overcoat and strands of white hair wriggled from under her headscarf. Her face was deeply lined and Kath judged her to be very old. At the sound of Kath's footsteps, she turned and glared at her.

"Excuse me madam," Kath said. "I'm afraid this is a crime scene. You shouldn't be here. If you could make your way to the main gate and give your name to the officer there."

The old woman pulled her coat tighter around her small, hunched frame and scowled at Kath.

"You're walking on the graves," the old woman hissed. "No good will come of that."

Kath looked down at her feet. The graveyard was so crowded that it was hard to tell where one grave ended and another began. "I'm sorry, madam," she said. "But I'd like you to vacate this area, please. We're investigating a possible crime and I'd hate for you to get into any trouble."

The woman's nose wrinkled. "Trouble? I'm not in any trouble," she said. "I'm tending my Eric's grave."

"Well, I'm afraid I'm going to have to ask you to leave the cemetery," Kath said, glancing over to the officers at the gate, who seemed oblivious to her.

"No," the woman snapped, in a reedy, petulant voice. "I always come here and clear the weeds every week. Who d'you think you are, trying to stop me?"

Kath pulled out her warrant card. "Detective Inspector Kath Cryer, of the Merseyside Police madam. Now can you please leave the cemetery?"

A look of pure malevolence swept across the old woman's face. "I will leave Kathy Cryer, who walks on the dead and shows no respect, but you'll be sorry you upset them and me. Bad luck dog you. Ill will hound you. Ill health bite you!" She flicked her fingers at Kath as if she was shooing away a fly.

"Please madam," Kath said. "I must insist."

"I'm going, I'm going," the old woman said, patting the gravestone. "See you next week, Eric." She shuffled away, her foot scraping on the concrete of the path. Kath stared after her and gripped her wrist splint. It was nearly a year since she'd been caught in a shotgun blast but the aching wrist reminded her of that moment every day.

"Kath," Blake called. "You okay?"

She turned round to see Will at her shoulder. "Yes, fine," she said. "It was just that old..." She turned back but the woman had gone.

"It's a mess in there, Kath," Blake said. "Blood everywhere but no body. Get Kinnear to check A&E for any emergency admissions with a significant blood loss. I think a door to door might be in order too."

"Will do," Kath said, still staring across the cemetery. "What about us?"

"Us?" Blake said with a deep sigh. "We've got an appointment with our favourite psychopath, remember?"

CHAPTER 3

The trouble with serial killers is that they just aren't reasonable people. In fact, they are a total pain in the arse, especially if they have a fixation on you. Will Blake had reflected on this several times in the past few months when sitting opposite Joshua Gambles, known as the Scissor Man, killer of at least four people. For a whole host of reasons, Blake really didn't want to be here, staring into the bright, febrile eyes of this monster.

The interview room felt too small and brought the young man too close, even though there was a heavy table between them. Kath Cryer sat next to Blake, her arms folded and an unimpressed look on her face.

"So, Mr Gambles," Blake said. "We're here again to talk about the murders committed in Hilbre Grove."

Gambles scratched his scrawny black beard. "Do you have to be so formal, Will? We're like brothers you and I. Why hide behind that official façade?"

"Can you explain exactly how you lured Katerina Dragavei into number two Hilbre Grove?"

"I could," Gambles said, leaning forward, "but let's talk about something else first, shall we?"

"You know, you really should steeple your fingers or raise one eyebrow if you're going to perfect the Hannibal Lecter look," Kath Cryer said. "Otherwise you just sound like a creepy jerk."

Gambles flashed her a venomous glare. Blake suppressed a smirk and reflected that it was a good job Gambles waived his right to have a solicitor in the interview. The young man had too much confidence in his own intelligence, but he also had another motive for dragging these sessions out. That was why Blake insisted on bringing Cryer along; her sharp tongue kept Gambles on his toes and regularly punctured the man's inflated ego.

"Let's stick with Hilbre Grove," Blake said. "Katerina Dragavei."

"Aren't you curious to know what happened to your own mother?" Gambles said. "What she said in her final moments?"

"No," Blake said flatly, keeping his face blank. he wanted to throw the table aside and bounce Gambles off every wall until the little rat squealed. "Hilbre Grove, please Mr Gambles."

"Do you know about DCI Blake's mother, DI Cryer," Gambles said, sitting back. "She had dementia and wandered out of her house while Blake was out on a case. When he came back, she was gone. never saw her again. It was as if she vanished into thin air."

"Thanks Josh, but I do know," Cryer said, she squinted across the table. "Did you have egg for breakfast this morning?"

Gambles' face fell and he put a hand up to his beard.

"We know you were in number two, Mr Gambles," Blake said. "Your DNA is all over the kitchen and living room."

"If you know so much, then why are you questioning me about it?"

"Not my choice, really. Just tying up loose ends."

"Don't you want to know where your mother is, Will?" Gambles said. "I was the last person she saw."

"That's it," Blake said, standing up. "Interview terminated. I don't know why you carry on with this charade, Gambles. You have about as much idea where my mother is as I do. And you're right, we've got more than enough evidence to convict you. I'm done here. DCI Cavanagh can pick this up. Goodbye Mr Gambles, we won't be meeting again."

Panic twitched across Gambles' face. "Wait. What? No. You can't do this. I won't speak to anyone else..."

Kath stood up, tapping the end of some documents on the desk. "You always have the right to remain silent, Joshy," she said. She pointed vaguely to her chin. "You've still got a bit of egg... just..."

"Don't make fun of me, bitch!" Gambles snarled. "How's your wrist? I hope next time, they blow your self-satisfied, piggy face off."

Kath instinctively felt the splint on her wrist. "How rude," Kath said, recovering her composure. She turned to Blake. "You ready, sir?"

Blake nodded and Kath stuffed the files into her briefcase.

"Wait!" Gambles said, as they headed for the door. "If you leave now, you'll be sorry. I warn you."

"If I spend another minute in your company, Gambles, I'll be sorrier," Blake hissed. "You're a sick bastard and I've got better things to do."

"I'll give you one more chance, Blake," Gambles hissed. "If you don't believe me, check the personal belongings they took from me when they locked me up. Check them and you'll know I'm not lying."

Blake frowned. Gambles was a headworker. He delighted in tormenting Blake. He had spent years planning a series of murders just to set up the chance for he and Blake to be a double act:

Sherlock and Moriarty or some such nonsense. This sounded like more of his mind games.

"Just let the nice prison officers take you back to your cell, Gambles," Blake muttered.

"Ha! They didn't tell you, did they?"

"Tell me what?" Blake glanced at Cryer who rolled her eyes.

Gambles grinned. "Just check the inventory of evidence. You'll see. You'll be right back to see me."

"Unlikely," Blake said but he couldn't keep the uncertainty out of his voice. They shut the door on Gambles and walked back to the reception area.

Blake stopped by a drinks machine. "Want a coffee, Kath?" He said, sliding coins into the hungry slot.

Kath pulled a face. "Nah, sir, thanks. Dunno how you can."

"It'll give me the kick I need after the Josh Gambles Show in there. What's he on about, Kath?"

"He's winding you up, sir. You've done your best. It's a wonder the Super allowed you to interview him anyway, given the circumstances. If he won't co-operate with Cavanagh, that's not your fault."

"You're right, Kath," Blake said. "I'm tired of

Gambles messing with my head. Let Cavanagh have the pleasure." But he knew his words sounded hollow. Sooner or later, he'd open up the exhibits file for the Gambles case to check out if anything really was waiting for him there.

CHAPTER 4

All the way home that night, Blake's mind was pulled in two directions; one by Gambles' suggestion that there was some compelling evidence that would show Blake that the psycho had been with his mother when she died; the other was the missing Trevor Long. Blake couldn't get away from the niggling feeling that the evidence left there had been arranged. He hoped the whole thing was some elaborate hoax, baulking at the idea that someone might create a tableau and daub it with human blood.

He pulled up outside Rock Lodge, and sighed at the crumbling building. His parents had bought it as a project to renovate but his father had died before they could complete the repairs. His mother had been trapped in it for a further two years, rapidly deteriorating. In lots of ways, Blake hated the house; it held too many bad memories. In another sense, though, it was his one last connection with his parents, apart from the rusting Opel Manta that had belonged to his father, which Blake couldn't bear to part company with.

A light gleamed in the living room and he smiled; Laura was home. At first, Blake had found it hard to adjust to having to include her in his daily routines. He'd been single and alone for so long that, at first, everything she did seemed to jar on him. But as the weeks went by, they'd found an accommodation. Laura had her own flat in Wallasey in the north of the Wirral but spent a lot of time at Blake's. She seemed to like this arrangement and Blake rarely stopped at her place. She said she liked being so close to the river.

As he entered the house, he frowned. Normally Serafina, Blake's huge Persian cat was wrapping herself around his ankles, virtually tripping him up, as he opened the front door. "Hello?"

Laura appeared in the hall. "Hi," she said. "Busy day?"

He hugged her. "Yeah. How about you?"

Laura was a self-styled animal psychologist and worked with troubled animals. It was through Serafina that she and Blake had got together. "A nervous Dalmatian over in Raby and a cat that didn't like being groomed," she said. "By the way, I haven't seen Serafina since I've been here, and her food hasn't been touched."

Blake went to the back door and opened it, tapping her food bowl with a fork. "Come on, cat," he called. He always felt ridiculous yelling into the darkness. "Food."

"I hope she's okay," Laura said, biting her lip.

"Do you think it's a problem?" Blake said. "I mean, she's gone AWOL before…"

"I'm sure she'll be fine. She's got the cat flap to get in. I bet she's lying on someone else's sofa being hand-fed mackerel fillets as we speak."

Blake laughed. "I wouldn't be surprised. That's why her weight is a constant battle. Don't know who it is, though."

"Is she spayed? If she isn't, she could be off looking for a mate. She'll roam for miles if that's the case."

"I think she's spayed," Blake said. "I could check her vet records. Mum was pretty good at that side of things."

He turned to the fridge freezer that stood in the corner of the kitchen and pulled out a microwave meal, then he paused. "Have you eaten?"

"Ages ago. I don't know how you can eat this late."

Blake shrugged. "I'm starving. Busy day." As he clattered around the kitchen, Blake ran through his day. Laura looked troubled at the mention of Gambles.

"Are you going to check what was taken from him when he was arrested?" she said.

"Probably. I'm going to have to at some point, aren't I? It'll drive me mad otherwise."

"Just don't let him toy with you. I'd check tomorrow. See what the big deal is and then assess whether it's worth seeing him again."

Blake brooded in silence until the microwave pinged. "Yeah. This other case might keep me busy, though. A load of blood but no body anywhere. We have a name but that's about it and he could be the victim, or the attacker. God knows."

"Weird."

"It is," Blake said, wincing as he spooned hot rice into his mouth, "and I can't help but feel there's something fishy about the whole thing. I suppose we'll find out more tomorrow." He stared down at his microwave curry and wondered what revelations the next day would bring.

CHAPTER 5

DC Andrew Kinnear's initial searches had proved fruitless; nobody of the name Trevor Long had been admitted to any local hospitals in the last twenty-four hours and the area seemed to be something of a blind spot for CCTV cameras. He'd gone home dispirited.

The following morning brought a gift in the form of Gary Stott. He'd appeared at the front desk of Police HQ wanting to talk to a detective. It was only that Kinnear happened to be passing on his way into work, that he overheard the young man speaking to Madge, one of the counter staff.

"It's my friend Trevor Long. I'm very worried about him," Stott had said. "He didn't come home on Sunday night, and I've checked with his mum and he's not there and... and..."

"It's all right, Madge," Kinnear said, with a smile. "I'll have a chat with...?" He looked at the young man.

"Gary," he said, reddening. "Gary Stott."

"Okay, Gary, give me a minute and I'll see if there's a room we can use to have a chat."

A little later, Gary Stott sat nursing a cup of

coffee in a meeting room. He was a short young man, in his early twenties and seemed lost in his track suit top and baggy jeans. He had short-cropped blond hair and thick, bottle-end glasses with a heavy frame. Kinnear sat next to him at the table. "So, you said you were worried about your friend. Can you give me his name, again?"

"Trevor Long," Stott said, peering at Kinnear. "We share a flat but he hasn't been home since Sunday night and he missed his shift at work..."

"And where does he work?"

"The Aldi down in town with me," Gary said. "Roscoe, the boss, was fuming about it. Trev was on a warning anyway. He wouldn't miss his shift."

"He was on a warning?" Kinnear said. "Was that for missing work?"

Gary shook his head. "No. It was for... for something else. He never misses work."

"Okay," Kinnear said. "When did you last see Trevor?"

"He was going on an investigation. Sunday night. Wanted me to go but I was too tired, and we had work the next day..."

"An investigation? What kind of investigation was Trevor going on?"

Gary Stott turned the cup around on the table-top. "He was investigating the Sons of Sol," he said. "They're like a pagan group who worship up on Biddy Hill…"

"What? Where?"

Gary Stott frowned at Kinnear. "Bidston Hill," he said. "It's that big hill right next to the graveyard. You must have noticed it."

"Right," Kinnear said, feeling a little embarrassed. He lived on the other side of Liverpool and had a rough idea of the Wirral's geography but not an in-depth knowledge. Blake was always berating him for not knowing enough about the peninsula. "Sorry. I live over in Kirby. So why was he investigating these…pagans?"

Magnified by his glasses, Stott's eyes looked huge anyway, but they widened at this. "Human sacrifice," he whispered.

Kinnear felt his heart sink. "Really?" he said, trying not to sound too unimpressed.

Stott nodded, sincerely. "We've been watching them for a while now. They're a secretive gang who live a life based around the worship of the sun goddess, Sol…"

"And what form does this worship take?"

"Lighting bonfires and getting off their heads. They fight each other and sing songs…"

"It's a bit of a leap from that to sacrificing people, Gary," Kinnear said.

Gary Stott blinked at Kinnear. "Trevor had evidence that they make a blood sacrifice to the sun goddess every solstice. There's a carved image of the sun goddess up on Bidston Hill. That's where Trevor was going. They must have taken him."

"Right," Kinnear said, scribbling notes hastily. "So can you tell me what Trevor was wearing last time you saw him?"

"Light blue jeans, a Stranger Things T-Shirt and his coat."

"What colour is his coat, Gary?"

"Oh, it's one of them old army things. Like a combat jacket but it's dead old and faded. So it's a kind of light green. And he was wearing black boots, too."

"Thanks, Gary. Can you tell me all the places you think Trevor might go?"

Stott shrugged. "Not really. Like I said, I checked with his mum and he's not at home or work. So I don't know where he might be."

"Are you and he partners?"

Stott's eyes widened even more. "What? No! God, no! We just share the rent and bills. It's cheaper that way..."

"Could Trevor have met with someone else last night?"

"No. He was on an investigation he never sees...

anyone during an investigation. he says it isn't professional."

"Do you get involved with these investigations?"

"Yeah. I carry stuff or take pictures and video. I'm like his runner." Gary seemed to grow a little as he said this.

"And what might these investigations involve, Gary?"

"All kinds of stuff. We go into haunted houses. Look for UFOs and aliens. Expose secret organisations. That sort of thing. Trevor has a YouTube channel and we post documentaries there."

Kinnear blew out a long breath. "Okay. So, what did you do the night before last when Trevor went off on his mission?"

"Me? I watched a bit of TV. Then I went to bed. When I woke up, Trevor wasn't in. I got more worried as the day went by, especially when he wasn't at work. I went to his mum's house but he hadn't been there. I even went up on the hill but couldn't see any sign of him."

"So how come you waited so long before coming here?"

"Would you have believed me? You lot would have just sent me home, wouldn't you? Told me to wait a bit. See if he turns up. Well, I have waited and he hasn't come back."

Kinnear nodded. "True, but he's an adult, Gary. He could be anywhere. I've worked on cases where the missing person turns up weeks later having decided to go on an impromptu holiday."

Stott looked down at his trainers. "No, that's not like Trevor. I'm really worried about him. These guys are really hardcore. they throw axes and all kinds of shit."

"Who?"

"The Sons of Sol!" Stott snapped. "The pagans. They've got him. I bet they're going to sacrifice him. If they haven't already!"

"Okay, Gary, keep calm," Kinnear said. "Do you have any notes or a contact address for these pagans?"

"Trevor had all that in his bag. He took that with him. I bet they've destroyed all the evidence he had."

"Right. Let's focus on finding Trevor. If you can give me all his contacts and the name and address of this Mr Roscoe, the manager, perhaps we can get a clearer picture of where Trevor might be."

Trevor's social circle did seem to be pretty limited. Gary Stott reeled off a few numbers from his phone, adding addresses when he could remember them. Then he looked up. "That's it," he said.

"Great," Kinnear said, stabbing a full stop into his pad. "We'll follow these up and then we'll be back in touch for more detail, Gary. We might need to come and have a look in Trevor's room. Will that be a problem?"

Stott shook his head. "Should be fine. Can I ask a favour?"

"Go ahead," Kinnear said.

"Will you write me a note for work. Just to say I've been here reporting Trevor's disappearance? Only I'm late for work and Roscoe will nail my balls to the staff noticeboard if I don't have a cast-iron alibi."

*****

Serafina hadn't turned up for food before Blake had gone to work and he was beginning to worry. He'd gone outside to have a look around the garden and up and down the road. It was pointless, he knew, but he felt like he was doing something. So, just as he was settling down to work, the last thing he needed was a phone call from Jeff, his little brother.

There was something about Jeff that just pressed all the wrong buttons for Blake. His little brother was a writer and lived down in London. When he'd first got the book deal, Blake's parents had been so proud of him and maybe

Blake was a little jealous. But Jeff had shown his true colours when the book deals didn't keep rolling in. He frequently asked for loans from Mum and Dad; loans that never got repaid. There was always a big deal just around the corner. Phrases like 'lots of interest' or 'agent is excited' would get bandied around followed by a request for some money just to tide him over. Blake's parents gave without questioning and it set his teeth on edge. When their mother vanished, Jeff began pressuring Blake to sell the house with unseemly haste.

"Hi Jeff," he said, trying to sound casual. "How are you?"

"Is this a good time?"

Blake looked at the work on his desk and the emails flagged red on his computer screen. "Sure," he said. "You okay?"

"Yeah, I just wondered how long before the declaration gets processed..."

Blake breathed out for a count of four as Laura, his partner, had advised him. When Blake's mother had vanished, he was left living in the house without any way of selling it. Sustaining some forlorn hope that his mother might turn up safe and well, Blake had put off having her declared dead. He'd put off living a full life, too. "It shouldn't be long now, Jeff. I saw the solicitor a while back and filled in all the forms. There were a few glitches, but I think it'll be okay."

"Great. I guess you're as keen as me to get rid of that place, eh? Bad memories and all that…"

"Maybe," Blake said. In truth, he'd become quite attached to the house. Since he'd met Laura and she'd worked wonders on Serafina's psychotic behaviour, it felt more like a home.

"Only, I'm going to need a small cash injection soon and…"

"I wouldn't go taking out a loan on the strength of your share of the house, Jeff. Once the declaration about Mum is done, the house will take a while to sell and it needs a bit of work. I don't know how much we'd get for it."

The was a moment's pause. "Right," Jeff said. he sounded dejected. "It's just that the royalties aren't going very far at the moment and my agent can't seem to land any firm offers for my latest work. Lots of positive noises but no commitment. I've managed to get a couple of teaching jobs; writing workshops that kind of thing but the pay isn't much…"

"I'm sorry to hear that, Jeff but there's not a lot I can do. We can sell at a lower price for a quick sale, but it could still take months."

There was an awkward silence, as though Jeff was considering his next words carefully. "I'm thinking of coming up to see you," he said, suddenly. "Stay a while. I haven't been up there since... well... since mum went... There'd be room at the house."

Blake ground his teeth. "I don't know, Jeff. I mean, it's really busy right now. I wouldn't be able to take time off..."

"That's okay," Jeff said, not giving Blake time to formulate any coherent defence. "It's not like I don't know the area. You wouldn't have to show me round or anything. Besides, I haven't met Laura yet."

"Okay," Blake muttered. "Just let me know when you want to come up and we'll get a room ready." It wasn't as if he could deny Jeff a room for a short stay; it was as much his house as Blake's. The only other person who had a claim on the family home was their sister Rosie and she seemed to be lost up in Scotland living in some kind of Buddhist retreat.

"Great," Jeff said. "Give me a couple of days to get things organised here and I'll be up."

Jeff hung up and Blake stared out of the window. "Bugger," he said.

CHAPTER 6

Why is it, Blake thought, that all workplaces have at least one person who is always hungry, one that's always cold and one that is always just about to leave? Sitting in the Major Incident room before the Trevor Long briefing, he looked at Kath Cryer as she fiddled with her wrist splint and pulled her cardigan around her shoulders. Andrew Kinnear was eyeing a plate of biscuits brought in from a meeting earlier as he chatted with Alex Manikas. Vikki Chinn was currently filling in for Tev the exhibits officer, who was on sick leave, as she thought it would be good experience. Still, there was nothing wrong with a bit of ambition and Vikki was a great copper.

What about Manikas? Blake thought. He didn't know much about the young DC. Alex was quiet, attentive and kept his opinions to himself unless he thought they would help the investigation. A solid officer. He had a good sense of humour and was sociable but always seemed on the periphery. Maybe Blake should do something about that. More importantly, he had to find a way to start this meeting. Often he clapped his hands and instantly felt ridiculous; like a primary school teacher bringing the class to attention. Sometimes, he said, "Okay, people," but that felt awkward. Maybe he should tap a tea mug with a spoon as though he were about to make a speech at a wedding. In the end he found himself cringing, clapping and using the 'okay people' phrase all at once. It worked, though.

"Bit of a strange one, this," Blake said. "Andrew, do you want to give us the details?"

Kinnear nodded and turned to the whiteboard which had pictures of Trevor Long taken from various videos, and photographs of the crime scene. "Trevor Long, 24, a self-styled local paranormal researcher was reported missing this morning by his flat mate, Gary Stott. Early on, the day before, officers were called to Flaybrick Hill cemetery after the discovery of a large amount of blood, a coat and a boot belonging to Trevor Long. An axe was recovered from the scene, too. Amazingly, the blood has already been identified as human by the lab but we're waiting for more detail. The amount of blood at the scene would indicate a fatality. We don't know for sure that Long is dead, but, alive or not, we can't find him."

"What was Long doing in the cemetery?" Kath Cryer said.

Kinnear waggled his eyebrows. "Investigating a mysterious group called the Sons of Sol. They present themselves as a group of young people interested in an old way of life. Trevor believed they performed human sacrifice at their gatherings. There's no evidence for that but it sounds like they might be involved in a bit of drug dealing."

"You think Long stumbled on the drug dealing and they got rid of him?" Manikas said.

"One possibility, Alex," Blake said. "Apart from Gary Stott, are there any other friends or relatives?"

"Gary gave me a couple of contacts but Trevor doesn't seem to have been a big socialiser," Kinnear said. "I've arranged for someone to go and get some DNA samples from Trevor's flat. Tasha Cook is popping over to his mother's to see what she can find out."

"Any other evidence?" Blake said. "Mobile?"

Kinnear shook his head. "No mobile but a camcorder, tripod and recording equipment was found near the scene, too. We're waiting for the labs to extract any footage."

"Okay, so while we're eagerly awaiting to hear if the blood actually belongs to Trevor Long, we can have a chat with friends and family. Get a picture of who this bloke actually is and who might have been with him on Sunday night."

*****

Trevor Long's mother lived in a terraced house

in Birkenhead, not far from the entrance to the Mersey tunnel. These were small, well-kept red brick houses, squashed together and close to the river. Most of the old windows had been replaced with white uPVC frames and satellite dishes sprang out in front of many of the properties, but they still had a certain charm. It struck Kinnear that if he could carry on walking down this road and somehow walk across the river, he might encounter an identical street on the Liverpool side.

Shana Long was a pale, skinny woman with dark hair in a ponytail and teeth yellowed from years of smoking. When she opened her front door, Kinnear almost recoiled from the smell of smoke that oozed out of the house.

"I thought I told the other policewoman that I didn't know nothing. Anyway, you don't look like a copper," she said when Kinnear showed her his warrant card. Kinnear had heard this before, wondering what it was people expected. He fretted over it secretly, too. Was it his size? He was slightly heavy, something he was conscious of. Someone had once said he looked 'a bit too smiley' to be a policeman.

"I know you've spoken to the Family Liaison Officer already, Mrs Long but it would help greatly if I could ask you some more questions. I wonder if you could tell me the last time you saw Trevor?" Kinnear said, deciding that a direct approach would probably be the best way of skirting around the whole subject of whether or not he looked the part.

Mrs Long leaned on the door frame, took a long drag on her cigarette and blew a column of smoke into the air. "I've already said, to the woman haven't I?"

"I know, Mrs Long but…"

"Bloody hell, when I get hold of him! He's such an annoying little pillock."

Kinnear blinked and gathered his wits. "It was explained that we think he might have gone missing and may be seriously hurt. We found his coat and a lot of blood in Flaybrick Hill cemetery yesterday. We'd like to locate him at least to ensure he's safe."

"Yeah. He'll be fine," Shana Long said, pulling a face. "He always is."

"He's gone missing in the past then?"

"Not really but he gets himself into bother and always pulls himself out, somehow. I told you, he's annoying. He has been since he was a baby. Dunno what it is. You must have met people like that. They just get on your tits, like."

Kinnear nodded, thinking that if Trevor was anything like his mother, it was a wonder he had reached adulthood. "So, when was the last time you saw him?"

"About a week ago. Came scrounging money off me. I told him to fuck off. He's always short of cash. He wastes it all on his stupid videos and books."

"Right. And was he particularly upset by your refusal?"

"Nah. But he must have been pretty desperate to come and ask me for money. He knew I'd send him packing with a flea in his ear."

"Did he ever mention anything about the Sons of Sol to you?" Kinnear felt himself reddening. It sounded such a ridiculous thing to ask really.

Mrs Long looked puzzled. "Never heard of them. Are they one of his pet conspiracy theories?"

Kinnear frowned. "How do you mean?"

"He's full of them," she said, rolling her eyes. "Illuminati, bloomin' aliens, witches, you name it, he's always banging on about them. I told you. A waste of money."

"Sorry, I'm confused."

"He makes these daft videos on YouTube. Like the X-Files or that Ghost Hunters programme, only shit ones. He spent a load of money he didn't have, on cameras and sound equipment."

"I see and where did he get the money, if it wasn't his?"

Shana Long shrugged. "I dunno, do I? Not from me, that's for sure. He probably borrowed it from someone. He came here last Christmas with all the gear. Wanted to make a family video. I told him to piss off."

"Right," Kinnear muttered, thinking about his own mother and feeling desperately sorry for Trevor Long. "If he did have any problems, can you think of anyone he might turn to?"

"Not me, that's for sure. He didn't have many friends. Too annoying. I used to tell him, 'don't be such an annoying little shit and you might get a few friends.' He never listened, though. There was that speccy streak of piss... Gary. He shares a flat with him."

"Yeah, it was Gary who reported him missing."

"Doesn't surprise me. Follows Trevor round like a lap dog, that one. Dunno why. Trevor treats him like crap."

"Really?"

"Yeah. Makes him carry everything and bosses him round like he's his slave. I'd give Trevor a kick up the arse if he spoke to me like that. I'm surprised Gary puts up with it, to be honest."

"I see," Kinnear said. An idea forming in his mind.

*****

People often made the mistake of underestimating DCI Matthew Cavanagh. They heard his thick scouse accent and saw his sharp suits and assumed he was a brainless fashion victim. Like the old joke told by wools over on the Wirral: What d'you call a scouser in a suit? The accused. But they soon realised that there was more to him than met the eye. If he heard any comments like that, he'd put people straight. He was proud of his city and the people in it. Well, most of them; like anywhere, it had its fair share of scallies. Looking at Joshua Gambles across the interview desk, he got the distinct feeling that the young man was underestimating him.

"I'm afraid DCI Blake is unavailable from now on, Mr Gambles, so you have the pleasure of my company," Cavanagh said.

"I warned Blake yesterday," Gambles said. "I told him he'd be sorry if he neglected me. We have so much to talk about."

"Really?" Cavanagh said, giving a sidelong glance to his DS, Bobby Dirkin. Detective Sergeant Dirkin was a man of few words, a short, crumpled man but solid as a rock. "How about you share some of that with me?"

Gambles gave a snort of disgust. "You? Who are you? You are nobody. I don't remember seeing you on television."

Cavanagh smirked. "You mean the Searchlight programme? The one Blakey was on years ago?

All he ever did was ask punters if they'd seen various criminals caught on CCTV. It wasn't like he was saving the world."

Blake had been a police presenter on Searchlight back in 2007 and had done a brief stint in front of the cameras before the programme folded. It had been Gambles' obsession as a teenager and the root of his fixation on Blake.

"I wouldn't expect someone like you to understand," Gambles hissed.

"What's that meant to mean?" Cavanagh said, lowering his voice.

"You know," Gambles sneered.

"Thing is, Gambles," Cavanagh said, "you think you're the big 'I am' calling the shots here but I get to go home tonight and watch a bit of footie on the TV. You'll be stuck in a tiny little cell with... who's his current cell buddy, Bobby?"

Bobby Dirkin opened a file and flicked through it. "A bloke called Rufus Stock. Small-time burglar."

"Ah, right."

Gambles curled his lip. "That's no hardship to me. I hate football, anyway."

"Yeah," Cavanagh said with a chuckle designed to be annoying, "but I won't have to shit in the same bucket as Rufus, will I? That's classy, Joshy boy, classy."

"Have you seen this, boss?" Bobby said, making a pantomime of showing Cavanagh his notebook. The page was blank but Cavanagh nodded sagely.

Gambles frowned at them. "What?"

"Nothing," Cavanagh said. "Just an old acquaintance of mine. He got moved out of a secure unit down south for tearing a new arsehole in some nonce who'd got lippy with him. He's a near neighbour of yours at the moment. I'm wondering if I could have a word…"

"And I'm meant to be afraid. Is that the idea?"

Cavanagh shrugged. "Not really. It's all the same to me. Personally, I don't mind going through the motions, getting everything ready for court and raking in the overtime. Your non-cooperation makes the job of prosecuting you easier, to be honest. So, go for it. In the meantime. I'll have a word with my mate anyway. Not because I think it'll put any pressure on you, but just because I don't like you, Gambles."

"Kyle Quinlan," Gambles said.

"What?"

"Kyle Quinlan," Gambles repeated. "Find him. If you can."

Cavanagh glanced at Dirkin who shrugged. "Who's he, then?"

"That's for me to know and you to find out,"

Gambles said, grinning smugly. "See what you can dig up. You won't be sorry."

CHAPTER 7

All day, Blake had resisted the urge to check through the items taken from Gambles when he was arrested. He didn't want to play the madman's game. It would just be another wind-up. Another way for Gambles to rob Blake of yet another good night's sleep. According to initial psychological reports, Gambles saw Blake as his other half; when Gambles suffered as a child, he became obsessed with Searchlight, using it as a distraction from the violence and abuse in his own home. But Gambles was a narcissist who wanted something akin to the fame Blake had once experienced. Blake had rejected him, and now Gambles was trying to make Blake pay.

"Sod it," Blake muttered and jumped up from his desk, heading across the Major Incident room to DS Vikki Chinn's desk. Vikki had been working as exhibits officer for the case and so had access to many of the items that would be used as evidence in court.

She smiled as Blake approached her desk. "Hi sir," she said. "What brings you over to this desolate part of the office?"

Blake laughed. Vikki had been keen on taking on the exhibits role. It was a painstaking job and meant she was largely deskbound, but she liked it. "I just wondered if you had any details of the items that were taken from Gambles when he was arrested."

"Sure," Viki said, peering at the screen and typing in a code. "So, there was some cash. A bus ticket and some jewellery. Two rings; one was a wedding band and the other an engagement ring."

Blake's mouth suddenly felt dry. "Do you have a picture or a description?"

"Yep," Vikki typed in another keyword and two images popped up. Vikki frowned at Blake. "Are you okay, sir?"

"Those rings," he said. "They're my mother's."

*****

Kinnear's second port of call after Mrs Long, was Trevor's place of work. Aldi supermarket in Birkenhead. He'd tried to get Nathan Roscoe, the store manager to come to the station, but the man had said he was too busy and had arranged to meet Kinnear in his office at the superstore.

He parked the car in the superstore carpark and went into the shop. The place was heaving with shoppers and Kinnear couldn't get near the man at the checkout. A queue of shoppers scowled at Kinnear as he tried to interrupt the man, who seemed intent on sending a furious flow of items flying through the scanner and down the metal slide to a customer. In the end the man pointed to a woman who was stacking shelves.

Kinnear hurried over to her and tapped her on the shoulder. She looked blankly at him. She was pretty, with dark skin and delicate features. Bubbly black hair cascaded over her shoulders.

"I'm here to see Nathan Roscoe," Kinnear said, showing his warrant card.

The girl's face crumpled, and tears coursed down her cheeks. "It's about Trevor, isn't it? Gary told us about him going missing. Is there any news?"

"No, I'm sorry," Kinnear said, glancing round at the customers who rubbernecked at the whole scene. "Look, do you want to go somewhere quieter? You look very upset."

She nodded and dabbed at her eyes with a tissue. "I just feel so awful," she said. "I'll take you to Nathan."

Snivelling into her tissue, she led Kinnear through the shop to the back offices. One door had Roscoe's name on it and she knocked on this, not waiting for a reply before opening it.

Roscoe's office was tiny and dimly-lit; the walls plastered with charts and notices. He sat at his cluttered desk, leaning back in a swivel chair. He was thickset, with a goatee beard and thinning brown hair. His suit seemed too tight for him and he'd dispensed with a tie, leaving his crumpled white shirt open at the neck. Kinnear estimated him to be in his late twenties.

"Thanks, Alyssa," Roscoe said. He frowned at the girl. "Are you okay?"

"Yeah, it's just, Trevor and all that. You know," she said and left, shutting the door behind her.

"DC Kinnear," Roscoe said, leaning forward and shaking his hand but not getting out of his chair. "So have you found Trevor? We're all very concerned about him."

"I'm afraid we haven't located him yet," Kinnear said. "When was the last time you saw Trevor Long, Mr Roscoe?"

Nathan Roscoe leaned on his desk. "Day before yesterday at work."

"Gary Stott said that you'd had to have words with Trevor."

"Did he?" Roscoe said, pulling a face. "It wasn't anything serious. Trevor's a bit of a dreamer, to be honest. If you don't keep an eye on him, he'll be telling all kinds of wild stories rather than working. He'd been late for work the day before, too. So I thought I'd nip things in the bud. He wasn't in any big trouble, though."

"And how did he react to you reprimanding him?"

Roscoe shrugged. "He seemed a bit embarrassed but agreed to buck up his ideas. I wouldn't say he was particularly upset. I think he's used to it."

"Used to being told off? Why?"

"He's just one of those people," Roscoe said throwing his hands in the air. "Annoying. I'm sure you've heard it before if you've spoken to anyone else. He always manages to say the wrong thing at the wrong time. I had to keep him on shelf-stacking and in the back room as much as possible. Every now and then, he'd rub one of the customers up the wrong way and I'd have to smooth things over. He'd be more suited to a warehouse role, to be honest."

"What about Gary Stott?"

"What about him? He's a good worker. Punctual. In fact, you'd think that Trevor could get into work on time given his flatmate doesn't find it hard."

"Was there any tension between Gary and Trevor?"

"Tension? No. Stotty worships the ground Trevor walks on. Laps up those tales about aliens and ghosts. I'm pretty sure Gary covers for Trevor. I've no proof but I suspect Gary has done Trevor's work before now." Roscoe looked at his watch. "Now, if you don't mind, I need to do the rounds and keep an eye on what's going on."

Roscoe led Kinnear out to the front of the store where Alyssa was stacking shelves once again. "You okay now Alyssa?" Roscoe said.

Alyssa gave a brittle smile and nodded. "Yeah. Thanks, Nathan."

On his way out, Kinnear looked back. Roscoe was hugging the young girl. Nothing like a bit of hands-on management, he thought, wondering if hugs in the workplace were appropriate. His phone buzzed. It was DC Alex Manikas, one of Kinnear's favourite people; he was quiet, reliable and good company.

"It's that Trevor Long case you're looking at," Manikas said. "Something's come up."

*****

Superintendent Martin ran his fingers through his hair and let out a sigh of dissatisfaction. He was a tall, wiry man with a hawkish appearance. Blake thought he might have lost weight recently, which wouldn't be surprising given the chaos of the Gambles case. Gambles had engineered a perfect media storm, killing in a particularly vicious way, and even including a minor celebrity amongst his victims. "So the rings in Gambles' pocket were your mother's," he said. "And you're certain?"

"Absolutely, sir. The wedding band could be anyone's but the other ring with the emeralds in it was a one-off. I'd recognise it anywhere."

Martin looked at Blake. "How do feel about this, Blake?"

"I'm annoyed that nobody even thought that the jewellery might be significant, given that Gambles has been taunting me with the idea that he was the last person to see my mother alive. Matty Cavanagh should have thought of that."

"Fair enough," Martin said, nodding. "But what do we do? Gambles will only talk to you about this and you've said yourself that's not a good idea. Cavanagh may have been keeping it from you so you don't get mired in the case. There are a hundred- and-one ways Gambles could have come by those rings."

"But the most obvious one is that he took them from my mother," Blake said. "Which suggests that he knows where she is now."

"He'll torture you with this, Will, you know that," Martin said. "I can't condone it on an official level but I suppose if you choose to visit Gambles in a private capacity, I can't stop you. Just be careful."

*****

Back in the Major Incident room, Blake was glad to be distracted by Kinnear's excitement. Anything that took his mind off Gambles was welcome at the moment. DC Kinnear stood with DC Alex Manikas, staring at the computer on his desk.

"So, it seems that Trevor Long isn't the most popular man in the world. A conspiracy theorist and a self-styled paranormal investigator when he's not stacking shelves at Aldi in Birkenhead. He sounds a bit socially awkward but I wouldn't wish his mother on anyone."

"So far, so not very inspiring, Andrew," Blake muttered.

"That's what I thought," Kinnear said. "I felt a bit sorry for poor Trevor to be honest. But then, this turns up." Kinnear pointed at the screen and Manikas clicked on the video that was cued-up to play.

A night vision camera had been used to take the video so everything was in black and white. A thin young man with a straggly beard and lank hair stared into the camera.

"I'm Trevor Long. For thousands of years, Bidston Hill has been a centre for the worship of pagan gods. From witches in the Middle Ages to modern pagans, they've all been drawn to this mystical place... ow!" The narrator put a hand to his head and turned round, staring into the dark. "Who threw that? Come on! I can tell you're hiding out there."

The camera panned across the shadowy trees but nothing moved. "Wankers! Piss off and annoy someone else!" Trevor Long shouted. The video cut for a second and then returned to Long repeating his lines.

"I'm Trevor Long, paranormal investigator. For millennia, Bidston Hill has been the epicentre for the worship of demons, and all kinds of deadly deities. Witches, pagans and sun worshippers have gathered here on the darkest nights to celebrate... ow! For fuck's sake!" Trevor spun round again. "Who keeps doing that? Just stop it. We're trying to make a film here!"

The video ended abruptly again.

"Is all this relevant?" Blake said, glancing at his watch. "Only..."

"Just bear with us, sir," Manikas said.

The footage resumed but this time Trevor wasn't in view. Whoever carried the camera was running. The scene jogged up and down and all that could be heard was laboured breathing. "Oh God, oh God." Listening closely, Blake could hear more than one set of footsteps. Then the camera went to the ground and Blake watched as Trevor reappeared, running into the darkness and looking back once. A black shape followed him and then there was a horrible scream. Kinnear clicked off the video.

"The camera ran on but there was nothing more of interest."

Blake frowned. "Curious."

"It is," Kinnear said. "A dog walker found the camera the same morning the bloodstained coat was discovered. She saw the CSI down at the cemetery and handed it to them. they retrieved the footage and sent it over."

"So, Long was up on Bidston Hill making a film and then vanished, leaving a heavily blood-stained coat, his wallet and one boot down below in the graveyard. Any suspects?"

Kinnear almost shrugged but stopped at the last moment. "Long didn't have a huge circle of friends, sir," he said. "Most people I met described him as an irritant but his flatmate, Gary Stott is the only one who seems concerned about him. He reported him missing."

"Is he the camera man?"

"Stott says he wasn't with Long the night this was taken, sir," Manikas said.

"Stott told me that he didn't go up to Bidston that night because he wanted to be bright-eyed and bushy-tailed for work the next day. Apparently, Long had been getting some grief about punctuality."

"We know that there were two people up there that night for sure. In the final clip, Long is alone and being chased. So, either our camera man is chasing him, or he's vanished into thin air."

"Maybe run away, sir," Kinnear said. "What do

you think?"

Blake pulled a face. "To be honest, it all looks a bit odd. The video could just be Long's attempt at remaking Blair Witch. But the amount of blood on that coat and around the crime scene was quite staggering. Keep looking, Andrew." He looked at Kinnear. "Who was the dog walker who found the camera?"

Kinnear smiled; Blake was always niggling him about detail especially when it came to dogs. "Miss Zoe Plumb aged twenty-five. She was walking her Jack Russell terrier called Nipper. It was the longer legged variety."

"Great stuff," Blake said, grinning. "Have another word with this Gary Stott. He sounds like a prime suspect if any crime has been committed."

CHAPTER 8

Blake kicked off his shoes and slumped into the armchair without even bothering to think about food. He felt drained by the day. Laura had spent the day down at the RSPCA cattery, working and secretly hoping Serafina might turn up. Blake was worried about the cat, too, but there was so much stuff squirming around his mind that he found it hard to focus on one thing at a time.

In the end the first topic he lighted on was the focus for his discontent. In reality the least troublesome aspect of the day. "Our Jeff rang. He's thinking of coming up for a visit."

"Ooh, you'll like that," Laura said, smirking. She'd quickly picked up on the fact that Will and Jeff didn't get on.

"Can't wait."

"Give over, seeing him might do you good. You build up an idea of people in your mind when you don't see them for a while. You might realise he's not as bad as you make him out to be."

"Yeah, right. Anyway, I had a more unpleasant surprise today. Looks like Gambles was in possession of my mother's rings."

Laura put a hand on Blake's arm. "Oh, Will, that's awful. Does that mean...?"

"He killed her? I don't know. But it gives credence to his claim that he saw her before she died."

"Are you going to see him?"

"I'm going to have to, Laura. But in a private capacity. Cavanagh is officially in charge of the case."

"Just be careful, Will. You're dancing to his tune. I hate to see him doing this to you."

"Mum's out there somewhere. I have to find her if I can. And if that means visiting Gambles again, so be it."

*****

Kath Cryer was exhausted. She'd spent a whole day interviewing and catching up on paperwork. All she wanted to do was sleep. Her wrist ached, despite the splint and, as she drove home, she tried to tighten the straps that held it. A light rain smeared her windscreen, neither too heavy for wipers nor light enough not to bother. A car braked suddenly in front of her and she slammed her foot on her own brakes just in time.

All day, she hadn't been able to forget the old woman at the graveyard. Her milky eyes stared at Kath, whenever she paused for thought. Kath had popped out of the office to grab some food in

53

town. As she walked down from Canning Place, she thought she had seen the old woman in the crowd. She had hurried forward, pushing people aside but the old woman had vanished. Or never been there in the first place.

Her house was dark as she let herself in. She frowned and then remembered that Theo had his fitness class that night and usually went on for a pint with his mates. Sending a prayer of thanks heavenward, Kath dropped her bag on the floor. With any luck, she could get her pyjamas on and be asleep before Theo got in. She was so tired, she doubted he'd wake her. Stanley, their pug waddled up to her, wagging his tail. She picked him up and nuzzled the top of his head. "How you been Stan?" She muttered.

Stanley gave a crackling growl and Kath froze. He was looking over her shoulder. Placing him down, she turned and stared at the front door. it was hard to tell because the hall light was on and the glass in the door frosted but Kath could have sworn something moved outside. She opened the door but all she saw was her drive and the street beyond. A gentle drizzle still fell but so fine that you could only see it in the streetlights. She shook her head.

"I need sleep, Stanley," she said, closing the door. She went into the kitchen and stared at her blurred reflection in the dark, double glazed window. Stanley growled again and she glanced down. The dog stared up at the window.

Looking back, Kath gave a stifled scream and then a sigh of relief. The weary face staring back at her through the window turned out to be her own reflection. With trembling hands, she filled a glass of water and gulped it down. Was she losing her mind? Kath always prided herself on being a no-nonsense copper, but she could feel her scalp prickle. She felt her brow. Was there a fever? maybe she wasn't well. She was exhausted that was certain.

Dragging herself upstairs, she shut her bedroom door, threw off her clothes and slumped onto the bed. Almost instantly, she fell into a deep, dreamless sleep.

*****

If he was being completely honest with himself, Andrew Kinnear was actually enjoying the Trevor Long case because it was so interesting. Some part of him loved the sense of mystery that surrounded Long's disappearance. It was so weird; there was all that blood for a start. The camera that had been left behind on Bidston Hill wasn't cheap either. Manikas reckoned it would have cost over a thousand pounds. Long wouldn't just abandon that unless he was scared of something. It was still possible that Trevor Long would turn up after some embarrassing, drink-fuelled escapade. But a part of Kinnear hoped he'd been abducted by aliens or held captive by witches. He hoped Long was alive, of course but, on some childish level, he hoped for something a bit unusual, too.

Chris, Kinnear's husband, was marking books at the kitchen table when he got home. "There's a nut roast in the oven," he said. "Shouldn't be too dried out. I hope you haven't been eating biscuits all day, Andrew Kinnear."

Kinnear widened his eyes and tried to look innocent. "Me? Biscuits?"

"I'll take that as a 'yes,' then," Chris said, grinning. He was a curiously bony-looking man with a mop of blond hair.

"I'm still hungry," Kinnear said, opening the oven and making a pantomime of savouring the aroma of the food.

"God, you look like one of the Bisto kids on crack, stop it," Chris said.

Kinnear settled down with his food and flipped open the laptop, searching for Trevor Long on YouTube. It didn't take long. Many of the videos were talks to camera much like the aborted clip Kinnear had seen from the camcorder. They were amateurish efforts, full of mistakes and false starts. Long's delivery wasn't what you'd call slick or professional. In many of them, the public were all too eager to get involved but not in a helpful way.

"Here, outside Leasowe Castle Hotel," Trevor Long began, "there are tales of ghosts and..."

A small child on a tricycle shot past behind them, two fingers raised defiantly to the camera but Long hadn't noticed.

Even Chris stopped his marking and ended up sitting next to Kinnear chuckling. "Is this a parody?" Chris said, wiping his eyes.

By the end of the evening, they were propping each other up, weeping with laughter as Long stumbled through one awful video after another.

There was a link to another video not on Long's channel that just said, 'Perv Medium gets Broken Nose.'

*****

Trevor Long stood in the spotlight wearing a white suit a size too big. "It's like his mum bought it for him to grow into," Chris commented. Long held a microphone and had his eyes shut tight. In the darkened room, Kinnear could see the heads of the audience and a few pale faces behind Long. It was clearly the back room of a pub. Kinnear and Chris had been to one of these mediums for 'a bit of a laugh,' as Chris had put it. He knew that Chris didn't really believe in all that nonsense, but they had gone for fun. The medium was usually a little bit charismatic and had a good line in patter; being able to manipulate crowds as well as read them was key. Kinnear mused that what a good medium needed above all else were people skills. Long lacked charisma and the self-awareness to realise it.

"Total silence, please, ladies and gentlemen," he said. "Total silence while I make myself receptive to the words of the spirit world. The kindly messages of hope and love that we'll be receiving any minute now." He lowered his head and the audience fell silent. And waited.

"Timing's everything," Chris muttered watching as some members of the audience began to get restless. Someone coughed. Someone giggled.

Trevor Long lifted his head up. "I'm getting a name..."

"Yer certainly are," someone muttered off-screen.

"A David. Does anyone know a David?" Fifteen hands went up. "The surname begins with a V..." Fifteen hands went down.

"Bloody pound shop Derek Acorah," someone muttered on screen.

"Ah no... the v was the one in the middle of the name... my mistake... forgive me spirits... How about a K?"

One hand went up and Trevor sidled over to

the woman. The camera focused on her. She was young, maybe early twenties, with a strappy top on and long brown hair. Long slid his arm around her shoulder. "What's your name, love?"

"Uh oh," Kinnear said. "Look at the face on her boyfriend!"

"Doesn't look happy," Chris agreed.

Next to the woman was a brick wall of a young man, his hair cropped and muscles bursting out of his vest. Long seemed oblivious to the man's icy stare.

"Elise," the young woman said.

"Alice," Long said.

"No, Elise..."

"What does Dave mean to you?"

"I dunno anyone called Dave," she said. "You said Kay. My Aunty Kay passed over last month."

"I see," Long said, his arm draped in an unfortunate manner over the woman's shoulder so that his fingertips grazed her left breast. He hadn't noticed that she was leaning away from him. "Yes," he declared, sadly. "It was cancer, wasn't it?"

"No. She electrocuted herself with a toaster," Elise said. "Have you been eating onion?"

"But that's the message, Alice," Long said, leaning closer. "She doesn't want you to be sad because she didn't know it at the time, but she did have cancer. So she would have died anyway."

Elise stared in horror at him. "That's horrible," she said and looked down at his hand. "And stop feeling my boobs, you perv."

At this point the boyfriend leapt up. "You groping her?"

"No, I was merely... building up a rapport..." That was about as far as Trevor Long got before the boyfriend swung a punch. It sent Long staggering backwards into a nest of tables, blood fountaining from his nose. Glasses smashed and people cried out.

Long staggered to his feet but people were booing now and telling him to get lost. He stood, stunned for a moment and then a woman who wasn't Elise marched across the tiny space in the middle of the room and slapped him hard across the cheek.

Kinnear froze the video. "Now *who* is that?"

CHAPTER 9

All Blake wanted to do was punch the smug grin off Gambles' face. He sat in the visiting room and as Blake approached him, he noticed that Gambles had his fingers steepled and one eyebrow raised.

"Glad to see you're taking Kath Cryer's advice," Blake muttered as he scraped a chair from under the table and sat down.

"Isn't she with you?"

"This is a private visit. Otherwise I'd drag you over to the custody suite for interview."

Gambles gave that smug grin again. "I take it you've found out what I was carrying when you arrested me."

"I didn't arrest you, Gambles. A PCSO did. Never forget that."

"I won't, don't worry about that," Gambles hissed. True to his narcissistic personality, he had built into his plan the objective of being arrested by Blake. The idea was that Blake's TV credentials would serve to make Gambles notorious and talked about. Blake had short-circuited the whole thing by walking away and getting a humble PCSO to make a citizen's arrest.

"So," Blake said. "The rings…"

"Before you say anything more, Will, I just want you to know that I didn't kill your mother. She was dying. It was so cold that night and she only wore a dressing gown and a nightdress. So, I didn't hurt her in any way."

"And somehow, I'm meant to be grateful for that?"

"She was holding you back, Will. Look how much happier you are now, with your girlfriend and your cat. One big happy family."

Blake took a breath. "So, what did you do? Follow her? take her somewhere?"

Gambles shrugged. "I just followed her. I stayed with her. You should be glad she didn't die alone…"

"Go on."

"We walked and walked. It seemed like forever. It seemed like she just wanted to sleep. I ended up half carrying her, to be honest, but there was no weight. She was skin and bone."

"But you were on the old promenade. Where did you go?"

Gambles tapped the side of his nose. "I'll keep it vague if it's all the same to you. In the end I called a friend and we took her home."

"Who? Your favourite foster parent, Albert

Green?" Blake spat.

"I couldn't say," Gambles said. "She didn't last long, though. I knew you wouldn't believe me, so I took the rings as proof. I would have shown you them when I was arrested but you stormed off."

"So where is she? Where did you bury her body?"

Gambles massaged the bridge of his nose with his thumb and finger. "The thing about private visits is I can terminate them if I want to. You could have engaged with me when I wanted you to. Now it's all going to go wrong. You'll lose your girlfriend, your dear brother, even that mangy cat."

"What are you talking about?"

He signalled to the prison guard who came over to escort him out. "Believe me, Will Blake, pretty soon, where your mother's body lies will be the least of your problems."

*****

The atmosphere in Trevor Long's flat was a heady mix of Lynx body spray, Pot Noodle and a strange sweetness that Kinnear couldn't quite pinpoint. He didn't really want to, either. The main living room was a shrine to the paranormal. Posters of aliens, UFOs, ghosts and witches plastered the walls to such an extent that little of the anaglypta wallpaper could be seen. Books on the topic stuffed several bookshelves. Their tops were cluttered with models of spaceships, figurines of monsters from various TV series, animal skulls, half-burnt candles, packs of tarot cards and an array of cameras and computer cables. A thick layer of dust coated everything. In the corner of the living room sat an enormous television, with a DVD player and an old VHS. This was surrounded by a stockade of DVDs and videos.

With the curtains half-drawn the way they were, the whole room was dingy and depressing. Gary Stott sat on an old leather armchair that looked as though it had been run over by a steamroller. It suited the dilapidation of the room, though and the sofa next to it looked little better.

DC Kinnear looked at his notebook. "Is Trevor a drinker, Gary?"

Stott shook his head. "No way," he said. "He never touched the stuff. He always said it was a sign of weakness, drinking alcohol."

"Drugs? Any substance abuse?"

Stott shook his head. "No. Nothing like that. Why are you asking me this? Why aren't you going after the Sons of Sol?"

"Sorry, Gary but we need to establish exactly what happened and that always starts close to home. Do you mind if DC Manikas has a look in Trevor's bedroom?"

Gary Stott shrugged. "I suppose not."

Manikas nodded and slipped away quietly.

"So, Gary, did Trevor take his camcorder with him when he went to Bidston Hill?"

"Yeah," Stott said, blinking through his thick glasses. "Of course he did."

"Who was going to hold it for him while he spoke?"

"What?"

"We've retrieved a camcorder from the hill with footage of Trevor on it. It's evident that somebody was holding the camera from the slight wobble every now and then. Somebody must have been with him."

Stott pushed his glasses up to the bridge of his nose. "Well it wasn't me. So I dunno who it could be."

"Trevor doesn't have many friends, Gary. You must have some idea."

Stott shrugged. "Honest, I haven't a clue. Maybe it was someone he met up there. I thought he was going up there to film the Sons of Sol doing their thing…"

"Doing their thing?"

"You know, fires and chanting. Sacrifice. He

didn't say anything about needing a camera-man."

Kinnear shook his head. "That camcorder is an expensive bit of kit to leave on the hillside, Gary."

"I know. He must have been really scared if he dumped that and ran, mustn't he?"

"How do you know he ran, Gary?"

Stott's face reddened. "Well, it's obvious, isn't it? He was being chased by the Sons of Sol. He dropped it as he ran, didn't he?"

Kinnear decided to change tack. "A few months back, Trevor was attacked in a pub. Were you there that night?"

"Nah," Stott said. "I don't really like his medium act. It's a bit shit, to be honest and I get embarrassed. I've tried to tell him to drop it but he won't listen."

"So, who did he go with?"

Gary Stott shrugged. "I dunno."

"We've found video footage of that evening, too, Gary. Have you seen it?"

Gary suppressed a smirk. "Yeah, I have. Someone took it on their phone and posted it up on YouTube. It was on social media too for a while. Trevor was fuming. He tried to get it taken down but nobody listened."

"Maybe you can help us. After he gets punched on the nose, a woman walks up to him and slaps him across the face. Who is she?"

"I dunno," Stott said, looking at the ragged carpet.

"Oh, come on, Gary," Kinnear said, lowering his voice. "I can tell you know. Who is she? She looks upset. Is she Trevor's girlfriend? Was she cross about him groping the woman in the audience?"

"He didn't grope her. It was just an accident, that's all. If that caveman boyfriend hadn't gone off the deep end, it would have been fine."

"Who's the girl who slapped Trevor, Gary?"

"She was just some woman. Trevor went out with her a couple of times and then she dumped him after he got punched. I don't know her name. Like I said, I didn't go to that show and he wouldn't take me out on his dates, would he? That'd be weird. So, I don't know anything about her."

Manikas emerged from Trevor's room holding a ring binder. A piece of paper had been glued onto the front and the words, 'Sons of Sol' had been written in orange felt tip. "Looks like he was building quite a dossier."

"I'm telling you, they know what's happened to Trevor. It's them you want to be talking to. I wouldn't be surprised if they hadn't killed him."

*****

Matty Cavanagh wasn't happy, Blake could tell. There were little red spots on the man's cheeks and he was chewing rapidly on a piece of gum like he had something against it. The conference room they sat in was empty for another ten minutes and Matty had almost dragged Blake into it, the moment Blake had set foot in Police HQ.

"I thought you'd done with Gambles," he said. "I thought you'd handed him over to me."

"I had Matty but if I'd known about the rings, I might have thought differently."

"He's going to be a pain in the arse to manage, now. Thinking he's got one over on you and how he's, like, oh so clever."

"Those rings belonged to my mother, Matty. What did you expect me to do?"

"What everyone else in the country has to do, Will, leave it to the investigating officer to deal with."

Blake heaved a sigh. "I know, I know. I'm sorry, but if you'd told me about the rings in the first place…"

"How was I to know they belonged to your mother? they could have been anyone's. Just keep out of it from now on, Will, please. Gambles has been awkward. Like I say, we don't actually need him to talk, but his cooperation will speed up the case. Plus, he's going on about some other character now."

"Really?" Blake said. He still felt angry with Cavanagh, but his professional curiosity had been piqued.

"Yeah. Does the name Kyle Quinlan mean anything to you?"

Blake shook his head. "Nope. Do you think he might be another victim?"

"I don't know. But given that it's the only thing Gambles will say when I speak to him, I'm going to have to look into it."

CHAPTER 10

Blake knew he shouldn't be out of the office, but the day had fallen apart the moment he'd visited Gambles and he knew he'd get nothing constructive done. When Kinnear called him, he decided to head over to the Wirral and have a look around. Now, standing at the top of Bidston Hill, he felt like he'd made the right decision.

It was common land, once part of a private estate. A mixture of gorse, bracken and hardy grasses survived in the shallow soil that lay on top of the sandstone that was close to the surface on many parts of the Wirral. It was also one of the highest points on the Wirral. Blake stood with Kinnear, staring out over the peninsula, and across the River Mersey to Liverpool. "Hell of a view, sir," Kinnear said. The Hill ran down to a patchwork of green fields and houses which gave way to the denser housing of Birkenhead. Beyond that was the river and the docks over in Liverpool. Looking north, the sky and the sea stretched on forever.

"You can see why there's a lighthouse up here. And an observatory," Blake agreed. "So where was the camcorder found?"

"A bit further round. There's a Viking carving

of a sun goddess apparently. It wasn't far from there."

Blake nodded. "And was there any activity reported up here the night Long went missing?"

"We did a door-to-door on the houses along the foot of the hill. There was a lot of shouting between ten and eleven, according to Mrs Pelham who lives close by. But she thought it was just some youngsters, certainly not chanting or anything like that. I think the whole Sons of Sol thing is a bit of a fantasy spun by Long and Stott, to be honest, sir."

"Maybe we should have a word, anyway," Blake said. "Have you got a contact?"

"I have, sir," Kinnear said, with an embarrassed cough. "He's called Thor. Thor Magnussen."

*****

Jeffrey Blake had already booked train tickets when he phoned his big brother. He'd had no intention of asking Will's permission to come up to the Wirral and stay at his mother's house. It wasn't Will's property and Jeffrey was entitled to stay there if he so wished. Besides, he wasn't sure that Will would be very happy if he knew the real reason he was coming up.

The landscape rattled past in a constant cycle. Fields and hedgerows flashed by, then suburbs reasserted themselves, finally giving way to a town or city. He scribbled in his notebook, making little observations about his fellow passengers or an unusual building along the way. He glanced up and caught the eye of the girl opposite him. A student, he thought, too young for the likes of him. Maybe in his heyday as an up and coming novelist, he'd have been able to dazzle her with his tales of publishers' parties and celebrity gossip but not now.

He glanced at his reflection as they entered a tunnel. He wasn't bad looking for his age. He had the height that all Blakes inherited from their father and the bone structure that in a decade's time would make him look 'distinguished' or maybe 'well-preserved.' Will had that, too. That's why they'd singled him out for that ridiculous Searchlight programme.

"What are you writing?" The girl said, startling Jeff a little. He looked at her. She had purple hair tied in a ponytail, studs along one ear. Maybe he'd underestimated himself. Or maybe he'd overestimated her youth. Looking at her more closely, he noticed that she was probably more in her late twenties despite dressing like a teenage goth.

"Just making notes," he said, smiling mysteriously. "I'm a novelist."

"Really?" The woman leaned forward. "That must be fun. What have you written?"

Jeff hesitated. This was a question he hated most of all because few people had read his later works and his first novel had gone out of print. The usual response was a blank look. "My most well-known book was called *Quixote Junction*. It was a study of selflessness and self-absorption in the twentieth century..."

"Right," she said. The blank stare didn't go unnoticed. "What else?"

"Cinnamon and Blue? It was a series of short stories about different people at a dinner party," Jeff's voice trailed off as he saw the indifference creeping over her face. "I wrote a children's novel for Bloomsbury, you know, the Harry Potter people..."

Her face brightened. "Ooh, I love Harry Potter. What was your book called?"

"Elven Strike," Jeff said. "It was a classic fantasy. You know, a bit Lord of the Rings."

"No," she said. "Never heard of it. So do you live in Liverpool?"

Jeff shook his head. "I'm going to visit a friend. And do some research for what I think might just be a bestseller." He pulled a business card from his jacket pocket and handed it to her. "Here. I'm staying on the Wirral with my brother. Give me a call if you're at a loose end. I'll wine you and dine you. My treat entirely and you can brag to all your friends that you knew me before I was famous."

*****

To be fair to Thor Magnussen, he was as impressive in stature as his name suggested. For some reason, Blake had half-expected an undernourished, pale desk jockey when they'd agreed to meet him at Winston's Bookmakers in Hoylake. But Thor filled the counter, processing betting slips and exchanging banter with the punters. His look was at odds with the light blue shirt and smart trousers he wore; he had a long beard and hair shaven at the sides of his head but combed back over the top. Muscles rippled under the sleeve tattoos on each arm. He looked decidedly out of place here.

Winston's was a small down-at-heel place, clearly feeling the competition from the big betting chains. Screens dotted the wall showing odds or footage from a horse race somewhere in the country. Between these were posters displaying the odds for football matches and special offers on other ways to lose money. Stubby pens and betting slips littered the ledge that ran around the edge of the room. A couple of high tables stood in the middle of the room. A few disappointed men ripped up their slips as a horse charged through the finish line on the screens.

"I don't like betting shops," Blake muttered.

"Oh, I don't mind a flutter, sir," Kinnear said. "Grand National, usually. A bit of fun, really."

"Yeah," Blake said. "It's okay as long as it stays a bit of fun."

"Gentlemen!" Thor said as they approached the counter. "How can I help?"

Blake showed Thor his warrant card. "We called earlier. Is there somewhere we could talk in private?"

Thor seemed unperturbed and nodded. "Julie, can you keep an eye? I won't be a minute," he said to a tight-lipped, narrow-eyed woman who stood next to him. She nodded and Thor opened the door at the side of the counter. "Step into my office, gentlemen!"

The back office was as cluttered with paperwork as the betting shop and with Thor filling it, there was little space. Blake squeezed into a small wooden chair in one corner while Kinnear remained standing. Thor settled himself into the chair behind his desk. "So what can I do for you?"

Blake gave an awkward cough. "We'd like to ask you a few questions about the Sons of Sol, if you don't mind."

Thor spread his hands out in a way that said, 'I have nothing to hide.'

"Is Thor Magnussen your real name?" Kinnear

said, suddenly. Blake ground his teeth. For some reason, Kinnear couldn't help butting in and it usually derailed the interview. He'd spoken to the young DC about it before, but Kinnear didn't seem to take it in.

Thor pulled a face. "It is now," he said. "I changed it by deed poll a couple of years ago. Fabian Thorpe didn't quite cut the mustard with the rest of the tribe. Do you know what Fabian means? Bean grower. So, not only does it make me sound like a posh twat, it actually means I'm a peasant. No, Thor suits me fine."

"So, can you tell me about the Sons of Sol?" Blake said, regaining Thor's attention. "What's it all about?"

Thor gave a shrug. "Just a bit of fun, really," he said. "We meet and have axe throwing competitions, get drunk, wrestle, sing songs around campfires. That's about it, really. It's more a way of life."

"A way of life," Blake repeated. "And what about your religious views? Do the Sons of Sol get involved in that side of things?"

Thor looked confused. "Not particularly. Sol was a Viking sun goddess. We took our name from there but…" realisation spread across the big man's face. "This is Trevor Long's doing, isn't it? He sent you."

Blake glanced at Kinnear. "What makes you say

that, Mr Magnussen?"

"That little toe-rag's been stirring things up for us for months. It's like a vendetta. He tried to join us a while back. Pestered me something rotten. In the end, we let him come along to some of our meetings. He was a complete pain."

"In what way?"

"Saying inappropriate things to some of the women in the group. He wanted to film us for his YouTube channel, too. Some of the guys weren't really happy about that."

Blake frowned. "Why not? Surely you'd like anything that would bring new members."

"Not really," Thor said. "We're not looking for members. Long was lucky to get invited. We're more interested in fellowship than anything else and some of the guys were familiar with Long's videos. Have you seen them?"

Blake shook his head.

"Yes," Kinnear said. "I can see why you'd want to distance yourself from that. So, what did you mean when you said Long had a vendetta against you?"

"He started stalking us and filming us from a distance. He had this really expensive equipment with zoom lenses. Sometimes, he'd be that far away, we wouldn't even know he was filming us. Then the next day, there'd be a video of us around a campfire and Long going on about human sacrifice and shit like that."

"I imagine that would annoy you and your friends," Blake said.

"Of course it did. We're a peaceful bunch. We just like a horn of mead and a singsong, that's all."

"When you aren't swinging axes at each other," Kinnear said. "Did anyone in the group want to do more than sing songs or drink mead and forget all about it?"

Thor's face hardened. "Some of the guys wanted to rough him up but I wouldn't allow it. It was annoying. We started getting approached by all kinds of weirdos who believed Long. It was spoiling things."

"We'll need a membership list, Mr Magnussen," Blake said. "So we can talk to your friends. Tell me, did you have a meeting a couple of nights ago, on Bidston Hill?"

"What's this all about? Has something happened to Trevor?" He said, suddenly realising the direction the questions were taking.

"Trevor Long has gone missing," Blake said. "We're concerned for his safety."

"Really? My God. Look, we had a meeting up on Bidston Hill on Sunday night. Just to have a few beers and discuss future events, really. But we got there late, around ten and it was pissing it down. We went before eleven at the latest. I never saw Trevor and neither did anyone else as far as I know."

"And you didn't see or hear anything unusual?"

Thor shook his head.

Blake frowned at Thor. "Tell me about these axes you all seem so fond of."

"It's just a bit of fun, really. We have throwing competitions..."

"Axe throwing competitions?"

"Yeah," Thor said. "I run an event business offering axe throwing evenings 'Sons of Sol Axe Throwing Experience.' We do birthdays, corporate events, festivals, that sort of thing."

"So you carry these axes around with you. In public?"

"We're as careful with them at our social gatherings as we are for public events. It's just a bit of fun, like I said."

"Are any of your axes missing?"

Thor frowned. "No. Not that I know of. Why do you ask? What's this got to do with Trevor?"

"That'll be all for now, Mr Magnussen," Blake said. "If you could give us the names and numbers of your friends. We really need to locate Trevor Long."

CHAPTER 11

To say Will Blake was surprised to see his brother Jeff sitting in the living room with a cup of tea, was an understatement. It also didn't describe his annoyance and irritation at all. At first, Blake felt like turning his wrath on Laura for letting him in, but he quickly realised that Laura could hardly have left him standing on the doorstep.

"What the bloody hell are you doing here?" Blake said, before he could stop himself.

"Charming," Jeff said, smirking at Laura. "I'm pleased to see you, too, Will."

Blake scowled. "Sorry. It's just that, when you said you were thinking of popping up, I didn't think you meant immediately. I thought you said you had to sort some stuff out first. I haven't got a room ready or anything."

"No worries," Jeff said. "I can sort myself out. I know where everything is." He looked around. "I see you haven't changed much, so I suppose the sheets and duvets will all be in the same place as they always were."

"But why so soon?"

"I don't know," Jeff said. "I was at a loose end

and talking to you just made me think there was no point in hanging around."

Blake glanced over at Laura who was clearly enjoying his discomfort. "I see," he said at last. "So, how long are you planning on staying?"

"Even better," Jeff laughed. "Here's your hat, what's your hurry?"

"No, I didn't mean it like that but..."

"I'm not sure, Will. I thought I'd do some research for my next book while I was up here. I may need your help. It's a crime thriller. A sort of real-life thing but fictionalised a little. I could do with your expert input."

"Right," Blake said, his heart sinking. He looked around and then turned to Laura. "Did Serafina turn up?"

Laura frowned. "No," she said. "She wasn't here when I arrived, and her food hasn't been touched again."

"I thought you'd got rid of that cat," Jeff said. "It was mental."

"I got a personal animal psychologist, instead," Blake said, smiling at Laura. "Look, I'm going to pop next door and ask if they've seen her. Grab something out of the fridge, Jeff. Make yourself at home." The words almost stuck in his throat but he had no real reason to resent Jeff's presence. He went out into the twilight, looking over the river to the lights of Liverpool twink-ling across the water.

The house next door was massive. Blake wasn't sure how many rooms it must have; too many for the young couple who lived in it. Rock Park had been an exclusive dwelling for the rich and well-to-do back in the 1850s. A small estate of villas stretched along the banks of the Mersey, not far from the ferry. This meant that the merchants and traders of the city could live in luxury and be separate from their place of work. Many of the houses had fallen into dereliction over the years and been demolished. The council drove a dual carriageway through the park in the 1970s, des-troying even more houses. What was left was a ribbon of mansions running along the riverbank. Blake's former lodge house was small in com-parison.

He couldn't remember the name of the couple who lived in this house. Facts and details being his bread and butter, Blake felt slightly ashamed that he'd forgotten it, but they'd not long moved in, so he had an excuse. Knocking on the door, he subconsciously reached into his pocket for his warrant card, then snatched it away as a young man opened the door.

"Hi," he said. "Will Blake. I live next door."

The young man had a serious goatee beard and horn-rimmed glasses. He looked like a 1960s poet; all he needed was a beret and a pipe. "Oh, yeah, hi. I saw you on telly a while back. That psycho in Upton."

Blake gave a brief smile, trying to hide the irritation in his voice. He hated any mention of Gambles. "I was wondering, have you seen my cat? A big Persian thing, grey-blue with orange eyes."

The young man frowned and shook his head. "Why? Has she gone missing?"

Blake resisted the urge to be sarcastic. *No, soft lad, I just popped round to ask you what you thought of her.* "Yeah. She's been missing a couple of days now and I'm getting a bit worried to be honest."

"We'll keep an eye out," he said, "but we're at work all day, so..."

Blake thanked him and walked back to the lane. He wandered around a little, hoping to catch sight of her. He tried a couple of other houses but there was no answer. Blake didn't blame them; they were secluded and anyone calling at that time of night could mean trouble.

A shape slid through the bushes ahead of him and his heart leapt but a skinny, black cat emerged, stared at him with yellow eyes then ran off. Blake wondered how he'd become so attached to Serafina; it had only been a recent thing. In the first couple of years of his mother's absence, the cat had been a painful reminder of the tragedy. Literally. The cat had physically attacked him on numerous occasions and left foul smelling deposits for him to find with monotonous regularity. Blake had borne it because he saw it as a kind of penance for letting his mother down. Then Laura came along and that all changed. Now he saw Serafina for the character she was and maybe saw what his mother had seen in her. But now she was lost, and Blake worried for her safety.

He strode a little further along Rock Park, reluctant to go back to face his little brother. He felt bad for leaving Laura back there, but she didn't have any history with him and would probably get along fine. Anyway, he could search the area before it became totally dark. It always struck him as an unusual place, with the large houses, railings and grand gateways so close to the Mersey. He could walk a few hundred yards and see what remained of the shipyards if he wanted to. Every now and then, the line of villas would be interrupted by an empty plot where a building had collapsed or been demolished. A couple were surrounded by board fences or mesh barriers, just waiting to be developed.

People were settling down for the night; lights glowed behind curtains and front gates were closed. A smart-looking man in a pinstriped suit was just pulling out of his drive in his BMW when Blake held a hand up to stop him. He lowered the window.

"It's Blake, isn't it? You live down in the Lodge, right?" The man said. His silver hair was slicked back and a thick gold ring adorned his finger.

"Yes," Blake said. "I'm looking for my cat. Persian, big fluffy thing. We haven't seen her for a couple of days..."

The man frowned. "You're the second person to ask that question. Not about your cat but about a lost cat. The woman at the house up the way called round yesterday. They've lost their tabby. It's got a weird name..."

"The cat?"

"No. The house. I can't remember it offhand begins with a 'P.' I hope you find her." He drove off and Blake watched him go.

The house was called Penumbra, which Blake thought was something to do with eclipses as far as he could remember. Like the others, it was a large building but this one wasn't as smart as some; the gate squeaked reluctantly as he pushed it open. He walked up the drive, the scrunch of the gravel muffled by the grass growing through it. The gardens surrounding the house were overgrown but in a haphazardly tended way. Blake could see where some bushes had been cut back to let others push through. Here and there ugly statues of dragons and demonic creatures poked through the undergrowth. Blake wondered what kind of person would want them as a feature in their garden.

He looked up at the building with its dusty grey windows and cracked paint. Its state of disrepair reminded him of his own except he didn't have quite so many windchimes dangling in the porch. He knocked on the door and waited.

The woman who answered couldn't have suited the house better if she tried. She was in her early fifties with dyed black hair that spilled around her shoulders. Her long, patchwork skirt seemed to accentuate her height. Bangles and bracelets rattled on her wrists.

"Hi," Blake said. "I was wondering if you could help. I'm looking for my cat, a big Persian thing..."

"I've lost my silver tabby. They've been stolen!" she said without letting Blake finish.

"What makes you say that?"

"Your cat went missing two days ago. Yes? So did mine. What are the chances of two cats going missing on the same day? And I saw a van."

"A van?"

The woman nodded, tucking a strand of hair behind her ear. "Yes. A dark blue van. It was driving slowly and it made a few passes up and down the road. Very suspicious. I have the registration number written down. Do you want to come in?"

The living room of Penumbra was much as Blake had expected it to be; old furniture, a lot of cushions, beanbags and ethnic throws scattered around. The smell of incense hung heavily in the air. Blake felt positively lightheaded and the dim light provided by the numerous candles scattered around the room added to the sensory deprivation. The woman who invited him in had draped herself across the old sofa.

"So, you said you'd taken the number of this van," Will said.

"Yes," she replied. "My name's Gwen, by the way. You live down the road, in the Lodge, don't you? You're Will Blake. I used to watch you in Searchlight."

Blake heaved a sigh at the mention of the old TV programme; people often recognised him and brought it up. So often, it was the subject of hilarity at work or it was used as a stick to beat Blake with when things weren't going so well. "A lot of people did, apparently. So, the van number. If you pass it to me, I may be able to find out who it belongs to."

"Do you think you can find them? I've heard such terrible things about what happens to cats that are taken. Do you think it could be a dog fighting gang?"

"I really don't know," Blake said. "What did

your cat look like?"

"A classic silver tabby. Striped and grey, like a miniature monochrome tiger," she said and suppressed a sob.

Blake shuffled uncomfortably. "If you could get me the van number, I can try and get to the bottom of this as quickly as possible."

"Of course," Gwen said, jumping up and wiping her eyes as she hurried out of the room.

Blake looked around at the room while he waited. Piles of books sat alongside the tired-looking sofa and a number of wine bottles and empty glasses dotted the room.

A deck of tarot cards lay on a low coffee table. Blake picked them up. They were larger than playing cards, almost as if they'd been made for children. The backs were a deep purple, dotted with gold stars. He turned the top one over. It had a queen holding a sword.

"The Queen of Swords," Gwen said, startling Blake. "That represents a widow, an abandoned woman. Someone with experience who tells you the truth. Sound familiar?"

Blake half smiled. "Sort of. If you believe in this sort of thing..."

She took the deck from him and shuffled them. "If she's upside down, she represents bitterness, resentment and not learning from past mistakes. Draw another."

He took another card from the fanned-out deck and turned it over. "Five of Swords," he said.

"Someone is going to disappoint you," Gwen said. "They're going to put themselves and their career before your needs."

Blake laughed. "That could be almost anyone I know at work."

"One more. Then you have three."

With a shrug, Blake took one more card. "Knave of Swords. He sounds like a reliable person to know..."

"Upside down too," Gwen muttered. "Someone is playing mind games with you. They're spreading gossip and malicious news. I'd beware of them."

Josh Gambles sprang into Blake's mind and for a moment, his doubt was shaken. "In my line of work, that happens all the time," he said. "Anyway, do you have the number."

Gwen looked surprised. "Goodness, yes. I'd forgotten." She put the cards down and passed Blake the slip of paper with the van's number on it. "Don't dismiss the Tarot so readily, Mr Blake. It's a guide; a focus for your thoughts. Think about it."

"Thanks," Blake said. "I'll let you know how I get on..." He stuffed the paper into his pocket and hurried from the house.

CHAPTER 12

Andrew Kinnear sat at his desk, the fluorescent lighting hurting his eyes. It was late and he should have gone home hours ago but the files and some of the video footage that Manikas had found in Trevor Long's flat had held his attention. Magnussen had been insistent that Long was just a nuisance, making things up about the Sons of Sol, but the file made some serious allegations about them. The films Long made were of poor quality as they were often taken in the dark with only flickering bonfires for lighting. Kinnear had to agree that some of the screams on the footage were bloodcurdling but there was nothing to suggest that foul play had occurred. It just seemed like a bunch of overgrown kids getting drunk and larking about. On the other hand, an axe was found at the crime scene and the Sons of Sol were all about axes.

He sighed and sat back, pushing the file away from him. He didn't think he could count this as overtime, so he was sacrificing his personal life by being here. Chris had texted a couple of times, wondering where he was. Not that Chris nagged or seemed to resent it when Kinnear worked late. Chris was a teacher and spent enough of his own free time working. There was just something about the Trevor Long business; something that drew Kinnear in and made him more determined to solve the puzzle.

Thor Magnussen seemed affable enough. He was a fierce-looking man but Kinnear wasn't convinced he would harm Long. Kinnear had put the names and addresses of the Sons of Sol through Niche, the police database and it had thrown up a few hits. Some of the members had been involved in fights or on the edge of things as witnesses but there were no serious criminals in the group. Thor Magnussen or Fabian Thorpe didn't register at all.

Officers would be deployed to interview them if Blake managed to get a budget from the boss. Kinnear sighed and picked up Trevor's ring binder. Something slid from behind a sheet of paper in one of the poly pockets. It flopped onto the desk face up. It was an index card with a name and address scrawled in what Kinnear assumed to be Long's spidery handwriting:

Bev Campbell: 14, South Parade, West Kirby. (She knows)

He tapped her name into Niche but nothing came up. A brief Google search gave Kinnear some images from a school production of Pygmalion at the local girls' grammar school. Bev was listed as someone in the back row and could have been any one of eight bubbly-looking teenagers beaming at the cameras. This was a few years back.

A Facebook search narrowed it down to a young woman with bright red hair who appeared to be a student at Liverpool University studying Archaeology. "Okay, Bev," Kinnear muttered at the screen. "We'll try and see you tomorrow and find out what you know about Trevor Long and the Sons of Sol. Me? I'm going to see my husband now."

*****

Kath Cryer heard the scream from upstairs where she was just drying her hair after a shower. Dropping the hair dryer, she hurried downstairs to the kitchen where her partner, Theo cursed and stared at his bleeding thumb. "What did you do?" Kath said, grabbing a length of kitchen roll and wrapping it around Theo's red thumb.

"I was just opening a bottle of Bud and it exploded on me," Theo said. "It was like someone had shot it."

"Weird," Kath said, glancing at her reflection in the black kitchen window.

"Have you been shaking them up or something?"

Kath stared at him. "Oh yeah," she said. "I was sitting at work all day just quivering with excitement at the idea of shaking up your bottles of beer when I got home, wasn't I?"

"Okay, okay," Theo snapped. "No need to be like that... ow!"

Kath gave his hand another prod and pulled a face. "That's going to need stitching," she muttered. "Come on, soft lad, let me get dressed and I'll whip you round to the hospital."

Theo looked even more woeful. "Do I have to?"

"Flippin' eck, you big kid. I'm not having you dripping blood all over the house. I'm not looking forward to a night waiting in A&E am I? I'm knackered as it is."

She turned and stamped upstairs to get dressed. It seemed like everything that could go wrong was doing so in short order.

CHAPTER 13

DC Andrew Kinnear had always liked going to the seaside. As a child, his parents had frequently holidayed at a UK beach resort. The smell of the sea and the cry of gulls brought back fond memories and he often fancied moving somewhere on the coast. Chris, his husband, wasn't so keen. "Cold winds and storms. And seagulls nicking your chips. I'd rather be inland any day."

Now Kinnear stood outside 14, South Parade in West Kirby, he had to take a moment just to look out at the view. Most of it was grey sky fringed by the Welsh hills to his left. It was amazing, though. he didn't imagine he could afford one of the properties on this stretch of road, even if they were just large semi-detached houses. Still he could dream. A few dog-walkers wandered along the promenade but otherwise, the place was quiet.

He'd called Bev Campbell early that same morning and she'd readily agreed to see him. She had even said she'd pop over as she had lectures in the afternoon, but Kinnear fancied the trip over.

The first thing that struck Kinnear when Bev opened the door, was the mass of red hair and freckles. She looked as though she had been born smiling and had never stopped. "Hi, is it Andrew?" she said. "Do come in. My mum's out at the moment but my dad is out the back in his office shed if you need to talk to him."

"Right, thank you," Kinnear said, pocketing the warrant card he hadn't had to show. He followed her into the front room which was tastefully decorated in pastel shades. an old spaniel lay on the mat and gave a half-hearted tail wag when Kinnear came in but it didn't get up.

"Don't mind, Roly," Bev Campbell said. "He's getting too old to make a fuss over visitors, these days. So, you said something about the Sons of Sol on the phone." Kinnear noticed that her face clouded a little as she mentioned the name.

"Yes," Kinnear said. "I wondered what your connection with them is."

Bev pouted. "Nothing. I did go to one of their meetings but very quickly realised it wasn't for me."

"Why was that?"

She looked uncomfortable and rubbed her hands together. "I'm not a prude or inexperienced, and I don't really have a problem with people using drugs if that's what they want to do but I just don't want to be involved, that's all."

"I'm sorry," Kinnear said. "I'm a little confused. Are you saying the Sons of Sol use drugs?"

"I'm in my second year at University, detective. Studying Archaeology. I met Fabian Thorpe at a Fresher's event, and he invited me to one of their evenings."

Kinnear frowned. "What was Fabian Thorpe doing at the Fresher's event?"

"He was doing an axe throwing display. A few people were invited to have a go. Being interested in the Wirral's Viking heritage, I thought the Sons of Sol sounded fun."

"But they weren't," Kinnear said.

"No. They just got drunk and shouted at each other. Then somebody produced these magic mushrooms and it got a bit mental."

"Mental?"

Bev rolled her eyes. "Chanting and dancing. It was embarrassing at first," her voice faltered as she remembered. "It was scary after that. They staked a woman out on the ground and began cutting her. She was too stoned to notice."

"And what happened to the woman? Was she okay?"

"I don't know. I ran for it once it started getting hairy. It was clear these people were more interested in getting stoned than Viking culture."

"And did you call the police?"

Bev nodded. "I did once I'd got away from there but I never heard anything back. I'm not sure I was taken seriously."

"What about Trevor Long? Did you talk to him about this?"

"I was going to," Bev said. "He rang me and asked about the night I'd left. We arranged to meet but he never turned up."

"How did he find out you'd been to the Sons of Sol meeting?"

"He does this YouTube thing," Bev said and pulled a face. "It's a bit pants, to be honest but my friend watches it and, when he did one about the Sons of Sol, she left a comment. He followed it up."

"So do you think people get hurt at these parties or worse?"

Bev paled a little and her smile slipped. "I don't know. They do get out of control and there seemed to be a lot of drug-taking going on. I don't know much about it but there were a lot of people throwing up after taking the mushrooms. It didn't look healthy to me."

"And you haven't been near them since?"

"It was ages ago," Bev said. "I joined a proper re-enactment group run by people who do their research. They're all about education. A lot of them are members of the Archaeology department at Liverpool. They're lovely. It's like having a second family. And I'd steer clear of Fabian Thorpe or Thor Magnussen or whatever he calls himself, these days. He might look like a Norse god but he's an animal."

*****

DCI Matty Cavanagh sat with one foot up on his desk. He liked the way the sun caught the shine on his new tan boots. Liverpool had won their match against Chelsea last night and all would be well with the world if it weren't for Josh Gambles. DS Bobby Dirkin leaned against the wall, his back to the window and stared down at a sheaf of print outs. Cavanagh always thought Dirkin looked like he'd been put in some kind of crusher, like the ones used to turn cars into cubes of metal. The man was as wide as he was tall but it was all muscle. Cavanagh had seen Dirkin take down men twice his size. He'd watched him get up after taking a punch that would have floored most people.

Dirkin wrinkled his squashed nose. "Kyle Quinlan," Dirkin said, speaking out of the corner of his mouth in a thick, Bootle accent. "A record as long as your arm, sir. Assault, aggravated burglary, domestic violence. Not a nice man."

"So, he's doing time somewhere? D'you think that's where Gambles heard his name. Seems like a bit of a wild goose chase to me, Bobby."

Dirkin pulled a dismissive face. "That's up to you, sir," he said. "As a matter of fact, Quinlan isn't in custody at all. He just vanished."

"What d'you mean, he just vanished?"

"Regular run-ins with police, short stints in prison then nothing from 2014 onwards. He either left the country, changed his name or turned over a new leaf because there isn't a hint of him. Not a dicky bird."

"So what would his connection with Gambles be? Were they in foster care together? Did they do time together?"

"I thought about that, sir, and yes, it seems that Gambles and Quinlan were in the same prisons at the same time on four occasions."

"So it's possible that he and Gambles knew each other but why bang on about him now? What does Gambles want us to find out?"

"Like you say, sir, he could just be winding us up and wasting our time. It does seem odd that Quinlan stops all activity six years ago. It's not like he's an angel and he mixed with some pretty serious characters. Even if he'd changed his ways, I'd expect him to show up as a witness or person of interest in some other case but he doesn't."

"Has he been reported as a missing person?"

"Nope," Dirkin said. "Mind you, he came out of care, had no living relatives apart from a divorced wife."

Cavanagh stretched back on his chair and put his hands behind his head. "I suppose people do just drop out of life, Bobby. He could have been a smackhead or an alcoholic and drifted onto the streets. We'll have to ask for Mr Gambles to clarify what it is he wants us to find."

CHAPTER 14

The Major Incident room buzzed with activity as Blake's team gathered together to review what they'd found in the Trevor Long case. Blake surveyed the group. Kinnear and Manikas sat discussing something, while Kath Cryer stared off into space. She looked terrible. Vikki Chinn's stint as exhibits officer seemed to be at an end as Tev, the usual incumbent had returned from leave.

"Okay, people," Blake said. "It seems that the blood at the graveyard is Trevor Longs. Taking that into account, along with evidence from some key witnesses, we're treating this as a murder investigation. I want to keep that as quiet as possible for now, but the Superintendent agrees with me that there are too many factors to ignore in this one. So, where are we up to?"

"Door-to-door interviews didn't reveal much," Kinnear said. "It was such a foul night that most people were shut away and nobody saw anything. Trevor had a girlfriend and there's a video of them probably splitting up at what could probably be the world's worst spiritualist act. I get the impression that Trevor isn't a very popular person. Even his mother doesn't like him."

"Tasha Cook got nowhere with the mother. It's like she doesn't care or is in denial that her boy has gone," Alex Manikas said.

"Maybe we need to explain the gravity of the situation. That we think it's murder," Vikki Chinn said.

"I saw a woman called Bev Campbell this morning," Kinnear said. "She had dealings with the Sons of Sol and described Thor Magnussen as an animal. She said that there was a lot of drug taking in the group and she witnessed them torturing a woman."

"There's also the axe connection. The axe that was found at the crime scene is a," Blake looked at the report from forensics, "'replica Viking bearded axe but with a shortened handle.'"

"Maybe Gary Stott's insistence that they took Trevor isn't so far-fetched, after all," Manikas said.

"Except that the axe is clean apart from the blood. Forensics said they would have expected remnants of bone or flesh to be on the blade along with the blood but there was nothing. No fingerprints, either."

Manikas raised his eyebrows. "Strange, sir, but I still think it all points to Thor."

"You might be right, Alex," Blake said, "but we need to explore all possibilities."

"We've also got this video footage. I hope nobody is of a nervous disposition," Kinnear said, grinning and pressing play. They sat, arms folded watching Trevor trying to do his piece to camera and then him being chased. On screen, Trevor screamed, and Kath Cryer leapt up startled. "No!" She shouted.

"Jeez, Kath. Are you okay?" Blake said.

She looked around, bewildered. "What? Oh, yeah. Just gave me a jump, that's all. I'm fine. Honest." She sat down again, trying to ignore the sidelong glances and smirks.

"Don't watch many horror films, Kath?" Kinnear said, grinning.

"It just took me by surprise, that's all," Kath snapped. "If you must know, I was in A&E with Theo half the night after he cut himself on a beer bottle, the big divvy."

"Do you want to take a moment?" Blake said. Cryer was one of his best officers, a voice like broken glass but a mind twice as sharp. Blake had noticed that she had been struggling recently, since she'd been caught up in a shooting. Her physical injuries were superficial, but he worried that the experience had impacted her in other ways.

"No, thanks, sir, I'm okay," she said. "So... where did you say this came from?"

"A camcorder was recovered from Bidston Hill just above Flaybrick, the next morning," Kinnear said. "Expensive piece of kit, too."

Kath pulled a face. "On Tuesday morning. What? It had been out all night? It was chucking it down on Monday night. Biddy Hill is pretty exposed, isn't it? If it had got a good soaking, it wouldn't work. Unless it's an underwater one or something. How come the camcorder was working?"

Kinnear blinked at Cryer. "I don't know," he said.

Blake grinned. This was the Kath Cryer he knew and loved.

"Who found it?" she said.

"A woman called Zoe Plumb," he said. "She was walking her dog..."

"And it was just lying there?"

"That's what the statement says," Kinnear muttered, flicking through his notes. "The CSI team had no trouble operating the playback on it and, with the exception of Ms Plumb's, the only other fingerprints on it were Trevor Long's."

"Well he didn't film himself, we're already sure of that," Blake said. "The cameraman..."

"Or woman," Kath said.

"Or camerawoman may have been wearing

gloves..."

"Or might have been Zoe Plumb, sir," Kath finished. "Do you want me to talk to her?"

Blake nodded. "Yeah, have a word, Kath. See what you think."

"Is Trevor Long particularly well-off?" Vikki Chinn said.

"He's single with only his rent to pay and he has a job at a local supermarket. But his mum said something about him getting into debt to buy all the film equipment, so I guess not."

"So he must have borrowed money from someone to be able to afford the camera. Could we be looking at local money lenders making an example of him?"

"Could you explore that avenue, Vikki?"

"Of course," Blake said. "The prime suspect is the last person to see the victim alive, isn't it? In this case, that means the unseen camera man. I think we need to have another word with Gary Stott. Let's get our friend the thunder god in too, and have another chat."

Kath Cryer's first port of call was the toilets to go and splash some water on her face and wake herself up. They'd got back from the hospital late and Theo had been tossing and turning all night. She was low on sleep. Her wrist ached. On top of everything else, she was pretty sure she had a water infection. She just wanted to go home to bed. She leaned heavily on the wash basin and stared at herself in the mirror. She hated the jowls that were developing and the crow's feet around her eyes. A gym membership syphoned fifteen quid a month out of her bank account, but she rarely went.

The water felt cool and refreshing. Kath straightened up and adjusted the splint on her wrist. It felt worse lately. And she knew she shouldn't spend so much time obsessively straightening the Velcro straps that held it tight. but the anxiety that bubbled up from her stomach to her throat, choking off all breath was too much to bear if she didn't.

Blake had suggested counselling several times but she'd resisted so far. The last thing she needed was another appointment gumming up her, already busy, schedule. "Right Kath Cryer," she said. "Get a grip and let's go and shake this Zoe Plumb up." A movement behind her made her start and she turned, expecting to see someone coming out of a cubicle but, apart from her, the toilets were empty. Muttering to herself, and shaking her head, she hurried out.

CHAPTER 15

Thor Magnussen appeared quite happy to come into Birkenhead Station. Normally Blake would have left Kinnear or Cryer to interview him, but he wanted to see the man again for himself. There was something that had bothered Blake about Thor since their first meeting and he couldn't quite pin it down.

The sense of disquiet was amplified when Blake saw Thor's companion.

"Who the hell is that?" Blake said to Kinnear, who shrugged.

If the man was a solicitor, then Blake had never met him before and he looked like no solicitor, the detective had ever met before. The man was short and stocky with a mop of brilliant white hair greased back. His bronze tan contrasted starkly with his hair and the gold rings that glinted on his fingers. He wore a sharp suit and a pink shirt, open at the neck. Blake had no real interest in fancy clothing, he left that to the likes of Cavanagh, but even he could tell that the man's clothes were expensive and tailored to fit him perfectly. Despite all this show, Blake felt suspicious straight away. It was the darkened glasses that he wore even though the light was quite dingy in the old station. There was just something about his manner. He seemed to be assessing everything and everyone as he sauntered through to the reception desk; watching for threats and opportunities.

Thor Magnussen strode behind him like some kind of giant bodyguard and Blake wondered quite what their relationship was.

"Mr Magnussen," Blake said as they reached the reception desk. "I'm so glad you could make the time to come and speak to us again."

"No worries," Thor said, like an awkward teenager at parents' evening, and glanced at the man next to him.

"Harry Thorpe," the man said, extending a hand. "Fabian's father. So you're the famous DCI Will Blake. I used to love that Searchlight programme. You did that so well."

Thorpe's grip was tight and grasping; Blake wanted to check his watch once he'd shook the man's hand. "It was a while back, now, Mr Thorpe," he said, frowning. "Besides, I feel like I've heard your name before, too?"

"Probably from a couple of years back. I took your lot to the cleaners for harassment. A Detective Inspector Clements had something of a vendetta against me, I'm afraid. He was convinced I was up to all kinds of mischief. Money laundering, intimidation, loan sharking, even murder. I was shocked. Outraged. I'm a legit businessman. Anyway, it was all sorted out. I don't think Clements works for your lot anymore. I think he went off on gardening leave and never came back."

"Right," Blake said through gritted teeth. "let's get this over with, then."

"So," Harry Thorpe said, once they'd sat down in the interview room. "This is the second time you've wanted to talk to my son. Is this about Trevor Long?"

"Unless your son has some kind of problem that means he's not capable of answering, Mr Thorpe, it's him I'd like to speak to," Blake said.

"I think he's helped you all he can, to be honest but you can ask away."

Thor went pale and nodded in agreement. "Ask away," he said, trying to imitate his father's dismissive tone.

"Can we start by establishing your movements on Sunday night?"

"I told you, I met some of the lads up on Bidston Hill but it was pouring down. You couldn't light a fire or anything. We hung around for half an hour and went home. Nothing happened."

"Did you see Trevor Long at all that night?"

"No. It was dark. If he was there. I didn't know about it."

"You said that a number of your friends weren't happy about Long's videos about the Sons of Sol. Did any of them say anything about hurting him that night?"

"It was pissing down. The only thing we had in mind was getting in the dry. Trevor Long was the last thing on our minds. Really!"

"If it was so horrible up there," Kinnear said, "why didn't you just phone each other and cancel?"

Thor shrugged. "Point of honour, innit?"

"Sorry?" Blake said. "I don't follow."

"We make a point of keeping our meetings even if it's for a few minutes. Anyone suggested crying off and they'd be a laughing stock. So we met up and split up soon after everyone was there. Bjorn's always a bit late, so we ended up kicking around for a while waiting for him."

"And once you left there, where did you go?"

"I went back home…"

"I can vouch for that," Harry Thorpe cut in. "I saw him come back and go into his flat shortly after eleven. He has his own pad on our premises. It's a converted farm."

"Do you recognise this?" Blake said, sliding over a photograph of the axe found at the crime scene.

"Nice," Thor said. "It's a Viking bearded axe. Tasty bit of kit that. Why?"

"Does it belong to you or one of your friends?"

"It's not mine. You couldn't throw that axe. Normally, those axes have a longer handle. I don't think that would fly very well. All my throwing axes are simple hatchets. Wait a minute... why are you asking me about axes again?"

"Okay, Thor. I'm going to level with you," Blake said. "We have forensic evidence to suggest that Trevor Long is probably dead and we're conducting a murder investigation. This axe was found at the crime scene, covered in Trevor's blood. It's a bit of a coincidence, don't you think?"

"I think that's probably enough," Harry Thorpe cut in. "Unless you've got real evidence that links my son to the death of Trevor Long then you can stop it with the innuendo. We're here voluntarily, okay?"

"What about drugs, Thor?" Blake said.

"I'd prefer a cup of coffee," Thor said, emboldened by his father's interjection.

"You know what I mean. I've heard you and your friends are fond of dropping a few mushrooms at these gatherings."

"I wouldn't know about that. I've got a mushroom allergy. They make me throw up and go all blotchy, and that's the button mushrooms from the supermarket. I'm hardly going to be munching the raw magic mushies off the lawn, am I?"

"So nobody else in your group takes them?"

"I don't think so," Thor said. "I'm not in charge of their lives, am I? They might or they might not. I've never really noticed anyone who seemed stoned. We prefer a beer when we're not riding our bikes."

"You see, detectives, my lad's a good, clean-living boy," Thorpe said. "Surely you can see he has nothing to do with any of this."

Blake sat back in his seat. "Would you be happy to give us a DNA sample so we can rule you out of any further enquiries."

"No," Thorpe said. "He wouldn't. I know you people. The things your colleague did trying to frame me. If my son gives you his DNA, it'll be all over the next crime scene."

"With all due respect, Mr Thorpe..."

"You don't even have a body, do you?" Thorpe said, leaning forward. "You've got a whole load of forensic evidence but no body. Otherwise you'd have come out and said it. Plus, whoever killed Trevor Long would have left some DNA. You're thrashing around looking for someone to pin this on. Well, it's not going to be my Fabian.

Come on, son, we're leaving."

Harry Thorpe stood up and Thor trailed after him, shrugging and mouthing 'sorry' as he did.

The door slammed and Blake blew out a breath. Kinnear raised his eyebrows. "What d'you make of that, then, sir?"

"I reckon we have to tread very carefully with Thor or rather, his dad," Blake replied. "But then, if Thor is innocent of any wrong-doing, maybe he did the right thing. I knew DI Clements, the man who investigated Harry Thorpe and I hate to say it, but he was just the kind of bloke to sail a bit close to the wind. I've heard that Thorpe's as crooked as they come but I can understand why he's suspicious. Clements would have had no compunction about planting evidence."

"So you don't think Thor did it?"

"I don't know what to think, Andrew," Blake replied, staring at the door.

CHAPTER 16

Shana Long, Trevor's mother, clearly wasn't pleased to see DS Vikki Chinn and Tasha Cook, the family Liaison Officer. She scowled and pulled her dressing gown tightly around her shoulders. Vikki noted that it was past midday but tried not to make any kind of judgement.

"Can you come back later? Loose Women is on," Mrs Long said, flicking ash onto the front doorstep.

"I'm sorry, Mrs Long. Can we come in?" Tasha said. "We'd like to have a word about Trevor. It's bad news, I'm afraid."

"If you must," Shana Long muttered and walked back into the house.

They followed and Vikki tried not to wrinkle her nose at the smoky atmosphere and the smell of fried food that hung heavily in the air. Mrs Long led them into a small living room crammed with furniture. A leather sofa filled one wall and almost touched arms with the armchair pressed against the other. A low coffee table, buried in magazines filled the space in the middle of the room and an enormous TV dominated the third wall of the room. A thin light filtered in through the windows which were draped with nicotine yellow net curtains. They edged in, shuffling for lack of space and sat down on the sofa.

"You're wasting your time. I'm sure Trevor's okay," Shana Long said over the voices of the panellists on the TV.

"I'm afraid..." Vikki began then glanced at the intrusive screen on the wall. "Could we have the TV off, please, Mrs Long?"

"It's my favourite programme," she said, lighting another cigarette.

"Please Mrs Long," Tasha said. "It's really important."

Shana Long rolled her eyes. "God," she hissed, smoke billowing from between her teeth. "All right then." She stabbed a finger at the remote and the chattering stopped.

"So, you know that we've been concerned about Trevor's whereabouts for a couple of days now," Vikki began.

"You haven't found the stupid pillock's body, have you?" She said, her eyes widening. "That'd be just like him to go and get killed."

Tasha looked pained. "We haven't found a body as such but..."

"See, I knew he was fine. he'll turn up, you wait and see," Mrs Long said, sitting back in her armchair.

"We have found his coat and a large amount of blood which our scientists have established is Trevor's," Vikki said. "There's no way Trevor could have lost that much blood and still be alive without urgent hospital treatment. We can't find any record of Trevor having attended any local A&E or any other medical services that night. I'm afraid we're investigating his murder."

Shana Long took a long drag on her cigarette and silence filled the airless room. "You're going to have a job on your hands trying to work out who killed him, then, aren't you?"

Vikki frowned. "I don't understand."

"He was such a little pain in the arse, there'd be a queue of people wanting to murder him." Her mobile rang and she answered it. "What? No, I can't. I've got 'kin police here haven't I? They think our Trevor's dead. He's been murdered. I know, that's what I said. Yeah, see you." She hung up and nodded at the mobile. "My mate. She said the same."

Vikki glanced over at Tasha. "You told DC Kinnear that Trevor was 'spending money he didn't have.'" Vikki said. "What did you mean by that?"

Mrs Long scowled. "He was never any good with money. Always buying rubbish. Anyway, he bought all this film equipment, didn't he? He was gonna make a big documentary. Wanted me to lend him money but I told him to do one. He

117

might have got it from somewhere else."

"An illegal money lender? Would you know who?"

"No," Shana Long said. "And even if I did, I wouldn't grass them up, would I?"

"Even if they'd murdered your own son?"

"If he got himself murdered then he's only got himself to blame, hasn't he? If he didn't go around rubbing people up the wrong way, they wouldn't turn on him."

"Who else might have turned on him?" Tasha Cook said.

"Oh, they all do in the end, don't they? Girl-friends, his so-called mates, people at work. He doesn't help himself at all. I bet it was that Stotty. He had enough reason to turn on him."

"Really?"

"Yeah. Trevor always bossed the little fella round. Made him carry and fetch stuff. He even made Stotty miss a date with a girl from work so he could film some stupid video about a ghost in Birkenhead Town Hall. They got chucked out. They came over here afterwards and I could tell Stotty was fuming."

Tasha Cook frowned. "Forgive me, Shana, but you don't seem very upset. You do understand what we've told you. We think your son is dead."

Shana Long stubbed out her cigarette. "Yeah, I heard you," she said. "And I think I'd like you to go now so I can grieve for my son."

"I'm sorry, Shana," Tasha said. "I didn't mean..."

"Nah," Mrs Long said. "It's all right. I just need time to think."

"If you want, I can stay. I'm a Family Liaison Officer so I can keep you in touch with the investigation and raise any concerns you might have."

Mrs Long shook her head. "No. Can you just leave, please?" Tasha left a card on the coffee table and they let themselves out.

Once they were in the car, Tasha widened her eyes and puffed out her cheeks. "In all my years, I haven't seen someone react like that. I feel bad now..."

"Don't worry," Vikki said. "If Trevor Long lacks social graces, I think we know where he gets that from. If it's any consolation, I think there's more going on there than meets the eye."

Tasha started the engine and pulled off. As Vikki looked back, she glimpsed Shana Long staring after them, a phone pressed to her ear.

*****

The fact that Zoe Plumb lived on the other side of town from Bidston Hill and Flaybrick puzzled Kath Cryer. It was the first thing that struck her as she pulled up outside the red brick end terrace just near Birkenhead Park railway station. Zoe Plumb was a big, smiley woman in her early twenties. A bit too smiley for Kath's liking. A hairband fought constantly to hold back her wild mass of black hair. She wore jeans and a sloppy jumper.

"You just caught me," she said. "I'm on shift in an hour but I've got time to talk."

"Where is it you work?"

"Merryvale Pet Vets in Clatterbridge, you might have heard the advertisement on Radio City?" Zoe said. "We've got a pet crematorium, too..."

Cryer shrugged. "I don't listen to City that much. So, you found the camcorder on Bidston Hill on Tuesday morning, is that right?"

"Yeah, I was taking Candy, my neighbour's dog out for an early morning walk and stumbled across it."

"Was it just lying there on the grass?"

Zoe frowned. "Yeah. I wondered where it had come from. I looked around a bit but there was nobody near, so I thought it must be lost. I'd seen the police cars at Flaybrick cemetery, so I took it to them."

"Do you often walk your neighbour's dog?"

"I have the last couple of weeks. George, my neighbour, has just had an operation, so I offered to help out."

"Why did you go to Bidston Hill to walk the dog?"

"I like it there."

"Yeah but you live right by Birkenhead Park and you had work early that morning, so it would have been easier to step outside your front door and walk over to the park."

Zoe's face fell. "How do you know I was in work early that day?"

"You said in your statement that you'd come out early because you were due in work. It just seems like a schlepp across town to walk the dog, especially after it had been raining so heavily the night before. That reminds me. Was the camcorder wet, when you picked it up?"

Zoe shrugged. "I don't think so."

Cryer pulled a face and scratched her head. "Weird that, isn't it? I mean, I was up in the night. Bit of a water infection. It's doing my head in, you know? Up to the loo, oh, don't need the loo and then when you do go...ouch," she screwed her face up. "Anyway, I happen to know it was chucking it down that night. The camcorder should have been soaked."

Zoe blinked and licked her lips. "I just found it, that's all. I don't know if it had been there all night."

"Where were you the night before you found the camcorder?"

"Me? I- I was out with friends. We went to that new Italian place in Hoylake. You can check if you like. I don't know why you're giving me a hard time about this. I could have just left that camcorder there. I thought I was helping."

Cryer sniffed. "Yeah, okay," she said. "We're investigating a serious crime and I have to iron out any inconsistencies in the evidence. Don't get too upset. Do you know Trevor Long?" Kath watched Zoe Plumb closely as she asked the question. The young woman glanced down and clasped her hands together.

"No," she said. "No, I don't know him. Why? Who is he?"

Cryer made a note in her notebook and then put it away. "Just a person of interest," she said, standing up. "Thank you for your time, Ms Plumb. We may have to talk to you again to get more details."

Zoe gave a sickly smile and nodded, then led Cryer to the front door in silence. Once outside Cryer looked back at the house and saw Zoe peering at her from behind the curtains. "I see you, missy," DI Kath Cryer muttered. "You're up to something."

CHAPTER 17

Blake sat at his desk twisting a paperclip out of shape as he brooded over the interview with Thor Magnussen. Kinnear and Manikas sat expectantly, waiting for him to say something that would give them some direction.

"I reckon Magnussen's involved in this, sir," Kinnear said at last. "He has to be. There's too much evidence that points to him."

"Yeah," Manikas added. "The axe, the fact that his dad is up to all kinds of mischief..."

"True," Blake muttered. "But that doesn't make his son a murderer."

"Oh come on, sir," Manikas said. "There's no smoke without fire. Thorpe has been named as a person of interest in a number of cases. He's got loads of property that he rents out and it's well-known on the street that he's not a friendly landlord for a kick off."

"We need to tread carefully, though, Alex," Blake said. "I know Thorpe's crooked. Clements knew that but he underestimated just how clever Thorpe was. According to Clement's file, Thorpe should be locked up for murder, extortion, money laundering. And yet Harry Thorpe

managed to turn that all around and success-
fully sue the force."

Manikas frowned. "But if Thor did it…"

"We don't know that he did anything, Alex,"
Blake said. "We know that Long was a pain in
the arse and Thor didn't like him. Neither did
half of Birkenhead, it seems. There just happens
to be an axe at the scene of the crime. Thor or
Fabian or whatever he calls himself seems like a
big kid, which doesn't rule him out but it doesn't
rule him in, either. I'm just saying, we have to be
wary, that's all."

"What about the drugs angle? If Long had
evidence that Magnussen and Thorpe were involved in dealing, maybe that would be enough
reason to kill him."

"It's possible," Blake said. "Thorpe's capable of
that, I'm certain. Trouble is, I can't believe he'd
be so theatrical about it. He knows how investigations work, he made that clear at the interview. He'd just dispose of Long somewhere far
from here."

"Unless Thor botched it," Manikas said.

"I get the impression that Harry Thorpe
wouldn't trust his son to sharpen a pencil un-
assisted. I can't imagine him telling Thor to
bump Trevor off."

"D'you want me to see if I can do a bit more digging, sir?" Alex said.

"Yeah, but tread lightly, Alex," Blake said. "I don't want anyone getting their arsed kicked or worse for rubbing Harry Thorpe up the wrong way."

"Andrew, can you catch up with Gary Stott? He's still a suspect despite Manikas' enthusiasm for Thor."

"Will do," Kinnear said.

Blake watched the two men leave and turned to his computer. He was pretty certain he shouldn't be searching for registration numbers on company time for tracking down a missing cat. But it was *his* missing cat. If she had been stolen, it was a crime, right?

This heart sank when he discovered that the van belonged to an Emrys Evans who had convictions for animal cruelty. In addition, the man had been fined for keeping cats and dogs in insanitary conditions and selling stolen pets. He'd also run a puppy farm which had since been closed down. If you were a cat owner, this was the last person you'd want driving past your house.

Blake drummed his fingers on the table. Serafina had been missing for three days. He could wait until the end of the day to go and see this man, or he could do it now. He glanced out of his office at the Major Incident room. Heads were down, people were working. There was a pile of cases to review and other paperwork to look at, but Serafina could be suffering. Blake pulled a file and clicked on his computer. What if he'd sold her on? What if some scummy dog-fighting gang had got hold of her? Some of his work was urgent but it would keep. Serafina, on the other hand, might not. He pulled his jacket on and hurried through the office to his car.

*****

The problem with getting information about a secretive gang of pagans is that they're secretive, DC Alex Manikas thought. He started with a simple Google search for the name Fabian Thorpe and came up with the Sons of Sol Axe Throwing Experience website.

It was slick with videos of men and women dressed as Viking warriors hurling axes at targets. A huge banner headline read:

VALHALLA BECKONS!

A thousand years ago, warriors from the
North beached their long ships on the
coasts of the North West and pillaged
the whole region. But they met their
match on the Wirral. Find out why!

There was a Frequently Asked Questions section that reassured as well as excited, promising that by the end of the night, you'd be throwing axes 'like a berserker.' Manikas wasn't sure that this was a good thing. He had to admit, though, after reading the website, he fancied a night of axe throwing.

"Maybe I should do that," he muttered to himself. He picked up the phone and dialled the number on the website. "Hullo, Winston's Bookmakers," a deep voice said.

"Oh, hi. I think I've got the wrong number. I was looking for the axe throwing company... Sons of Something..."

There was a gentle chuckle. "Yeah, sorry, you're through to the right place," the voice said. "I'm Thor. How can I help you?"

*****

Gary, Trevor's flatmate had sounded irritated on the phone when Kinnear had asked to talk again, but he agreed. Now they sat in the cluttered flat again, Kinnear scribbling in his notebook.

"The thing is, Gary," he said. "We're treating this as a murder, now. We suspect that Trevor is dead. We found his blood-stained coat in Flaybrick Hill cemetery and nobody could lose that much blood and survive."

Gary looked like a sulky teenager and kicked his heel into the carpet making an irritating bumping sound. "I dunno," he said. "I told you. It's them. The Sons of Sol. They were up on the hill that night and Trevor was filming them."

"It could have been any number of people, according to Trevor's mother," Kinnear said. "Why wasn't he very popular, Gary?"

Stott shrugged. "He was just a bit different, that's all," Gary said. "Didn't always read social situations right or take account of other people's feelings. But he was shit hot on his paranormal knowledge..."

"Okay, I need you to think really carefully. Apart from the Sons of Sol, who else might want to harm Trevor? Because, if I'm being honest, it sounds like you were the last person to see him alive and your alibi is paper thin."

Gary Stott's eyes widened. "You think I'd hurt Trevor? He was my best friend!"

Kinnear raised an eyebrow. "That may well be Gary, but somebody was up on that hill with Trevor. We know that for a fact and if it wasn't you, then who was it?"

"I don't know."

"What did you watch on TV the night Trevor went missing?"

Gary looked non-plussed. "What? I don't know I... just some rubbish..."

"You're going to have to do better than that Gary," Kinnear said. "What was on? What did you watch?"

"Netflix," Gary said. "Yeah, it was that Tiger

King..."

"Doesn't that woman's husband goes missing in Tiger King?"

Gary's face fell. "Carole Baskin," he said. "Yeah."

Kinnear looked at Gary. He was like a kid. Totally out of his depth. "Did Trevor ever look into department 23?"

"What?"

"Department 23. It's a shadowy police department. They're a group of trained hackers and computer analysts who work for the police."

Gary's eyes widened. "Really? No, I've never heard of them."

"Like cyber ninjas, Gary. They're based in Bootle. Now if I go to them and say, 'what was Gary Stott watching on Netflix on Sunday night?' they'd be clicking away at the keyboard for a few seconds and BAM! they'd come up with that information, what you ordered for your tea and what your favourite Pornhub videos are."

"I don't..." Gary started to say but his voice faded.

"So you better tell me the truth now Gary," Kinnear said. "All it takes is a phone call to department 23."

Gary Stott chewed his lip. His eyes flicked from Kinnear to the TV to his laptop. "Okay," he said at last. "I went up there with Trevor and I filmed him doing some introductions, but someone kept throwing stuff at us. probably kids mucking about."

"Why didn't you tell me this in the first place?"

"I don't know. I was worried about Trevor, but I knew you'd think I had something to do with him disappearing if I said I was up there with him that night."

"So what happened then?"

"I got fed up. These kids kept shouting out when we were trying to record, and Trevor was getting more and more angry. It was chucking it down, too. I was soaked, so I said I was going home but Trevor wanted to go and find the Sons of Sol. We had a bit of a row about it and I told him he could stick his camera and dumped it."

"So you had a row with Trevor. Did it get violent?"

"No," Gary said. "I just went home in a sulk, that's all. I watched Tiger King when I got home and then I went to bed. Honestly. You can have your department 23 check that out."

"Maybe I will, Gary. Maybe I will. Is there anything else you want to tell me?"

"Please, I didn't hurt Trevor," Gary said. "You've got to believe me. He was my best friend."

"Who else was up there with you that night?"

"Nobody. Honest. I'm not lying."

"I think there was someone. How come the camcorder turned up the next morning bone dry?"

Gary blinked and swallowed hard. "What?"

"We found Trevor's camcorder the next morning and it was in perfect working order. How do you think that's possible? It was pouring down on Sunday night as you said."

Gary looked pale but he folded his arms and tightened his mouth. "I don't know. Maybe the Sons of Sol stole it off him and then dumped it because it was evidence. I left early. I wasn't there."

Kinnear saw that Stott had closed up; he wasn't going to get any more out of the lad yet, but something told him his hunch was right. There had been another person up there that night. If they found out who that was, they might have Trevor Long's killer.

CHAPTER 18

The Wirral is a relatively small place being around fifteen miles long and seven miles wide. And yet there are still small pockets that seem to have been untouched by the modern world Here and there, down a rough lane, between a couple of fields or behind an industrial estate, you can stumble across an old farmyard or a cottage that looks like its inhabitants haven't left the premises for decades. Emrys Evans' home was one such place.

On a little patch of scrubland, trapped between the railway and the north coast of the Wirral, Evans' house stood surrounded by scrap cars, old railway carriages, wooden huts and run down stables. The tyres of Blake's old Opel Manta squished through mud and he winced at the thought of the old screws and nails that might lay beneath the surface.

Evan's house itself was a ramshackle affair. The windows were part dirty glass and part hardboard. It had been painted white once, long ago, but chunks of cladding had fallen off revealing weathered brick. Slates clung onto the roof at haphazard angles, and a cracked chimneypot smoked on top of a stack that had a sapling growing out of it.

Blake climbed out of his car and picked his way through the rubbish that littered the yard. He curled his lip at the sound of barking and meowing. This man had been banned from keeping animals so many times it had become meaningless to him. Blake thumped on the door so hard it nearly collapsed. It scraped open and a ferret-eyed middle-aged man with a puffy face covered in stubble peered out. "Yeah?" he said.

"DCI Blake. Emrys Evans?"

The man's eyes widened and he tried to slam the door shut but Blake rammed his foot in the way.

"Would you mind stepping outside please?"

Emrys Evans turned to bolt back into the house. Blake followed him into a stinking, dark room. Evans opened another door at the back of the room, but Blake had caught up with him, grabbing the collar of the man's grubby tweed jacket and pulling him back.

"Get off me, that's police brutality, that is," Evans yelled. "I'll 'ave you for that!"

"I'll show you brutality if I find you've hurt my cat!" Blake snarled and slammed Emrys Evans down into a motheaten armchair. The whole room looked like it needed gutting and its contents throwing into a skip. Boxes of dogfood formed a huge tower in one corner of the room, looming over the sofa and an ancient, square television. Blake blinked in puzzlement at a wall of what looked to be microwaves and old VCR recorders stacked against another wall. The place stank of smoke and grease and dogs.

"Y-your cat?" Evans stammered. "Oh, bloody hell."

"Yeah, Emrys, you picked on the wrong moggy this time," Blake snapped. "A grey-blue Persian, orange eyes. where is it?"

"I don't know. I haven't picked one up like that. I'd remember it if I had. Worth a bloody fortune, they are."

"So what were you doing down at Rock Park the other night?"

"Rock Park? Where the hell's that?"

"You were seen, Emrys. Your reg number was spotted."

Evans scraped his fingers over his stubbly beard. "All right, I admit, I'd had a tip off that there were some cats to grab."

"A tip off?"

"Just some bloke. A friend of a friend. Phoned me up and told me there were some class cats around there. But I swear to you, I didn't find a big Persian cat. You can look if you want."

"Yeah, I do want," Blake growled. "I don't believe you further than I can throw you. And now, I'm getting kind of curious about how far that might be, Emrys. So, show me what you've got."

*****

Telling Zoe Plumb about the water infection had been a ruse to make her uncomfortable but Kath Cryer hadn't made it up. She'd felt rough since Sunday night but on Monday, she'd felt worse. She felt cold one minute and boiling the next and wondered if it was affecting her in other ways. The movements in the corner of her eye, the general feeling of anxiety and restlessness. She'd gone home early, after phoning the GP who had promised to call her back for a telephone consultation. She glanced over at Blake's office as she passed but it lay empty. Kath doubted he'd ever had to leave early because of water works trouble and felt bad right away. Blake had known more than his fair share of hard times without illness adding to it. Anyway, he was a man, right? What was it her mum used to say? 'Men get sick, women get on with it.'

By the time she got home, she was desperate for the toilet. Theo lay on the sofa, shivering, a blanket pulled over him. A detective film played out on the telly but he wasn't paying any attention.

"What's up with you, you big wuss?" Kath said,

as she came out of the bathroom. When she came out, she peered at him. He looked grey and sweat beaded his forehead. His skin felt cold.

"I feel crap," Theo croaked. "My thumb is thumping and I'm sweating like a pig. I think it might be infected."

But Kath had her phone out already. "I'm calling an ambulance," She said.

*****

Emrys Evans shuffled across the yard and Blake resisted the urge to push him face down in the mud that covered the place. Blake could hear the dogs and puppies yapping and cats meowing, clearly in distress. He'd never really thought himself as an animal person and his strength of feeling surprised him. Maybe the first time Evans had been pulled up by the law, the man had made a mistake thinking he could look after so many animals; but to be repeatedly convicted of cruelty and then to be caught stealing animals from their homes was low in Blake's book. Often the crimes he dealt with were criminal on criminal; gangs taking their anger out on each other, people settling scores. Sometimes it was hard to tell who the bad guys were. Sometimes, through sheer carelessness or stupidity, people got themselves mired in crime and became victims. Animals had no control over their destinies, they couldn't make choices about these things. That made Evans a monster in Blake's book.

He watched as the man opened a wooden stable door and switched a light on. A wave of noise hit Blake. Dogs barked and cats cried from small steel cages stacked on top of each other. Blake scanned them all for Serafina or for the silver tabby but couldn't see either. A sea of eyes stared back at him and he felt his anger rising.

"How can you do this?"

Evans' face sagged. "I dunno, detective, it's just business. Got to make some money, see?"

Blake pulled his phone out. "Well, money's going to be the least of your problems. I'm calling backup and the RSPCA so they can get these poor creatures returned. I hope they take this place off you."

"You think these beasts will be missed?" Evans snapped, his eyes hardening. "Oh yes, some little girl might cry, oh boo hoo. But then they'll just buy another. Parents will replace them without a thought, won't they? Half of them are probably insured in case they go missing, anyway..."

Blake gave Evans a long, silent stare. "D'you know what? I think you might be a flight risk. I'm going to have to use the cuffs." Something jangled in Blake's head though, like Evans had tripped an alarm. Something Evans said resonated with him, but he wasn't sure what.

Thor Magnussen swung the axe, his right arm spinning like a windmill and then he let go sending the deadly weapon spinning through the air. It buried itself into the target board with an impressive, deep thud.

DC Alex Manikas clapped and nodded. "Well done. You're an expert."

Thor grinned and shrugged. "Practise I suppose," he said. "You have a go." He handed Alex the axe.

They stood in an old barn that had been converted into a playroom. Everything an overgrown teenager needed lay in this huge cavern: a snooker table, a huge TV linked up to a computer, games consoles, beanbags, kegs of beer and, at one end, a long gallery for throwing axes at a target. The whole place was part of a farm on the edge of Thingwall, a village that had been swallowed up by the suburban sprawl in the middle of the Wirral. The farm complex clearly belonged to Fabian Thorpe's parents and was more residential than a place of work. The yard was cobbled and the outhouses repurposed into flats and garages. When Alex had pulled in and parked next to a row of BMWs, he questioned why Thor Magnussen worked behind the counter at a bookmakers.

"I've never done this before," Alex said, weighing the axe in his hand.

"If you stand legs apart to begin with," Thor said. "Feel the weight of the axe and hold it above your head."

Alex held the axe above his head. "I feel a bit mad," Alex said.

"Mad is good," Thor said, slapping Alex on the back. "Now when you're ready, take a step forward and bring the axe down, release it when your hands come to eye level and see what happens."

Alex lunged forward, bringing his hand down. The axe whirled from his grip and stuck into the target. "All right!" Alex yelled.

"Nice one," Thor said. "You're a natural. So, who will be at this party?"

Without really thinking about it too carefully, Alex had made up a cover story about wanting the axe throwing to be the centrepiece of a party. "It's a works do, so there'd be a mix of people. Younger and older. Women and men. Would that be okay?"

"Sure," Thor said. "We've got all different weights and sizes of axe. Here, have another go." He handed Alex another axe.

Alex looked over his shoulder at the long-handled Viking weapon that leaned against the raw brick of the barn. "What about that one?"

Thor laughed. "I like your style. Reckon you can handle it?"

"I've got the blood of Achilles running through my veins, mate," Manikas laughed. "I was named after Alexander the Great."

Thor picked up the axe and Alex took his jacket off. The axe weighed a ton and Manikas wondered if he'd even swing it over his head. He hefted the weapon above his head and then gave a roar swinging the axe high and then bringing it down. The weight of the axe took over and Alex flipped it so that it spun towards the target. Miraculously, it buried itself into the board. Thor clapped and gave Alex a high five.

"Nice one!"

"Thanks," Alex said. "That felt great, actually."

"It's liberating isn't it?"

"Yeah. You forget everything but the axe and the board. It's like, I don't know, like tapping into some ancient instinct."

"Exactly!" Thor said. "Like the blood of your ancestors is suddenly pumping through your veins." He paused for a second. "So, what is it you do?"

"Signs," Manikas lied, thinking of his father's business over in Liverpool. "I'm in accounts for a company that makes signage for things, events, businesses, all kinds of things really."

"Cool," Thor said, stroking his beard.

"It's a bit boring, to be honest," Alex said. "Some days, I feel like screaming. I envy the guys going out there hanging the signs up or posting the billboards."

"I know what you mean," Thor said. "My dad's got me working in one of his betting shops. It drives me up the pole."

"But you've got this," Alex said, waving at the axes.

Thor shrugged. "Yeah," he said. "It's hard to scale up though. I can do little events, make pocket money really. I mean, no offence."

Alex smiled. "None taken, mate. I'm made of sterner stuff than that."

Thor frowned at Alex for a second, then threw the axe in his hand. It whirled through the air and stuck next to the double handed one Alex had thrown. "I like you, Alex," Thor said. "You've got warrior blood in you. Like me. Have you ever heard of the Sons of Sol?"

Alex shook his head and then made a play of remembering something. "Other than the advert for your axe throwing thing. Hey, wait a minute, yeah! I saw a video on YouTube about you. Some nerdy guy with specs, what was his name? Tony L…"

"Trevor Long," Thor said, his face dropping.

"Yeah, that dick head caused us a few problems. Spreading lies about us. He's sorted now, though."

"Sorted?" Alex said, looking quizzical.

"Let's just say, me and a few of the brothers put him straight," Thor clapped his hands and grinned again. "Don't believe a word in those videos. We're just fun-loving, action and adventure types."

"Sol," Alex said. "Isn't that something to do with the sun?"

"Exactly, my friend. Let's have a beer and I'll tell you about a big event that's kicking off tomorrow night. You might want to come along. It'll be wild. I think you'll like it."

CHAPTER 19

It was late by the time Blake got back home. Emrys Evans continually denied knowing anything about Serafina and the silver tabby and, eventually, Blake believed him. The man had no reason to keep their whereabouts a secret. He wasn't going to be able to sell them where he was going, and he confessed on the spot to selling a load of other animals. Blake was still no nearer to finding out what had become of his cat.

Laura met him at the door, expectantly, her face dropping when he shook his head. "I've put up posters all around here. And I've posted a note through every door in the area, asking people to check their garages and sheds to make sure Serafina hadn't been accidentally locked in."

"Great," Blake sighed. "It's likely that's probably what's happened."

"Or she's been run over," Jeff said, pouring a glass of red wine for Will.

"Thanks Jeff, you're my rock," Will said, giving him an appalled look but taking the wine anyway.

"Well, you have to accept it as a possibility,"

Jeff said, with a shrug. "Apart from the missing cat, how has your day been?"

Blake gave Laura a sidelong glance. "I think the day has mostly been about my missing cat, Jeff. You wouldn't believe some people. I went to this guy's place, an old farm. It was disgusting and he had dogs and cats in tiny cages."

"Old man?"

"Yeah," Will said.

"Probably got all kinds of mental health problems, poor bugger," Jeff said. "Not really his fault."

"I wouldn't say that, Jeff. He's had numerous convictions for animal cruelty and keeps coming back for more."

"Isn't that the definition of madness? Doing the same thing time and again and expecting a different result."

"That may well be but the people I deal with who are cruel to animals are often cruel to humans too."

"Have you told your tarot woman about the van?" Laura asked.

Blake shook his head. "Not yet." He'd mentioned Gwen to Laura when he'd returned from his search that morning. The moment he'd mentioned the tarot cards, he'd felt foolish. Laura had been interested in what they revealed but

Blake dismissed them and said he couldn't remember what cards he'd drawn.

"I'll go and talk to her if you want," Jeff said, sounding sleazy and making Blake wince.

"Really, Jeff? You sound like Leslie Philips. You should have said, 'ding dong' just to complete the effect."

Laura looked puzzled. "Who's Leslie Philips?"

"And to think, I made you lasagne for dinner," Jeff said, pretending to look hurt.

"Thanks Jeff, and it's tea when you're up north," Will Blake muttered. He felt guilty about his feelings towards Jeff. His brother irritated him but he couldn't pin down why. It might have been because he was the apple of his mother's eye, despite Jeff's frequent cries for financial assistance. Blake didn't really resent the money; he earned plenty of his own but hated the idea of scrounging from family members. He'd lent Jeff money himself. Maybe it was a combination of Jeff's exalted position in his parents' eyes and the infantile way he squandered cash that did it. Or maybe it was the insensitivity with which he used people. He knew that Jeff would quite cheerfully go round and try and get into Gwen's bed. Jeff had no shame.

They ate in silence at first. Blake tried to make some positive noises about the food but they stuck in his throat. At last, Jeff said, "So tell me about Joshua Gambles, then."

Blake spluttered, almost spraying red wine all over his brother. "Gambles?" Blake said, dapping his chin with a napkin Jeff had found for him. "He's a murderous psychopath, fascinated by himself and also has a history of cruelty to animals as I recall."

"Fascinating."

"No not fascinating, Jeff, horrible. If you'd seen what he did to those people. Laura knows first hand what he's like."

Laura nodded. She'd been attacked by Gambles and had managed to fight him off but it had left her shaken. "Yeah, he's a monster, Jeff."

Jeff took a gulp of his wine. "But what makes a person like that tick?"

"He wanted to be infamous. Notorious, even. And he took four people's lives just to get into the papers."

"We all want fame, though, don't we, Will?"

"No," Blake muttered. "Not all of us. I had a brief taste and it did me no good at all. In fact, if I hadn't been on the Searchlight programme, Gambles would never have fixated on me."

"He'd have found another focus, though, surely," Jeff said.

"Anyway, let's talk about something else,"

Laura said, hoping to diffuse the tension. "What's your next book about, Jeff?"

Jeff gave an enigmatic smile. "I couldn't possibly say. It would ruin the magic if I told you. Seriously, I can never talk about my work while I'm writing. It breaks the spell."

"Breaks the spell," Will snorted. "What? Are you a wizard now, Jeff?"

Jeff's face fell. "I don't see anything to laugh at, Will. You tell me about your latest case."

"No. It's confidential. I'm not allowed to."

"That's not why you keep schtum, though is it, big brother? You think if you talk about it, you'll jinx the case. You won't catch the bad guy or solve the crime or whatever. We all believe in a bit of magic, Will."

Blake shrugged. He felt needled because Jeff was right. "The difference is, Jeff, nobody cares if you never write a book again. Whereas if I don't solve a case, somebody gets away with murder, or even worse, dies. Anyway, I'd better go and tell Gwen the bad news." He stood up and stalked out of the room.

*****

"At least you tried," Gwen said, giving Blake a hug of thanks after he'd apologised for not having found her silver tabby. She wore a silk dressing gown and a flowered scarf held her long,

147

flowing hair back.

"Which still leaves me wondering where both cats are. I mean, logically, if they both went missing on the same night, it seems unlikely that they both had an accident of some kind."

"You still think someone took them?"

"I think they might be trapped in some-body's garage or shed. Maybe they were fighting and ended up somewhere they couldn't escape from."

"Or maybe they found food and didn't notice when a door closed."

Blake nodded. "Serafina's a devil for food. She will eat until she bursts."

"An angelic name for a cat," Gwen said.

"So I believe," Blake said. "My mother named her."

"The other William Blake, the poet, used to see angels in the trees," Gwen said. "And devils on his staircase."

Blake shuffled on the doorstep uncomfortably. "Yeah he also did a spot of naked gardening, I'm led to believe."

"Maybe you should try it, sometime," Gwen said, arching one eyebrow. "Could be liberating."

Blake could feel himself blushing. "I think I'll pass on that, to be honest. Let me know if anyone contacts you. Have you put any letters out around the area?"

"No," Gwen said. "I hadn't thought of that. I'll find some paper. I've been out and about, dowsing with hazel rods but found nothing, sadly."

"Dowsing? Isn't that what people do to find water?"

Gwen's eyes glowed. "You can dowse for anything, Mr Blake if you have the gift."

"Right," Blake said. "Goodnight, then." He turned and walked back up the road, but he could feel Gwen's eyes on his back all the way.

*****

Andrew Kinnear was going to be in trouble with Chris again, but he felt like he was onto something. Gary Stott had said that nobody else was with Trevor and him on the Sunday night, but Kinnear was sure he was lying. And a sudden thought had struck him as he sat in the car outside Trevor's flat, but he knew that there was no point going back and asking. He'd get no more sense from Gary Stott tonight. The young man had clammed up and wasn't about to start blabbing.

Instead, Kinnear got his mobile out and brought up the YouTube film of Trevor getting punched. He knew which pub it was because it said in the description: 'Pervy medium gets punched in the nose and then slapped by girl-friend at the Connaught Arms. LOL.'

According to Google Maps, the Connaught Arms was just down the road. Kinnear was certain that someone would remember that night and may know who the girl was. Trevor seemed to have a limited circle of friends. If he could find the girl, maybe she could shed more light on what he was like. It might help, or it might just add to the list of people who wanted to harm Trevor. Not that it needed lengthening, there seemed to be few people who had a good word for him. After checking the exact location of the pub, Kinnear started the car and headed up the road.

There was nothing particularly special about the Connaught Arms; it was a typical pub on the edge of town, struggling to keep afloat. Huge TV screens clung to every wall showing the current football match playing out on Sky Sports. Menus offered cheap food during the week, and even cheaper Sunday dinners. The pub had accumulated the trappings of various makeovers through the decades and now they seemed to compete with each other; rustic barstools upholstered in chintz fabric clashed with laminate flooring and chrome rails along the bar. Music merged with the sports commentary and Kinnear wondered how anyone found this a pleasant atmosphere. Enough people seemed to, though.

The bar was lined with young men swilling pints of lager. Older couples took to the dark oak tables in nooks and crannies around the edge of the pub.

Kinnear made his way to the bar and asked for the manager. A young man with a skinhead haircut and black spacer earrings came over. "Charlie," he said, shaking Kinnear's hand. "What can I do for you?"

"I wondered if you could give me a bit of background about this incident," Kinnear said, showing Charlie the YouTube clip.

Charlie's face darkened. "Mate, I told the little prick that was on him. He's not made a complaint, has he?"

"No," Kinnear said. "So did Trevor come back to you about this?"

Charlie rolled his eyes. "God, yeah. He tried to get me to pay him compensation. He said he'd been assaulted in my pub so it was my fault."

"And you told him to…"

"Do one. Yeah. He brought that on himself. Trevor wasn't a very good medium, to be honest. I had doubts about letting him do an evening, but he pestered me so much I agreed just to shut him up. Then he got a bent nose for his troubles. I barred the guy that hit him. Don't want any trouble here."

"What about the girl who slapped him? Do you know who she is?"

"That was his girlfriend, Zoe," Charlie said and grinned. "She wasn't at all happy. I can tell you."

"Zoe? Do you know her surname?"

"Yeah. Plumb. Zoe Plumb."

*****

Kath Cryer's phone kept ringing. She looked at it the first time, saw it was Kinnear and killed the call. Theo looked terrible and was shivering as he leaned heavily on her. A nurse hurried past and Kath grabbed her, almost letting Theo topple over. "I'm sorry but could we see a doctor? My boyfriend is slipping into unconsciousness and I'm really worried about him."

The nurse looked alarmed and nodded. "I'll get someone," she said and hurried away. Kath watched her disappear from the waiting room and into the A&E ward. She'd been here many times herself, in a professional capacity, collecting drunks and drug addicts in the past. The phone rang again. This time she answered it.

"Hi Andrew, not a great time right now."

"Zoe Plumb," Kinnear said.

"Yeah, the girl who handed in Long's camcorder. What about her?"

"She's Trevor Long's girlfriend."

"What? I knew there was something dodgy about her."

"I'm bringing her in tomorrow. Can you be there, ma'am? I'd love you to give her a grilling."

Kath looked at Theo who was sliding off the plastic seat. "Yeah," she said. "I'll do my best. I'm with Theo at A&E right now, he's really not well."

"Oh no, Kath. I'm sorry. What's up with him?"

But before Kath could answer, Theo slid onto the floor, curling up and shaking as he went into a seizure.

CHAPTER 20

DCI Matty Cavanagh dearly wished there was some way he could wipe the smile off Josh Gambles' face but he couldn't think of anything that might do it. The man was right where he wanted to be; everything he'd done had led him to this point. Gambles had become a celebrity apparently worthy of miles of newsprint. Already there were blogs springing up speculating on his state of mind and revelling in any detail of the murders that might inevitably leak out. Gambles knew this, Cavanagh was certain; he also knew that the CPS would want to build a watertight case and, even though Gambles was clearly guilty, any slip up that lessened his sentence or created a loophole would be disastrous. By not cooperating, Gambles was drawing out the anticipation. By the time the whole thing came to court, there'd be a feeding frenzy amongst the journalists and the psychopath would be world famous.

So here they were again in a tired interview room with plastic beakers of lukewarm coffee and a few cardboard biscuits.

"Kyle Quinlan," Cavanagh said. "You knew him in prison."

Gambles raised one eyebrow and clapped his hands. "Bravo, detective."

"He lived a life of crime, in and out of trouble with the law until 2014 and then vanished. So what happened to him, Mr Gambles? Are you saying he's another of your victims?"

"Oh dear," Gambles said, looking disappointed. "I thought you were onto something. Honestly, I'm not here to spoon feed you. You're meant to be detectives. You find things out."

Cavanagh scratched his head and glanced at Bobby Dirkin who sat impassively next to him, writing everything down, despite the fact that they were recording the interview. Bobby had a perfect poker face but Cavanagh knew that he'd relish giving Gambles a good kicking right now. "I'm sorry we aren't mind readers, Mr Gambles," Cavanagh said. "And, contrary to popular belief, we don't spy on everyone…"

"Oh I know that," Gambles said, laughing. "Otherwise you'd have caught me months ago. Probably before I'd even got started. I'll try and help you but, I'll be honest, even I'm speculating about some of this. I first met Kyle Quinlan when we were kids. I don't know what he'd done but I'd just blinded a kid in high school. Stuck a pencil in his eye. Didn't blind him literally but he's probably partially sighted to this day. Maybe I did him a favour; he'll have a blue badge and benefits…"

"Yeah, let's just stick to the story, Gambles," Cavanagh said. "I don't want any of your wry observations about life the universe and the price of chips."

"As you wish," Gambles said. "Anyway, Kyle Quinlan stopped me from getting killed. I must have said or done something to the meanest kid in that secure unit, I don't know. One minute I was eating my dinner, the next, I was on the floor having the proverbial kicked out of me. Then Kyle Quinlan was there, fists and feet flying. I don't know why he joined in; maybe he didn't like bullies or maybe he wanted to show who was top dog. We ruled the roost after that and, whenever we met up in prison again, we had each other's backs."

"Touching," Cavanagh said. "Your knight in shining armour. So what happened to him?"

Gambles shrugged. "We'd meet up every now and then on the outside when we could but ours was a loose affiliation based on mutual need. Neither of us needed friendship. I heard he'd settled down, found a woman. I thought nothing of it but then another of his acquaintances got in touch with me, asking if I knew where he was. They told me he'd vanished off the face of the earth."

"So, you did a little digging yourself?"

"Nope. I was curious, to be honest, but by that time, I was too busy plotting my grand schemes to bother with poor Kyle…"

"*Poor* Kyle?" Cavanagh said.

"Let's just say I've done some research since and I suspect something terrible has befallen him."

"What exactly?"

Gambles sighed. "I don't know, do I? Honestly. What's the point of having a dog and barking yourself? You're the coppers. Go and find out."

"You think we'd go on a wild goose chase on your word?"

"You already have. And it's not a wild goose chase," Gambles said. "Do whatever it is you do. Don't you track down last known associates and previous employers, that kind of thing? I heard he got married. You could check that."

Cavanagh looked at Bobby Dirkin, who shook his head.

"I tell you what, Gambles," Cavanagh said. "If I do what you ask, and look into Quinlan's whereabouts…"

"His employer, wife, yes," Gambles said.

Cavanagh nodded. "Right. If I do that, will you cooperate with us and tell us everything about what you did and why?"

"Full cooperation," Gambles said. "I'll confess to everything. But I suspect your investigation might go in some interesting directions."

*****

Zoe Plumb sat, dabbing her eyes with tissue and sniffing. Kinnear was only human; he didn't like making people cry. His main regret, though, was that DI Cryer wasn't there to turn the thumb screws on her. Kinnear knew he wasn't as good at playing tough.

"You say you found the camcorder on Bidston Hill without realising that it was Trevor Long's. Didn't it even cross your mind once that it could be his?"

"I don't know. I haven't got a running inventory of his belongings, have I?"

"No, but it's quite a machine. There aren't hundreds of them kicking around Bidston. It's a model used by professionals and you knew Trevor was always filming around the Hill. Surely you could have put two and two together."

"It was early in the morning and I was walking the dog."

"Yeah, I spoke to DI Cryer about that and she thought that was most unusual."

Zoe shrugged. "I can't help that, can I?"

"Oh come, on, Zoe. You cross town to walk

158

your neighbour's dog for the first time in ages and stumble across a high-end camcorder that just happens to belong to your boyfriend..."

"Ex-boyfriend. Trevor and I haven't seen each other for months."

"Even so. It all sounds a bit far-fetched."

Zoe Plumb narrowed her eyes. "It's a small town. What is it I'm meant to have done, exactly?"

"We're just trying to understand what happened to Trevor, that's all Zoe and, to be blunt, you've been lying to us."

"No I haven't."

Kinnear shook his head and opened a file. "According to DI Cryer's notes, you denied knowing Trevor Long and said, 'who is he?' when you were asked. Why did you do that?"

Zoe's face hardened. "If you knew Trevor Long, you'd deny any knowledge of him. The man's a walking disaster area. Always putting his foot in it, always upsetting people and always getting into trouble."

"So much so that you'd deny any knowledge of him to an officer of the law?"

"Yeah."

"You said you went to an Italian Restaurant with friends. Can we have some names and addresses?"

"Of course you can. I was with Caroline Maston, Sally Martin, Bev Campbell…"

Kinnear looked up from his notepad. "Bev Campbell? Can I have her address, please?"

"South Parade, West Kirby, why? Look what's going on? Has something happened to Trevor?"

Kinnear weighed-up how much to tell her, wondering if the shock might loosen her tongue. "Earlier in the week, we found Trevor's coat soaked in his blood. A large quantity of blood but no body. We're assuming that Trevor is dead and treating that death as suspicious. And, to my mind, you're behaving suspiciously, too, Ms Plumb. So, shall we start again?"

*****

Blake sat at his desk and frowned at the computer screen. Manikas stood to his left, leaning on the desktop, looking crestfallen. Alex had hurried in with news of his conversation with Thor Magnussen and the chance to go to a gathering that night.

"Honestly, Alex, what did you expect me to say?" Blake said. "It's pretty basic stuff. You can't just phone a suspect up and pretend to be someone else. It's entrapment. Imagine the fun Harry Thorpe would have with that!"

"But he said that they'd 'sorted' Trevor Long

for making those videos."

"Yes, but if pushed, our friend Thor would just say they'd had a word with him or even roughed him up. It doesn't amount to an admission of murder. Frankly, I'm wondering what's got into you. You're normally more level-headed about these things."

"Thor trusts me, sir," Manikas said. "He was really keen to show off. It'll be a great chance to gather information about Trevor Long."

"It might, but any information or evidence you gathered would be inadmissible in court. Any defence lawyer would ride a coach and horses through a case built on you casually turning up to a Sons of Sol meeting pretending to be an accountant from your dad's firm. From what I've seen, Thor Magnussen is little more than an overgrown teenager, but that doesn't make him any less unpredictable and it doesn't mean he isn't a threat. Harry Thorpe managed to get DI Clements sacked for his role in trying to fit Thorpe up. Thorpe took the force to court. What part of all that works with your current plan? Or are you looking for a new career?"

"Sorry sir, I just thought..." Manikas began.

"Stay within procedure, Alex," Blake said. "Vikki Chinn is speaking to a contact who might have info on Trevor's debt situation. Go and assist her. It might keep you out of trouble." Manikas looked like a kid who'd had his favourite teddy bear taken off him. Blake watched as Alex left the office and wondered if Thor Magnussen wasn't the only overgrown teenager in these parts. He just hoped Manikas had listened or there'd be Hell to pay.

CHAPTER 21

Detective Sergeant Chinn leaned against the back door of the Golden Sunrise not far from Trevor's flat. This takeaway was in a row of shops at the intersection of two roads. They were old and brick built. The smells of cooking and the voices calling food orders to each other made her suddenly nostalgic for her parents' restaurant. They'd sold up and retired now and Vikki had never had any desire to follow the family tradition. But just then, she missed the hustle and bustle. She could see through to the front of the shop where people queued for fish and chips, kebabs, fried rice, anything that meant they didn't have to cook on a Friday evening. She'd left Manikas stewing in the car. The man hadn't stopped grumbling about Blake 'cramping his style' over some suggestion Alex had made about the investigation of Thor Magnussen. Vikki had only been half listening but whatever Alex had suggested it didn't sound entirely sensible. Vikki was surprised, Alex was normally such a reserved character who didn't go in for flights of fancy. Right now, she had more important things to think about; sweet talking her informant for one.

Lee Wan leaned against the back wall of the

shop, flicking cigarette ash into the grid. The back of the shop was closed in by a small walled yard, with a disused outside toilet in the corner. Huge wheelie bins bursting with paper and smelling of rotten food dominated the tiny space. "Haven't seen you for a while, Vikki," Lee said, ruffling his fingers through his thick, black hair.

"Probably a good thing, that," Vikki said, raising one eyebrow. "You been keeping out of trouble?"

He was a young man; good looking with a cheeky smile that could get him anything. Or almost anything, and that was the trouble because, more often than not, Lee wanted everything. His madcap get-rich-quick schemes had landed him in trouble more than once and Vikki had come to his rescue. Which meant that he owed her. The great thing about Lee owing her was that he didn't mind paying the debt in local knowledge and gossip.

Lee rolled his eyes and backheeled the wall gently. "I don't get chance to get into trouble," he sighed. "My dad is making me work like a dog. Anyway, I need to get back or he'll be onto me for smoking. What do you want?"

"What do you know about Trevor Long?"

Lee smirked. "He's a professional dipstick. Have you seen those crap videos he makes?" Lee wobbled his fingers in the air and made a Twilight Zone noise. "Beware the flesh-eating rats of Wallasey sewers…"

Vikki couldn't help laughing and reminded herself that Lee was a master of charisma and charm. "He's the one."

"He's gone missing hasn't he? Left a puddle of blood behind but no body. Weird. But then it would be with X-Files Trevor, wouldn't it?"

"Any ideas?"

Lee glanced back into the chippy and then leaned towards Vikki, beckoning her to come closer. Vikki leaned in. "Aliens," he said and fell back against the wall, laughing loudly.

Vikki folded her arms. "Very funny," she said. "And there's me thinking you had your finger on the pulse of the underworld around here. Clearly not. Maybe Mr Lee Wan has spent all his time frying fish and doesn't have his ear to the ground anymore."

Lee stopped laughing and frowned. Vikki knew his weak spot, his ego. He thought of himself as a street warrior, a hustler who knew everything that went on and was always one step ahead. Any doubts about his street cred were like a dagger to his heart. "I heard something," he said, airily. "He owed money bigtime."

"I'd heard that too," Vikki said, shrugging to

show she was unimpressed. "Who did he owe money to, that's what I don't know."

Lee Wan gave a secretive smile. "There's only one person stupid enough to lend Trevor Long money, and that's Emilio Ogden. He hangs around Winston's up in Hoylake just waiting to lend money to the desperate and self-destructive. Drives a ridiculous, pimped up Fiat Punto. I heard he lent Trevor a rather tidy stash."

*****

Blake had made himself cheese sandwiches, but the temptation was to head into town for lunch and find some comfort food; the greasier the better. He stared at the limp brown slices that clung to the fluorescent orange slab of plastic. It was meant to be a healthy option, but he wasn't convinced. If Jeff was cooking every night, Blake suspected his waistline might start expanding. As much as he resented Jeff's presence, the man could cook.

And why the hell was Blake so concerned about that cat? The thing could look after itself. Anyone daft enough to take it in would be bringing it back soon enough. That's what he told himself, anyway. Another truth was that he couldn't bear for something else he cared about to just wander out of his life, never to be seen again.

Cavanagh popped his head round the door, breaking Blake's train of thought. "Hi, Matty.

How did you get on with Gambles?"

"Don't talk to me about that streak of piss," Cavanagh said. "Leading me a merry dance over this Kyle Quinlan character. If I find him, then he'll talk to us. I wonder if it's worth pandering to him, to be honest."

"You'll have Bobby Dirkin onto it, won't you?" Blake said, pulling Cavanagh's leg gently. "You just have to sit back and file your nails."

Cavanagh snorted. "Yeah, right. Gambles gets under your skin, doesn't he? I mean, I've met some creepy bastards in my time, but he takes the biscuit."

"Takes it, cuts its throat and buries it under your floorboards, mate," Will agreed. "Be careful doing whatever he wants. Chances are, you'll find Quinlan, only for Gambles to bring up another demand or condition."

"Yeah. I'm gonna have a look into his last employer and see where it goes from that but I'm not getting bogged down. If Quinlan is pushing up the daisies somewhere, someone else can dig him up."

"So, was there anything else?" Blake said. Cavanagh was a bit of an office wanderer, treating work as part of his social life. He didn't have any ties or responsibilities so he could burn the midnight oil and spend the day nattering.

Cavanagh clicked his fingers. "Oh, yeah. I just wondered; have you got a double, Blakey?"

"A double? No. Why?"

"It's just that I was coming out of the prison today, after seeing Gambles and there was this guy who looked the spit of you."

Blake frowned, fighting the sudden sense of unease that had gripped him. "Really? Like a carbon copy?"

Cavanagh grinned. "Nah, more like you from an alternate universe where you'd become a Geography teacher and never worked-out. Bit of a goatee beard... you okay, Will?"

Blake swallowed down the oath that nearly burst from his lips. "Yeah, fine," he said. "Weird, eh?"

"I thought it was you for a second. You know when you almost shout out to someone and then realise it isn't them? Ah well. Better get on."

Cavanagh vanished out of sight and Blake jumped up, dragging his jacket off the back of his seat. He needed to get home and quickly.

*****

For some reason, Alex Manikas was reluctant to come into Winston's Betting shop, which puzzled Vikki. "What if Thor's there? He might recognise my voice. It's better if he doesn't see me, too."

"What are you on about, Alex?" Vikki had snorted. "Is this still your undercover idea. Get that right out of your head, mate. The boss said no."

"I know, I know. I just think if he clocks the whole team, then we'll never have any covert advantage, will we?"

Vikki pulled a face. "Covert advantage? What d'you think this is Mission Impossible? Get your arse out of the car, Tom Cruise and follow me."

At one point, Winston's Bookmakers would have reeked of smoke as well as quiet desperation and disappointment. To Chinn, there was something a bit sad about all these men putting their cash on other people's glory in the hopes of winning a little for themselves. She knew plenty of people in her family who enjoyed a flutter. 'If you don't gamble, you don't know how lucky you are,' as her uncle was always saying. Mind you he lost his business and was always looking over his shoulder. Vikki's father had always been very anti-gambling and she had taken her lead from him. Looking around now, she felt vindicated.

Emilio Ogden was a shaven-headed stick insect. He had huge eyes and wingnut ears and was crouched at the back of the shop, sitting on a tall stool, watching a screen. It was clear that he was as involved in the race on the TV as any of the other punters. Thor Magnussen was nowhere to be seen which Alex seemed pleased about. Vikki wasn't bothered; she wanted to focus on Emilio.

There were a few glances as she walked across the room but nobody made any comments. "Emilio Ogden?" she said, pulling out her warrant card. "DS Vikki Chinn. Can I ask you a few questions?"

Ogden leapt up and threw his handful of betting slips in Vikki's face. He barged past, knocking her into Alex who stumbled backwards, taking her with him. Vikki rolled her eyes and started up after him as he crashed through the door into the street. People outside yelled and Vikki heard a car horn blare. The daylight dazzled her for a second and she paused, getting accustomed to it before scanning the street.

Across the road, Ogden was dodging between the shoppers and running towards a bus that was about to pull away. Vikki could hear Alex panting behind her as she sprinted diagonally across the road, skipping round a van that screeched to a halt. Ogden was tall, with a long stride but he lacked any fitness. Vikki trained in the gym and closed on him quickly. She intercepted Ogden just as he got to the back of the bus, putting a hand on his arm.

"I just need to talk to you," she said.

Ogden swung a fist at her but only managed to

punch the back of the bus. He gave a squeak of pain and stuffed his fist under his arm, grimacing in pain.

"Fine," Vikki snapped, swinging the man's arm up behind his back and pressing him against the bus. "Emilio Ogden, I'm arresting you for assaulting a police officer. You do not have to say anything but, it may harm your defence if you do not mention when questioned something which you later rely on in court. Anything you do say may be given in evidence. Do you understand?"

"You got him," Alex gasped as he caught up with them.

Unfortunately, the bus driver was blissfully unaware of the scuffle going on behind him and pulled off. Ogden pitched forward, with Vikki right behind him. He landed heavily with a grunt and lay still as Vikki wrapped the cuff round his wrists. "Honestly," she panted, "all I wanted to do was to talk to you. Why d'you have to make things so complicated?"

CHAPTER 22

Rock Lodge was empty when Blake arrived home. There was no sign of Serafina, Jeff or Laura and the house felt empty in a way it hadn't for some time. Blake made himself a cup of tea and went out into the front garden.

Across the river, he could see the suburbs of Liverpool spread along the far shore and, higher up the river, the Anglican Cathedral and the Beacon were visible. The more Blake thought about it, the more he wondered if he really wanted to sell up and move. He wasn't rooted here; he'd grown up further down the coast in a small village called Eastham. This was the last place his parents had settled and it brought him bitter memories but somehow, he felt connected to them in this house.

He walked down the drive to the old promenade and glanced left and right, half expecting Serafina to leap out of the bushes and come stalking up to him. Instead, a taxi pulled up and Jeff climbed out. His face fell when he saw Blake waiting at the gate and he turned back to the taxi driver, making a play of paying him and getting a receipt.

"Been busy?" Blake said, as Jeff sauntered up to

him.

"Just a bit of research in town," Jeff said, with a shrug. He held up a bag. "Did a spot of shopping, too."

Blake followed him back up the drive and into the house. "A friend of mine asked if I had a double, today," he said as Jeff placed his bag down. "He saw someone who had a striking resemblance to me at the prison he was visiting."

"I always said you should be behind bars," Jeff said, with a feeble grin.

"Yeah, this person was a bit thinner than me with a goatee beard, Jeff," Blake said. "Do you want to tell me what you were up to. I'm praying it's not what I think it is."

Jeff reddened. "I don't see that it's any of your business what I'm working on."

"You're writing Josh Gambles' life story, aren't you?"

"I'm not beholden to you..."

"That's why you were quizzing me about Gambles last night," Blake said. "You've been to see him today. How is that even possible?"

Jeff shrugged. "He's allowed up to seven visits per week while he's on remand..."

"I didn't mean that, I mean how can you sit in the same room as that man, when you know what he's done."

"How can you?" Jeff said.

"It's my bloody job!"

Jeff gave him a look that was meant to say, 'it's my job too.'

"No," Blake said. "You don't *have* to interview him. You could write a book about any number of things. I've backed away from the case because it's too close to me. He killed a man I know, Jeff, a friend." Gambles had murdered TV personality Ross Armitage a member of the Searchlight cast.

"All the better for me to get to understand him then," Jeff said. "Gambles gives me the low down about his motivations and we all get to find out why he committed those terrible murders."

"It just trips off the tongue for you, doesn't it Jeff? 'Those terrible murders,' like they were unfortunate accidents. If you'd been there, seen those bodies, smelt the decay. Do you know that smell, Jeff? It's like a sewer smell, only much more gamey, iron and rottenness in it too. It crawls down your throat like a living thing. I wake up thinking I can smell it sometimes. Gambles is a monster. Stop seeing him."

A disturbing light glowed in Jeff's eyes. "Don't you see? Insights like that would make this a ground-breaking book. The two sides of the story. The gritty detail…"

"Stop!" Blake snapped. "There are no two sides. Just the fact that Gambles took four innocent lives, and left numerous other people traumatised. Good, blameless people, Jeff. They'll never get over what they went through. You can't write a book that glorifies or even makes a monster out of Gambles. Either way, he wins."

"How can I not write this? I'm the only person who can write it."

"I didn't want to do this, Jeff but you don't know the half of what went on in that case or the real reason I can't be involved. Gambles was probably the last person to see Mum alive. He had her wedding and engagement ring in his pocket when he was arrested."

There were many ways Blake expected Jeff to respond, shock or disbelief, for instance, but Jeff's words pulled the rug from under his feet.

"I know," Jeff said, looking Blake squarely in the eye. "I know."

*****

The old woman leaned in close and leered at Kath Cryer. Kath could feel her closeness, smell her rancid breath, and see her crooked, yellow teeth. "Bad luck dog you. Ill will hound you. Ill health bite you!" The woman hissed, filling Kath's vision. "Bad luck dog you. Ill will hound you. Ill health bite you!"

"No," Kath pushed at the old woman, feeling an unusual strength in the old crone's shoulders. "Leave me alone! No!"

"Ms Cryer," said a voice that she half recognised, but the old woman's words echoed over it. "Ms Cryer, you're having a bad dream."

Kath snapped her eyes open. She was in a crowded waiting room, twenty-five pairs of eyes staring at her. She reddened and blinked around her. A nurse had hold of her shoulder and Kath was gripping her arm. Her chin felt wet and she absentmindedly wiped the slobber away from the corner of her mouth with the back of her hand. "God!" she said. "I'm sorry. I was dead to the world. Had a bad dream."

The nurse smiled and handed her a fresh tissue from her pocket. "Don't worry, Ms Cryer," she said. "Theo is asleep now. We've had some tests back but we can rule out sepsis."

Kath nodded. She felt punch drunk. She'd followed Theo round the hospital all day as he went through test after test: lumbar punctures, blood tests, scans and so on. "Can I see him?" She said, staggering to her feet.

"Are you okay?" the nurse said, steadying her.

"Yeah, just knackered," she said straightening out and rubbing her throbbing head. "Where is he?"

The nurse led her through the busy hospital corridors. "We've settled him down in a side room."

They walked on and Kath glanced into a side ward, flinching when she saw a mottled arm and a spray of white hair. An old lady lay in the bed nearest the door, she raised a hand and smiled. Kath gave a brittle smile back and hurried on.

"It might be best not to go in," the nurse said at the door. "He's had a long day."

Kath peered in through the window. Theo lay on his back, drips snaking into his arm and pillows propping him up. Monitors flashed but he was oblivious. "God, I wish I could just go in and have a snooze myself."

"Are you sure you're okay?" the nurse asked again.

Kath sighed. "Do you believe in curses?"

The nurse looked puzzled. "Not really, no. Why?"

"No reason," Kath said. "It's just a water infection, that's all."

"You've been staggering around the hospital all day feeling terrible?"

Kath shrugged. "You just do, don't you? Like I spent most of last week sitting in a patrol car with no toilet in sight. You need a cast iron bladder for some jobs."

The nurse gave a sigh of sympathy. "Tell me about it. Come with me," she said and marched up the corridor so fast that Kath had trouble keeping up with her. Kath followed her through the hospital again until they came to the reception desk of an out of hours clinic. The nurse leaned over to the receptionist and whispered something. The receptionist nodded and typed a few details into the computer. Then the nurse turned back to Kath. "You're next to see the doctor. He'll give you some antibiotics. Hopefully, that'll clear things up."

Forty minutes later, Kath came out of the clinic with a prescription for antibiotics. Even though she hadn't actually got the medicine or taken any, she felt a bit better already. Then she saw the van parked across the back end of her car. "You've got to be joking," she muttered.

*****

If Emilio Ogden was worried about being in the Birkenhead custody suite, he didn't show it. A solicitor had turned up after one phone call and now he sat, slouched in his chair facing DS Vikki Chinn and DC Alex Manikas.

"Can you explain why you ran away from me earlier on today, Emilio?" Vikki said.

"Police brutality, isn't it? I thought you was

goin' to hit me," Emilio said, grinning over at his solicitor who gave him a pained look back which screamed, 'you don't have to say anything.'

"Have you been hit by the police before, Emilio?"

Ogden shuffled in his seat. "No but I seen it on telly, didn't I?"

"Well," Vikki said. "Now I can ask you the questions I wanted to ask you back at the betting shop, can't I?"

"No comment," Ogden said, breaking into a broad, gormless grin.

"Do you know Trevor Long, Emilio?"

"Who?"

"Trevor Long. You know, he's got a YouTube channel about ghosts and aliens. You must have heard of him; he's a local celebrity."

"Oh, him. Yeah. What about him?"

"Know him well?" Manikas said, leaning forward.

"Not really."

"You do know him, though? You've met him."

Ogden glanced at his brief who rolled his eyes.

"Yeah," Ogden said, misinterpreting his solicitor's implied advice.

"How did you meet him?"

Ogden shrugged. "He was in the betting shop one day, that's all."

Vikki frowned. "He travelled all the way from Birkenhead to place a bet in Hoylake? Seems a bit odd to me."

"Yeah. Funny, isn't it what brings people into that shop?"

The solicitor winced as if to say, 'what part of 'don't say a word,' didn't you understand?'

"Yeah," Manikas said. "Hilarious."

"You might not be aware, Mr Ogden but Trevor Long went missing on Sunday night and a lot of his blood was found splashed around Flaybrick Hill cemetery the next morning."

Ogden looked like he'd had a bucket of ice poured down his back. "S-so?" he stammered. "What's that got to do with me?"

"We understand that Trevor borrowed a significant amount of money from you several months ago and hadn't paid it back."

"Who told you that?"

"It doesn't matter where we got that information from. What interests us is where you get money to lend out in the first place and what you do to clients who don't pay their debts."

"You think I killed him because he owed me money?" Ogden said, blinking in disbelief.

Manikas picked up a file. "You've got form, Emilio, threatening behaviour, extracting money with menaces. It would be right up your street."

"Except, you put your finger on it right away, didn't you? Where would I get that kind of money? I'm skint."

"That's not what we've heard, Emilio. We've heard you're the go-to man for cash handouts. As long as you can pay the interest."

"Behave, I couldn't even spell interest, let alone work it out."

Vikki sighed and looked at Manikas. "Looks like we're going to have to charge him with murder, then, DC Manikas. Turn his home over, take his car in for checking, that kind of thing..."

"My car?" Emilio Ogden said in a low voice. "I've just had the skirts done."

"Probably have to pull it apart. Forensics make a hell of a mess," Manikas said, pulling a long face. "Could be cash stuffed in the wings or the ceiling. Might be drugs in there too."

Ogden scratched his chin. "Can I have a moment with my legal guy?"

CHAPTER 23

Jeff's case stood in the hall. Blake had packed it for him. Now Blake stood, holding the front door open, while Jeff leaned against the stair bannister, arms folded. Laura watched the pair of them in utter disbelief.

"Honestly, I've just spent an afternoon with a two-year-old spaniel with more sense than you two and it spends its day chewing electricity cables," she said. "What is going on?"

"Jeff is just leaving," Blake said. "He's no longer welcome in this house."

"Will thinks he can throw me out but actually, the house is as much mine as his. So he can't throw me out and I'm not going."

"Then you're going to be standing in the hall for the duration of your stay, Jeff, because I won't let you go any further."

"What are you going to do? Beat me up? Imagine explaining that to your boss in the morning, DCI Will Blake. Or would you make it look like an accident?"

"Will one of you just explain what's going on?"

"He's Josh Gambles' official biographer, Laura," Blake said. "Took it upon himself to visit the twisted bastard today, just to get started. Preliminary notes, I dare say. Tell me Jeff, are you going to include Gambles watching Mum die and then hiding her body? Or maybe speculate about whether he actually killed her? Don't be thinking he will tell you anything except what he wants you to hear."

"Really?" Laura said. "Is that true?"

Jeff scowled at Will. "If I don't write it then somebody else will and who better to do the job than someone so close? Maybe, once I have his confidence then he'll reveal Mum's whereabouts. He swears that he didn't kill her."

"And that makes it okay does it?" Blake's voice was low and icy cold.

Laura put a hand on Jeff's arm. "Jeff, can't you see what Gambles is doing? Gambles is a manipulative mind-screwer. In the twinkling of an eye, he's managed to drive a wedge between you two and he isn't even here. If you think you're going to get anything out of him, then you're deluded. He'll lead you on down a path that will ruin you and everyone you love."

"He doesn't love anyone but himself," Blake muttered. "Doesn't think of anyone but himself."

"Is that so?" Jeff snapped. "And what have you done apart from mope around this house for the last two or three years? Have you noticed, Will, everyone leaves you, in the end. You've spent more time searching for that bloody cat than you ever did for Mum."

At that point Blake lunged, fist flying towards his younger brother.

*****

Emilio Ogden looked nervous and fidgety when Vikki Chinn and Alex Manikas returned to the interview room. His solicitor had obviously tried to put pressure on him to keep quiet, but the young man was too concerned about his car. Vikki thought back to Lee Wan's comment about Ogden not being too sharp and found herself agreeing.

"Look. I just arrange things. It's not my money..."

"What do you mean, you arrange things, Emilio?" Vikki said.

"People come into the shop, get a bit short of cash when they've lost money and come to me for a bit more cash."

"So if it's not yours, whose cash is it?" Manikas said, but he'd already guessed.

The solicitor shifted in his seat, trying to re-mind Ogden of the consequences of spilling the beans.

"It's all right for you," Ogden muttered at the solicitor. "It's not you that gets picked up by the feds, is it? I've had nothing but grief and now they're going to pull my car apart. It's not fair. I don't get paid enough for this crap."

"Whose money do you lend out then, Emilio?" Vikki said.

"It's Harry Thorpe isn't it? he bungs me a few thou' and I lend it out. Thor keeps the tally but if anyone comes looking for who lent the cash, it's me they find," he looked ruefully at the desktop. "It hasn't been a bed of roses, to be honest. I'm one of those fall guys, I think that's the word, isn't it?"

"So you're saying you lend money to punters at the betting shop on behalf of Harold Thorpe, the shop's owner?"

"Yeah, Thor's his son, isn't he? Doesn't want pretty boy Thor or Fabian, to use his proper name, to get rumbled, does he?"

"And if someone can't pay the money back?"

"They get a visit from those mates of Thor's – the ones who think they're Vikings..."

"The Sons of Sol?" Vikki said.

"Yeah," Ogden muttered. "I always thought Sol was a beer but it turns out it's something to do with the sun." He sniffed and wiped his nose. "Can I go, now? Are you gonna take my car?"

Vikki shook her head. "I don't think we need to impound your vehicle, Emilio. But you'll have to stay and make a written statement."

"God," Emilio groaned, like a grumpy teenager who'd just been given detention. "I hate writing stuff down."

Vikki glanced at Manikas who shook his head. Ogden obviously didn't realise how much information he'd given away. Whether it would give them enough for a warrant to investigate Thorpe's finances wasn't clear. In any case, that would take months. Alex smiled to himself. Surely it must have been Thor and his gang who killed Trevor and he knew just how to prove it.

*****

Blake hadn't expected to find himself lying on his back on the hall floor when he lunged for Jeff but that's where he was. At first, he thought Jeff had brought him down and he lay there blinking in disbelief. But it was Laura who loomed over him. He'd been on the receiving end of her right hook once, by accident, and that had shown him that she could handle herself, but she'd put him down like a professional.

"Will, keep calm," she said. "I'm sure Jeff didn't mean any of that. Did you Jeff?"

But Jeff's face still burned red. "Every bloody word," he spat. "D'you know your trouble, Will? You blame the world for your own faults. You see me as some kind of wastrel, drifting through life writing fanciful little stories that don't sell when really, I'm out there hustling every day. Teaching writing workshops to eager wanna-bees with no talent or inclination to put a modicum of effort in. They think they can buy everything. I'm proofreading terrible, terrible books that nobody should ever have to read. And you? Everything falls into your lap but you look at it as though it's a curse."

"Really?" Will groaned as the breath came back into his body. "That's what you think? At least I was here when Mum needed me..."

"Yeah, right, only because things had gone tits up with your own life. Where were you when they moved into this pile of crap? I helped them move, even though I'd advised them not to buy it. I knew it would be the death of Dad after his first minor heart attack... oh, you didn't know about them, did you?" Jeff stroked his beard theatrically. "Where were you, now? Oh yes, over in Manchester with your TV friends..."

"That's not fair."

"Isn't it? You see, all that time you were preening yourself on TV and Rosie was up in Scotland, bloody well 'finding herself,' I was here, by their side. You forgot that, though, didn't you? In your version of things, they were struggling with no help and you came to the rescue. Brave Sir Will! And you know what really sticks in my craw about all that? All the time I was taking

Dad to the hospital for his tests, who did they talk about? Whose name sprang to everyone's lips? Will Blake, that lovely lad of theirs on the TV, 'Oh, Mr Blake, you must be so proud.' And I'd stand there smiling and nodding along with Dad. It made me want to puke."

"It wasn't like that…"

"How the fuck would you know, Will? Barely a phone call in all that time. Oh yeah, you'd pop over for birthdays, Christmas and Easter but every now and then? One phone call would have helped. But you were too wrapped up in your own little world. D'you want to know the reason my last book stalled? I was up here helping Mum and Dad, just like I did all the time."

"I was here when they needed me…"

"Yeah and I wasn't. I had cancer, Will. Bloody breast cancer. I didn't even know blokes could get it. I thought I was a goner."

"Jeff… I didn't know…"

"No," Jeff said. "You never know, do you? You just wallow in your own self-pity, not realising that everyone else is coping with their own shit too." Jeff snatched up his case. "Thanks for packing for me, Will. On second thoughts, I wouldn't stay another second in this mausoleum. I will write Josh Gambles' book and maybe I'll find Mum before you do. Maybe I won't but I'm not going anywhere. I'll be around. I've let my flat out and the rent will easily cover my expenses here. Good luck finding the cat, Will. It's all you're good for."

Jeff turned and slammed the front door behind him.

*****

He might not have been a member of Mensa, but even Emilio Ogden didn't need it spelling out by his solicitor. Unfortunately for Emilio, his solicitor was paid for by Harold Thorpe, Thor Magnussen's dad. Everything he'd said in that interview would go straight back. Emilio had fucked up bigtime and needed to make himself scarce. Which is why he was driving down the Welsh Road and leaving the Wirral. It was Friday night and the inevitable tailback of caravans, cars and lorries had formed early. Emilio sat, twitching in the driving seat of his Fiat Punto, not listening to the music that thudded from the bass bins that filled the back shelf of the car. he just wanted to blot out any thoughts that might creep in. He was going to Towyn. Nobody would find him there.

Glancing in the wing mirror, he gave a whine of disappointment. A bike was drawing closer, its rider, hairy and built like a gorilla. Or a Viking warrior. Another pulled up on the passenger side and smiled into the car. Emilio couldn't see his eyes for the shades he wore. But it wasn't a nice smile.

CHAPTER 24

Once, when Alex Manikas was a teenager, he'd stolen a big bottle of Metaxa from his father's drinks cabinet. He'd done it because it was the only way to get invited to a house party being held by some of the coolest kids in his school. He remembered a feeling of guilt and a premonition of doom as he knocked on the front door of the cool kids' house. It turned out to be a really bad idea as the unconscious bodies and pools of vomit littering the lawn attested to by the end of the night.

That feeling of dread returned to him now as his taxi pulled up on a dark roadside somewhere in Thurstaston. The taxi driver looked back at him as he took the money. "You sure this is the right place? Only there's nothing but fields here."

"Yeah, thanks," Alex said, trying to sound confident. "Don't worry about the change."

The car drove off and Manikas looked at the instructions on his phone. There was a five-bar gate just a little along the fence which he had to climb over and then head across the field for the treeline.

Living in Liverpool, Alex wasn't really familiar with the area, so he'd read-up on it a little. Not far from this field was a huge sandstone outcrop and local beauty spot. The centrepiece of this heathland was Thor's Stone where most people thought the area got its name from. It seemed that this link to the thunder god might be wishful thinking. Magnussen had told Alex that his father owned some of the land next to the common and that was where the party was taking place.

Blake's words boomed in Alex's head as he trudged over the field, six pack of lager in hand. He shouldn't be here. He should have stayed at home with a few beers and the TV. This was a fool's errand and he'd been explicitly told not to come. If Blake found out, Alex would have his proverbials nailed to the front of Canning Place HQ. Alex stopped. He could back out now. Nobody would know. Magnussen, or whatever his name was wouldn't be particularly bothered. It made sense.

A flame flared across the field and a bonfire blazed into life. Dark silhouettes flitted through the light. Distant shouting drifted across the field. "Sod it," Alex muttered and strode towards the fire.

The hulking figure of Thor Magnussen sitting on a felled tree trunk filled one side of the fire. A girl with long blonde plaits, a tight leather jacket and leggings cuddled up close to him. Nobody else in the group quite had Thor's physique but they were all big lads with thick, long beards, partially shaven heads, and wearing leathers. Dotted amongst them were similarly dressed women, with long plaited hair and runic tattoos. The Viking biker look made Alex feel a little out of place in his hiking boots and North Face jacket. There must have been around fifteen Sons of Sol around the fire and a few daughters, too. They glared at Alex as he stepped into the circle of firelight.

"Alex!" Thor roared, jumping up and sending his girlfriend backwards over the tree trunk. "Brother! You came!" He rushed over and wrapped Alex in his thick arms. Alex was tall but not as bulky as Thor. "My friends. Meet Alex, another seeker of light and truth! The blood of the Spartans runs in his veins!"

Alex gave a self-conscious grin and a short wave. "Erm. Hi."

The assembled Vikings stood as one and raised their cans, mead horns and bottles. "Huzzah!" They all roared.

"Cheers," Alex said, raising the hand that held the six pack.

"Come and sit down," Thor said, returning to the tree trunk. "This is Hilda…"

"Sarah," the woman said, giving Alex a wave. "I'm Sarah."

Thor pursed his lips for a second. "Hilda's your Viking name. It means fighter…"

"It makes me sound like an old lady," Sarah said. "And it's silly."

"Enough!" Thor said. "Alex, tonight, you'll see some great warriors battling and competing for the Golden Flagon." He pointed at a sack and Alex could just see the handle of what looked like a trophy of some kind poking out.

"Right," Alex said. "You don't mind if I just watch, right?"

Thor gave him a crafty look. "You were a natural with the axe throwing, you know. You should have a go. You might win."

Alex gave a self-deprecating shrug. "I doubt it. Beginner's luck, I suspect."

"Nonsense! Who will challenge Alex Axe-bearer to a throwing competition?"

"I will!" A gruff voice said. A man who was as wide as he was tall, stepped up. His beard shone red in the firelight and a leather tunic stretched across his stomach.

"Bjorn Braveheart! May you prove a worthy opponent," Thor said.

"Really, I don't think…" Alex began but the group began chanting Alex's name. they led him into a thicket where a throwing gallery had been hastily erected. It was little more than three walls made from plaster board, but a human figure had been drawn on the far wall at the end of the gallery.

Alex was jostled to the entrance of the gallery and an axe was thrust into his hand. Some of the slaps on his back were a little too hard but he felt like a hero. Holding the hand axe at eye level, he took a single step forward and swung it at the target. The axe glinted in the firelight and buried itself in the head of the target with a satisfying thud. Equally satisfying were the cheers around him. Bjorn nodded in approval and picked up the next axe. He barely moved, just took one shuffling step and then the axe hurtled through the smoky air nestling itself beside Alex's. A roar went up and Alex clapped.

"Second axe!" Thor cried. Alex felt his heart thudding now. He was trying to stay detached and professional, but the excitement of the moment and his own competitiveness was getting to him. An image of Blake scowling across a desk at him on Monday flashed through his mind and the axe went wide, hitting the shoulder of the target. The crowd groaned. Bjorn's axe found its mark, sandwiching Alex's first one in the head. Bjorn gave Alex a grin and a gold tooth glinted.

"Best of three!" Thor declared, holding up a fist.

Bjorn nodded and Alex threw his final weapon. It whirled through the air and seemed to slow before smashing into the head section, sending Bjorn's axes clattering to the earth. The Sons of Sol gave a cheer.

Heaving his final axe, Bjorn took a step forward. He seemed off balance and stumbled as he threw. The axe hit the target somewhere in the groin area and everyone groaned.

Thor stepped into the gallery and grabbed Alex and Bjorn's wrists. "I declare it to be a draw!" He said, raising their arms. Everyone cheered and clapped. "Get the drinks!"

Alex's stomach lurched. "No, really," he said. "I've got a busy day tomorrow. Overtime. I'll need a clear head..."

"Relax," Thor said, passing him a can of low alcohol beer. "It's one of yours." He winked and passed it to him. "To Alex and Bjorn! Warriors both!"

"Alex and Bjorn!"

Bjorn took a long swig from a pewter tankard and smacked his lips, challenging Alex to do the same. Alex took a long gulp from the can and smacked his lips.

"So, this is what you do for fun, eh?" Alex said, trying to open up some kind of informative conversation.

Bjorn nodded. "Sometimes. Sometimes we sing if Valdur brings his guitar. He's our bard."

A slight man with long blond hair gave a modest nod and a wave. He seemed as self-conscious as Sarah about all the theatrics surrounding the Sons of Sol and Alex began to seriously doubt that any of these people could be involved in a killing.

Sarah approached Thor and whispered in his ear. Thor's eyebrows shot up and he smiled, narrowing his eyes at Alex. "We have lots of ways to entertain ourselves, Alex. Let me show you one of our more extreme sports."

Flanked by Bjorn and Sarah, Alex followed Thor out of the thicket and back towards the fire. A small, pathetic figure dangled from the arms of two burly men. Alex recognised him instantly. It was Emilio Ogden.

CHAPTER 25

Slipping back behind Bjorn, Alex pulled his hood up and slipped his hands into his pockets, just praying that Emilio wouldn't recognise him. The young man had his own concerns at the moment as Thor's two henchmen held him off the ground, his legs pedalling the air.

"I've heard some bad things about you Emilio," Thor said, his voice laced with disappointment. "Rumour has it that you've been squealing to the police."

Ogden's eyes widened. "Who me? I wouldn't do that Thor, you know I wouldn't. I'm not a grass."

Thor punched him hard in the stomach and Ogden slumped in the grip of the two men. "That's not what the brief my dad sent for you told us. Apparently, you told them everything to protect that heap of junk you call a car."

"Honest, Thor, I never said a word. Even if I did, it was only to get out of the station. I wouldn't stand up in court and say that, would I? Come on, mate, I'm sorry. I won't do it again."

Thor thumped him again. "I think it's too late for all that. All you had to do was keep schtum but no. You wet your pants, didn't you?"

"Please, Thor. I'm begging you. Don't hurt me anymore."

"Take him to the throwing gallery. Let's see who can give him a close shave."

The two men dragged Emilio towards the edge of the woods. Thor slapped Alex on the back. "You see, Alex, now we have a live target."

"You aren't going to…?"

"We're going to teach him a lesson."

Emilio craned his neck back at the sound of Alex's voice. Alex locked eyes with him and gave his head a faint shake, hoping Emilio would pick up on the message not to blab.

They dragged Emilio Ogden to the end of the gallery and tied him at the wrists and ankles so he was spread against the wooden wall. "D'you know what the Vikings used to do to traitors, Ogden?" Thor said, tossing an axe up in the air and catching it again.

"Something horrible?" Ogden guessed.

"Cut their back open and pull their rib cage and lungs through so they looked like wings. It was called a Blood Eagle," Thor let one of the axes fly and Emilio screamed as it buried itself in the wall beside his head.

"Please stop!" Ogden screeched.

"I don't think you've learned your lesson,"

Thor said and hurled another axe. At first Alex thought Thor had hit him. The axe cut through Ogden's coat and pinned it to the board.

"Don't hurt me! I'll do anything!"

"Stop squirming around or I might actually hit you," Thor said. The third axe struck home between Ogden's knees. Thor picked up another axe and offered it to Alex. "Your turn."

"No, really," Alex said, raising a hand.

"Come on, Alex, show some steel!"

"Listen!" Ogden yelled as Alex took the axe. "Thor! Let me go and I'll tell you something. Something really important."

Alex threw the axe, letting it land wide of Ogden. "Keep still, you idiot!" Alex said.

"He's trying to shut me up!" Ogden shouted. "He's a bizzy! His name is DC Alex Manikas. He arrested me today!"

Thor frowned and turned to Alex. "You're a copper?"

Without pausing to answer, Alex launched himself past Thor and made a run for the field and, beyond that, the road. Suddenly, the world turned upside down and strong arms wrapped around Alex's waist. Bjorn had brought him down with a crunching rugby tackle. Three more men joined in the scrum, grabbing at Alex's arms as he punched out and pinning him to the ground.

"Tie him up," Thor said. Soon, Alex stood in front of Thor, bound hand and foot. "So what was all this about being an accountant? You under-cover?"

Alex shrugged. "You better let me go or you'll be in deep trouble Fabian."

Thor's face paled and he back handed Alex across the face. "I hate that name. So, what shall we do with you?"

"You could let me go," Ogden wailed from the axe wall. Bjorn whispered in Thor's ear and a nasty smile spread across his face.

"Now there's a thought," Thor said, going over to the fire and picking up an old iron coffee pot that sat in the edge of the ashes. He poured the contents into a tin mug. "Hold him."

Someone grabbed the top of Alex's head and Bjorn squeezed his cheeks until his eyes watered and he had to open his mouth.

"Some nice mushroom tea," Thor said. He grinned and poured the liquid from the cup down Alex's throat. It was warm and tasted earthy and bitter, like soil and something else he couldn't quite place. Alex spluttered and choked as the liquid went down.

They threw him on the ground. "What was that meant to do?" Alex said, his voice still hoarse from coughing. A sharp pain cramped his stomach and he doubled up. For a moment, he thought he was going to vomit but then that passed, and his head became light.

"Put him in the pit," Thor said. His voice sounded distant. "Let him enjoy the trip down there."

The fire swayed back and forth in the darkness. He felt hands on his arms and then he was weightless, but he wasn't sure if he was being carried or if he was flying. Then he landed. He was pretty sure he should be in pain, as he lay in the bottom of a deep hole.

Time flew by in what seemed like seconds; events flickering in and out of existence. He fell in and out of consciousness. Moments of darkness followed moments of wakefulness. He lost all sense of what was real and what was a dream. Somehow, even at the bottom of the hole, he could still see the Sons of Sol. Maybe he imagined it, as he listened to the sounds. Maybe some magic had transformed him into a tree, and he stood looking down on them all.

Men wrestled by the fire, bodies twisting and glistening. Shouting and cursing hurt his ears. Somebody vomited. Somebody sang and played the guitar. Drums thudded and people danced. Alex watched it all like a bemused, distant observer. Sometimes he was a ghost-white owl in the branches looking down, sometimes he was a thorn-backed hedgehog in the nettles watching feet scuffle near his eyes.

Then he stood on top of Thor's Stone, a huge sandstone block with the whole of the Wirral spread around him. His feet and toes crept into the solid rock like the roots of a tree, stretching down and the bedrock of the whole peninsula was part of him. Worms crawled through the soil and creatures snuffled and burrowed in the sandy dirt. Brambles twisted through the bushes and plants. And Alex knew the age of the place; its antiquity. He saw long ships rowing up the Dee, barns burning in the distance. He heard the cries of the dying and saw buildings rise and fall. And he knew that the bones of the dead lay everywhere and he knew every one of them by name. But something was amiss. Someone wasn't where he should be. Alex frowned.

The hill fell away, and he was back in the pit. Thor's face closed in on him. "You'll be fine, mister policeman," he said. "We'll take care of you."

Panic filled Alex as liquid entered his mouth, choking and filling his belly. A cold stagnant water with that same earthy taste and smell. and then Alex was sick and as he vomited, he felt as though he was being drawn up on a rope high into the sky and at great speed. and he thought he saw Trevor Long standing by the fire, covered in blood, pointing and laughing at him. Everything began to melt and run like wax. Then DC Alex Manikas succumbed to darkness and oblivion.

CHAPTER 26

Birds chirped outside Kath Cryer's window but it was way too early and, to her, it sounded discordant and angry. She'd heard somewhere that birdsong was basically a cluster of challenges, warnings about territory and sexual advances. Translated into human, she surmised, most dawn choruses would be like a gang of Cro-Magnon builders shouting abuse and innuendo from scaffolding. She sipped her coffee, grimacing and wondering how it had managed to go cold so quickly.

She'd phoned the hospital and been told that Theo was comfortable, which was what they always said. They weren't going to say he'd been in terrible pain all night, were they? Kath supposed they had to say something. At least she had antibiotics now. After a lot of hunting, she'd found the idiot who had blocked her car in the hospital carpark. He'd cost her an extra hour's parking but she didn't have the time or the energy to try and get it out of him. She just flashed her warrant card and he shifted the van pretty damn quickly then. One trip to an out of hours chemist and she had her prescription. She'd also popped into Asda to get a gallon of cranberry juice. She hated the stuff but decided that whatever might work was worth trying.

Her wrist throbbed too. She straightened the splint and squeezed it, giving herself a momentary release from the pain. Some days she wished she'd let Kinnear take the blast of the shotgun and not thrown herself in front of him. Then maybe it would be him lying awake at night trying to ignore the gnawing pain in his arm. She instantly felt bad. Tomorrow, she'd shake herself up. Hopefully the antibiotics would kick in and she'd be able to get a grip of this Trevor Long case. She had a good idea what was going on but hadn't had chance to check her theory out with Blake.

The ceiling above her creaked and Kath looked upward. Another creak and then a muffled thump as though somebody was walking around upstairs. "Go away," Kath muttered, her heart thumped. "Leave me alone."

A louder bump made her flinch and then another made the light fitting vibrate. Kath suppressed a shriek. "Stanley!" she yelled. It was bound to be the dog. That pug was forever sneaking upstairs when he knew there was a 'not on the bed' rule. Stanley's claws clicked on the kitchen tiles and then he appeared in the living room, wagging his tail. Kath felt cold. Her scalp prickled as the ceiling reverberated again.

"That does it," she said, rising unsteadily to her

feet and striding out of the room into the hall. She paused at the foot of the stairs looking up. The house seemed alien and hostile; as if it had taken against her for some reason. Bad luck dog you. Ill will hound you. Ill health bite you. Could a house have ill will?

"Get a grip Kath Cryer," she muttered, pulling a can of pepper spray from her handbag. She wasn't really sure when she'd procured the spray. She must have signed for it at some point, but her head was fuzzy and memories out of focus. For the last twenty-four hours, she'd been living in a hazy dreamworld. Although the day was dawning, the grey twilight hadn't penetrated the house yet. Kath switched the hall light on and headed up the stairs.

The fifth stair creaked as she crept up towards her bedroom. She paused. It felt like the house had held its breath and was listening too. She continued up to the sixth step, the seventh, eighth, ninth.

Her head was above the floor level of the landing now and she could see the three bedroom doors, all shut tight. The bathroom was wide open. Something scratched at the back of her bedroom door. Like a long, fingernail or claw scraping against the wood; scratch, scrape.

Kath froze, gripping the bannister rail for a moment.

Scratch, scrape.

She listened for what was behind that noise.

The house listened too.

Nothing. The noise stopped.

Kath crept up tenth, eleventh and twelfth step, the thick carpet muffling her tread. Silently, she reached the door and gripped the handle. Taking a deep breath, she turned the handle and barged into the room.

The world became a flurry of screeching and fluttering. Kath felt claws against her cheek; wings pounded the air and battered at her face. She scrabbled at the wall for the light switch to banish the darkness but dreaded what she might see.

With a click, light flooded the room, dazzling Kath for a second. She blinked and the room fell into focus as a glossy black crow hopped across the duvet and, with a final indignant caw, flew out of the open window. Ornaments, tubes of cosmetics, clothes and boxes of toiletries lay scattered across the room. All were christened with a smearing of bird muck. The light fitting swung back and forth; its shade crooked.

Kath stared at the carnage. Half the stuff on the floor had been in cupboards she was sure and she knew for certain that she hadn't left the window open. Kath Cryer slumped onto the end of the bed and put her pulsing head in her hands.

*****

Will's phone rang as he sat at the breakfast table staring into a bowl of cornflakes. He hadn't been particularly hungry; Jeff's stinging critique had robbed him of a night's sleep and a morning's appetite. He stared at the phone, half tempted to ignore it but then he noticed Superintendent Martin's name on the screen and snatched it up.

"Sorry to call you at home, Will but I need to give you a bit of a heads up on Harry Thorpe," Martin said, briskly. "I believe you were talking to him the other day." The Superintendent was a hawkish man who didn't suffer fools gladly. By and large, he treated Blake well but he couldn't help needling him about the Searchlight days every now and then. It didn't help that Blake had recently been involved in two high profile cases that had caught the attention of the nationals, bolstering Martin's mistaken suspicion that Blake was something of a publicity addict.

"Yes, sir," Blake said. "His son is a suspect in the Trevor Long murder. He came in voluntarily."

"Tread carefully with that one, Will," Martin said. "Thorpe has been a thorn in our side for far too long."

"He made me aware of his success in the courts against us," Blake said. "Don't worry, sir, we're doing everything by the book."

Martin coughed. "Yes, well. On a need-to-know basis, Thorpe is part of a larger investigation by the National Crime Agency and the Serious Fraud Office. It seems he's quite a big player nationally in terms of money laundering and fraud and linked to numerous other notables in organised crime. They don't want their investigation messed up. It's all quite covert and hush hush at this stage, apparently."

Blake rolled his eyes. The Superintendent sounded as though he was almost salivating with excitement at the idea of the NCA conducting an undercover operation on their patch. "No, sir, I understand. We do have to go after his son if it looks likely that he killed Trevor Long, though. I can't tie my officers' hands on a case this serious."

"Of course you can't, Will. I'm just letting you know so you can be cautious. Thorpe has other associates. We don't want news reports getting out and putting the wind up them."

So that was it. Martin didn't want Blake to go rushing off to the media and seeking the limelight again. "We've been asking the public for help with locating Trevor Long, sir but only on a local basis and there have been no named suspects. It shouldn't be a problem. You know me, sir. I'm allergic to publicity."

"If only that was true, Will." Martin hung up

and Blake slumped back in his chair and pushed the bowl of soggy cornflakes to one side.

*****

The first thing Detective Constable Alex Manikas became aware of was the biting cold. He was shivering uncontrollably and didn't need to open his eyes to know that he was naked. He could feel damp earth beneath him and rough twigs and thorns stabbed his flesh, but he didn't have the strength to move. He forced his eyes open a crack, wincing at the painful, dazzling light that flooded his vision. Every limb ached and his mouth felt and tasted like dry earth. Looking up, he could see a brilliant light. At first, he thought it was still night-time and it was an arc light. He shook his head and rubbed his eyes, realising that he was at the bottom of a deep pit with sheer walls.

He tried to remember what had happened the night before, but it was a confusing mixture of images; some of them bizarre and twisted. He knew he'd really thrown axes with Bjorn, but after that? Then it all came back; Emilio giving him up, trying to get away. The mushroom tea they forced him to drink. Alex looked at his arms and legs. They were filthy as though he'd been crawling through mud. His whole body was just as smeared. How did this happen? A lead weight filled his stomach. Blake would have his bollocks for this. He was finished in the force and it wasn't as though he hadn't been warned. That's if he ever got out.

The silhouette of a head peered over the entrance to the pit. "You're awake," said the figure. "Eat some butties. You'll feel better." A packet of service station sandwiches came hurtling from above and Alex fumbled the catch. The sandwiches bounced off his head sending a stabbing pain through him.

"You had a busy night," the voice said and followed up the observation with a chuckle.

"You better let me out of here," Manikas said. "You know I'm a police officer. They'll be looking for me. The whole thing was being recorded."

"Even when you were bollocko naked, howling like a wolf?" the voice said. "No. I think you came on your own and nobody is looking for you. And I think nobody will find you even if they do."

The silhouette vanished and Alex felt a rush of panic. He was alone and helpless.

CHAPTER 27

Rather than spend time brooding, Laura suggested that Blake joined her to search for Serafina. Blake shrugged. "It's been almost a week, Laura. I mean if she's trapped anywhere then she's dead. If she's been taken, she could be anywhere in the country. God anywhere in the world by now. I hate to say it, but I think we've lost her."

"Really?" Laura said. "So, you're just going to sit there and mope? Was Jeff right then?"

Will glared at her. "No," he said, then looked at the floor. "Yes. He was right. I was so self-absorbed in those days. I was a dick. I've told you before, I don't deserve to be happy."

"Spoken like a true dick," Laura said. "You can't change the past, Will Blake but you can acknowledge your shortcomings and move on."

Will looked at her. "Just shrug and move on? You think it's that easy?"

"No, but it can be done, Will. You think you're the only one who has regrets and guilt? The past doesn't exist anymore. Only in your own head. You can punish yourself forever, but it won't bring anyone back or undo anything that's happened in the past. All you can do is to try and learn from any mistakes you've made and not let them happen again. If you ask me, this self-pity is harming Serafina's chances right now. Or are you just storing up things to feel bad about in the future?"

"That's a bit harsh."

"But it's true unless you do something."

Blake stood up. "Okay then. Let's go and find that bloomin' cat."

An awkward cough made both Will and Laura jump. Gwen stood at the open front door, dressed in a red kaftan. "Sorry," she said. "I didn't mean to interrupt…"

"No, that's all right. Laura, this is Gwen, her cat is missing too…"

Laura shook Gwen's hand. "Right," she said. "The silver tabby. We were just going to have a look around. Would you like to join us?"

Gwen shook her head. "No, I've been dousing all week and the cards aren't auspicious for today. I may go and recharge with some meditation and crystals." She paused and looked around the hall, a troubled expression on her face. "I hope you don't mind me saying but… this house…"

"Yeah?" Will said.

"It's so full of negative energy," she said. "Bad

things have happened here. I can tell."

"It hasn't been the happiest of households," Laura said. "I don't know how long you've been standing there but you could gather that from what I was saying to Will just now…"

"No," Gwen muttered. "Things have happened here long ago before Will's mother and father arrived. This was a sad house before the recent incidents."

"Okay," Will said. "Thanks Gwen. We'll try our best to cheer it up by finding the cats, shall we?"

Gwen smiled. "I'm sorry, I didn't mean to darken the mood," she said. "It's just that sometimes, I get a feeling about a place. We all do, don't we? Some sixth sense that tells us this isn't a good place to stay."

Will raised his eyebrows but he couldn't completely dismiss the idea; he'd stayed in a few hotel rooms that gave him the heebie-jeebies and he couldn't explain why. Besides, Rock Lodge hadn't been the happy home his parents had hoped. And who knew what had happened in the decades before that? It was an old house. "Yeah, well, hopefully, I'll get it up on the market soon and be done with it." He pulled his jacket off the pegs by the door. "We were just heading out Gwen. We'll let you know if we find anything, okay?"

Laura watched Gwen wander back up the road.

"Now she's a strange one. Dousing? Auspicious cards?"

"I thought you were a big fan of all this new age crap," Blake said, putting his jacket on and following Laura out of the house..

"I meditate, Will," she said, laughing. "There's a pretty strong collection of studies that have shown meditation to be beneficial. That doesn't mean I'm a great advocate of crystals, dousing and contacting the spirit world."

"Fair enough," Blake said, with a shrug. "Anyway, she's as mad as a box of frogs, so..."

"Pretty, though," Laura said, raising her eyebrows. "I can see why you jumped in to rescue her cat."

Blake managed a grin despite the morning's events. "Oh, give over. Honestly, anyone would think you were jealous, Laura Vexley."

"No chance. You're punching way above your weight with me, pal," she said. Then she frowned. "Something about her is a bit off though."

"See? Jealous. Like you were with the hairdresser, the other month."

"Behave," Laura said. "No, there was something she said that struck me as odd, but I can't for the life of me put my finger on what it was, now."

An old woman wrapped in a bright red waterproof, shuffled up to them and Blake realised it was Mrs Inchley from the top of the road. There weren't many houses but some had extensive gardens and so the road was quite long. Mrs Inchley had been a resident for more years than anyone could remember and had been a friend of Blake's mother.

"I've lost Merlin," she said, without even a greeting. "Have you seen him?"

"Is Merlin a cat, Mrs Inchley?" Blake said. "Only we've lost Serafina, too."

"Yes, oh I'm sorry to hear that, William," the old woman said. "Merlin was black, long-haired. Only had him a couple of months. He went missing last night."

Blake frowned. "Seems strange."

"What does?" Laura said.

"Another cat going missing so soon after Serafina. To my mind, that points to someone taking them or trapping them deliberately."

Mrs Inchley put a hand to her mouth. "Oh my."

"It's all right, Mrs Inchley, Will's just thinking aloud. Nothing's certain."

"No, we arrested a man who had been stealing cats in the area recently but he's under lock and key now, so he doesn't have Merlin," Blake said. "Besides, most pets are stolen as part of a burglary, sweeping them up off the street would be a bit hit and miss."

"Then where are they, William?" Mrs Inchley said.

"If they'd all disappeared on the same day, I'd maybe have said they were miles away by now. But I think they're local, maybe stuck somewhere or trapped deliberately…"

"Oh dear," Mrs Inchley said.

"Don't worry, Mrs Inchley, we'll do everything we can to find Merlin for you," Laura said. "Will is a detective. So, think, Will. If this was an abduction, what would you look for?"

Blake scanned the street. "House-to-house and CCTV," he said. "We'll start there."

*****

From feeling like he was getting somewhere, DC Andrew Kinnear now thought he was back to square one. Thor Magnussen was nowhere to be found. He wasn't at the betting office and the woman there told Kinnear that he was 'off on one of his jaunts' and wouldn't be in until Monday. Not only that but Emilio Ogden had gone missing, too. His car wasn't parked outside his house, Emilio wasn't picking up and ANPR spotted his Fiat Punto heading into Wales.

"Bugger," Kinnear muttered.

DS Vikki Chinn sat next to him at the desk in the Major Incident Room. "It's like herding cats," she said. "I feel like arresting them all for... God! I don't know... for something!"

"Without Ogden, we can't really lean on Magnussen," Kinnear said. "He'd better only have gone on a day trip to Talacre."

"Do you really think either Ogden or Magnussen are capable of murder?" Vikki said, frowning.

"Despite his comedy name, I don't think Thor Magnussen is as harmless as he seems." The phone rang interrupting Kinnear's line of thought. He watched as Vikki nodded and scribbled on a pad.

She put the phone down. "A body has turned up," she said. "Male, young. Better let the boss know. It sounds like it could be Trevor Long."

CHAPTER 28

Gorse Meadow Caravan Park in Thurstaston was a quiet settlement of around twenty-five privately owned static caravans. They stood, shielded from the road by a tall, clipped leylandii hedge. Signs all around the site reminded everyone that it was private. It was a beautiful location; right on the top of the cliffs, looking out across the Dee Estuary. Kinnear could see the Welsh hills, Hilbre Island and the distant horizon dotted with wind turbines. Most of all, Kinnear was always impressed by the sky on this side of the Wirral. Whether it was because of the buildings or just the lie of the land but even on the banks of the Mersey, the sky didn't seem as big. Here, it dominated the landscape. He could understand why anyone would want to live here.

A small crowd of residents, all in the twilight of their lives, stood gawping at the busy CSI officers dressed in their white coveralls.

Kinnear, similarly clad, stood inside the caravan frowning at the scene. The mobile home was unremarkable; reminding Kinnear of many he had stayed in on childhood holidays. One end held a table surrounded by bench seats that converted into a bed. The middle of the caravan was a kitchen area with a gas hob, a small fridge and a sink. Behind Kinnear, a narrow corridor led to a bedroom and a shower room. But there was no body.

"PC Mark Robertson was the first responder," said a constable, who identified herself as PC Irwin. "He went with the victim to the hospital to gather more evidence. I stayed here."

Kinnear frowned. "Victim? Not dead then?"

"No," the police officer said. "We thought he was at first but then we realised he was breathing still. An ambulance had been called when they called us."

"Any ID?" Kinnear said.

PC Irwin shook her head. "The neighbours heard shouting and came out to see a woman with dark hair and a man in a red hoody jump into a green hatchback and drive off. I'm afraid initial descriptions are a bit hazy, most of the residents were just starting the day and by the time they'd got to their windows to look out, the car was disappearing."

"Make? Model? Registration?" Kinnear said, forlornly.

Irwin shook her head. "Sorry."

"So the victim," Kinnear said. "Description?"

"Male. Mid to late twenties. Stocky, five foot seven, brown hair, beard. There was no obvious signs of trauma, no bruising or blood loss. He was just lying on the floor, unconscious."

"Right," Kinnear said. "Who's the best witness?"

Irwin pointed out of the window towards an old man leaning on a stick as he stood with the crowd. He had swept back silver hair and an impressive walrus moustache. "The gentleman out there, a Mr Gilchrist seems to have seen the most."

Kinnear left the caravan and ducked under the tape. After taking off his coveralls, he approached the old man. "Mr Gilchrist? I believe you have some information."

"I'll help if I can," he said, glancing at his neighbours. "Can we go inside?"

"Sure," Kinnear said. "Lead the way."

Gilchrist's caravan had a similar layout to the one next door but everything seemed more permanent and lived-in. Kinnear couldn't pin it down exactly; maybe it was the bookshelves, or the magazines piled on the table but it struck him straight away that the caravan where the body had been was a temporary residence. This was a home.

The old man leaned his stick against the wall. A small terrier lay curled up in a basket at his feet and didn't move other than to wiggle one ear as he settled himself into an armchair. "So," Mr Gilchrist said. "Where do I start?"

"Who lives in the caravan next door?"

"Trevor Long," the old man said, rolling his eyes.

"I'm sorry?" Kinnear said. "Can you describe him?"

"Who? Long? I can do better than that. I can show you one of his dozy YouTube videos. The lad's a barmpot..."

"So, you're saying that Trevor Long, the conspiracy theorist, lives in the caravan?"

Gilchrist looked puzzled. "He doesn't live here full time," he said. "His grandad, Len, used to own the caravan but when he died, Trevor took it over. I think Len left it to him."

"But I understood that Trevor lived in a flat in Birkenhead," Kinnear said.

"Oh, most of the time, yeah," Gilchrist said. "Not having a car makes this neck of the woods a bit inaccessible for Trevor but he kept the caravan on. He comes down most weekends. He's been here all week as far as I know. He doesn't come out much. Just sits inside watching telly or playing those video games they're all mad about these days."

Kinnear blinked. "He's been here all week? Mr Gilchrist, haven't you heard the news at all?"

"Don't bother with it myself," Gilchrist said, with a dismissive shrug. "I've got my books and music. Gave up listening to how the world's gone mad. Why, should I have?"

"We've been investigating Trevor Long's murder for most of this week."

Gilchrist raised his eyebrows. "Well, I can assure you, Trevor Long has been alive, swigging beer and watching TV in that caravan for the last seven days."

*****

Blake couldn't believe what he was hearing as he stood in Rock Lane. "Are you certain it's the same Trevor Long?" he said.

"Yes, sir," Kinnear said. "Mr Gilchrist identified him as the one who made the videos. Long's caravan was stuffed full of cans and microwave meals for one. He was clearly planning to be holed-up for some time. It looks like we've been had."

"Some kind of elaborate hoax, then. Wasting police time. Pull that girlfriend in. She's clearly an accomplice. I'm not having them thinking they can give us the run around like that and get away with it. How about Long? Has he woken up yet?"

"I don't know. I haven't heard from the officer who accompanied him to the hospital," Kinnear said. "I'm on my way over to Arrowe Park now."

Blake pocketed his phone, shaking his head. "You wouldn't believe the half of it," he said to Laura. "The murder victim whose body we couldn't find has only turned up alive."

"Do you need to get to work?" Laura said. "I can keep knocking on doors."

Blake shook his head. "No. The Superintendent would go off on one if I put another overtime claim in. Vikki Chinn and Kinnear can sort this one out."

"Why would anyone pretend to have been murdered?"

"Plenty of reasons, I suppose. If you owe a lot of money or just want to change your life. From what I understand, Trevor Long was a bit of a fantasist anyway. Maybe he wanted to enhance his image in the world of paranormal investigation. As I say, there's a whole world of weirdness out there; none of it to do with ghosts or aliens. It's just the great British public. Let's go and find Serafina and Merlin."

People had been surprisingly helpful as Laura and Blake had made their way around Rock Park and Rock Lane which ran through the old estate of huge houses. Blake's warrant card helped. Many residents recognised Blake from recent newspapers or, more annoyingly, from Searchlight all those years ago. So far, they'd had access to all the CCTV they'd asked to see but nothing came of it.

They came to the end of the road, not far from Gwen's house. On the other side, clipping an immaculate privet hedge with a pair of hand-shears, stood a man in his sixties. He struck Blake as an outdoor type. The sort of person who has kept in trim by gardening, pushing barrows and wrestling nature into line day in, day out, come rain, hail or shine. He wore blue overalls that bore testament to someone who worked with care and precision. They weren't covered in paint but had the evidence of it here and there; small spatter patterns rather than swathes. Amateurs always had huge blotches and streaks up the legs or arms.

The man turned as they approached him and Blake saw a closed face, suspicious, glittering eyes and a letter box mouth. His silver hair was cropped close to his head and his skin was tanned nut brown by years of work outside.

Blake flashed his warrant card. "Hi, I'm Will Blake, this is Laura Vexley, we live just down the road in the Lodge..."

"I know who you are," he said, the corners of his eyes crinkled in suspicion.

"We're looking for our cat..."

"Three cats, actually," Laura butted in. "Mrs Inchley's cat has disappeared too..."

"Bloody cats," the man said, still gripping the shears, the blades pointing directly at them. "Crapping in my borders. Worse than dog shit. Dogs don't bury their crap, do they? At least you can step over dog shit."

Blake looked up at the CCTV camera on the corner of the man's house. "We think someone might have taken them. Some of the neighbours have let us look at their CCTV footage to see if there's any evidence of where they've gone."

The man shrugged. "Good riddance, I say. Do you know how many birds cats kill every year? Millions of them. I hate them."

"So, can we have a look at your CCTV?" Laura said, clearly pushing her luck.

"No," the man said.

"But Gwen, just over the road has lost her cat. You might have something that could help..."

"Her?" the man snorted. "Didn't even know she had a cat. If she's so bothered, how come she's not out looking with you? She's a nutcase, that one. Have you seen what's growing in her front garden?"

"Sorry?" Blake said, giving Laura a sidelong glance.

"Deadly nightshade, hemlock, monkshood, digitalis. It's a poisoner's paradise, that place. You want to steer clear."

"Right," Blake said and looked beyond the man into his drive and front garden. It was immaculate. Everything cut in sharp angles and planted in regimented rows. The lawn was striped from frequent mowing. To the side of the man's house stood a large potting shed, with a strong wooden door. "Well, thanks for your time. Sorry to bother you," he said, dragging Laura away.

"Horrible man," Laura hissed as they headed back down the road. "If anyone's harmed the cats, it's going to be him."

"Just because he doesn't like cats, doesn't make him a suspect," Blake said. "There was something about him, though. He strikes me as a controlling sort of person."

"It was funny what he said about Gwen..."

Blake grinned. "Here we go again. You said the same about her yourself. Just jealous, that's all."

"I am not," Laura said, digging him with her elbow. "But she is odd."

"We're all a bit odd. I said that before, didn't I? How does the song go? People are strange."

"What's her cat called, then?" Laura said, coming to a halt in the middle of the road.

"What?"

"Tell me her cat's name."

Blake frowned. "I-I don't know... it's a silver

tabby…"

"Exactly," Laura said, "and what was the first thing Mrs Inchley said to you?"

"She said, 'I've lost Merlin,' something like that," Blake said. "Yeah, that was it. I don't know what you're getting at, Laura."

But Laura was staring down the road to Blake's front gate. "Who's that standing outside your house?" she said.

DCI Matty Cavanagh stood next to his car and as they drew near, Blake could see he was twitchy and agitated. Whatever it was he had to say, it wasn't good news.

CHAPTER 29

It hadn't been so long that Alex Manikas had been stuck in this deep hole but it felt like an eternity. The sun shone above but down in the pit, the shade and the dank soil walls summoned up a chill that seeped into his naked body. He smacked his forehead. What an idiot he'd been. Nobody knew he was here. He hadn't let anyone know where he was going. If only he'd listened to Blake and stayed the hell away. Now, even if he was rescued, he'd be in big trouble. He stared up at the edge of the pit. It wasn't as deep as he'd first imagined; when he'd woken up, he'd felt as though he was at the bottom of a deep well. He reckoned that the top of the wall was probably only four or five feet higher than his head. It was deep enough though.

He looked at the corners of the hole, wondering if he'd be able to wedge himself in one of them and climb up. It was a possibility but the sides crumbled when he pushed at them. the whole thing might collapse if he wasn't careful and bury him alive. Alex shivered. Was that what would happen? Would they just bulldozer a ton of earth on top of him and he'd never be found?

A scuffling noise saved Manikas from his dark thoughts and he looked up. Two heads appeared over the lip and peered down. "Company for you, Spartan," Thor's voice said.

"Let me out of here. You've had your fun. It's only a matter of time before my mates at the police station come looking for me..."

Alex's words were cut short by something big and heavy being thrown down. It blotted the light out and Alex barely had time to press himself against the wall of the pit. Soil and clods of earth rained down on him. It hit the earth with a thud and someone groaned. There, lying on the floor, was Emilio Ogden, his pale flesh showing welts and bruises. He squirmed and stared at Alex with one bloodshot eye, the other was blue and swollen shut.

Alex pulled the young man into a sitting position. "Are you okay?" he said. Ogden tried to say something, then ran his tongue around his mouth and spat. A couple of teeth fell into the mud, surrounded by a clotted parcel of spit and blood.

"I think so," he said and gave a bloody grin. "Where there's no sense there's no feeling, that's what my old nan used to say. Where are we?"

"At the bottom of a hole," Alex said. "Thanks to you."

"Me?" the lad said. "Why is it my fault? You

threw an axe at me."

"I deliberately missed, you idiot. Looks like they weren't as impressed by you ratting on me as you'd hoped."

"I tried to run away from them when you made a break for it, but they caught me and beat me up. I've been chained up to a bloody tree all night."

"We're still on the field, then," Alex muttered. "There's a chance we can escape."

Emilio stared at him. "Are you off your head? We're stuck at the bottom of a bloody big hole. How are we going to escape?"

"Trust me, Emilio," Alex said. "I'm not waiting around to find out what they've got in store for us. We're getting out."

*****

What worried Blake the most was the fact that Matty Cavanagh looked so concerned. The man usually struck Blake as shallow, and a little devil-may-care. Even in the toughest cases, Cavanagh made it clear that it was just work. He had perfected that sense of professional detachment. But then, Cavanagh had been working with Josh Gambles and that worm could get inside anyone's head and twist things up.

Cavanagh sat in Blake's living room on the sofa with a mug of coffee. He sipped at it and turned the mug around in his fingers and then sipped again.

"Are you okay, Matty?" Blake said.

"Yeah," he muttered. "It's that bloody Gambles, isn't it?"

Blake glanced over at Laura. "Laura, can you give us a minute?"

"No," Cavanagh said. "I need her here."

"Really? If it's police business, surely she shouldn't be listening in…"

But Cavanagh was ready to launch into his story. "You know we've been working on Gambles, trying to get a confession out of him and tidy this up in record time to minimise the publicity. Well, he mentioned a name. I think I told you."

"Kyle Quinlan, yeah," Blake said. "What about him?"

Cavanagh just nodded over to Laura who sank slowly into an armchair, her eyes wide. "That's what I wanted to ask Laura," Cavanagh said. "What about Kyle Quinlan?"

*****

Andrew Kinnear hurried over to Arrowe Park Hospital as quickly as he could. It was a Saturday and he'd expected the roads to be quiet, but the roads were busy; Shoppers were heading for Liverpool, Cheshire Oaks Outlet Village or further afield to the Trafford Centre. When he'd finally got to the hospital, he couldn't park at first as it was visiting time and the whole place was rammed with cars.

At last he found the side room where they'd placed Trevor Long. Constable Mark Robertson stood outside the door, his arms folded. He was a tall man, with a dark beard flecked with grey. He struck Kinnear as sharp and alert. "Any change?" Kinnear said, after showing his warrant card and introducing himself.

PC Robertson shook his head. "The medics think he's been given some kind of tranquiliser. They found a puncture wound on his neck. No other obvious signs of injury, though and they ran some tests for internal injuries, but he seems clear."

Kinnear shook his head. "He hasn't come round at all?"

"Nah," PC Robertson said. "Dead to the world."

"Not dead," Kinnear muttered. "That's the point. Are we okay to go in and have a look at him?"

Robertson shrugged. "Nobody's said we can't."

The light in the room was subdued. A machine flashed at the side of the bed, showing various numbers that Kinnear didn't understand. Drips ran down from a stand into Long's arm and he lay on his back, for all appearances still and dead. But as he drew nearer, Kinnear could see the man's chest rising and falling slightly.

"Told you," Robertson said, giving Kinnear a jump. "Totally out of it."

But DC Andrew Kinnear wasn't listening anymore. He stared down into the face of the man on the bed. A face he recognised straight away. "*That* is not Trevor Long," he said.

CHAPTER 30

Laura Vexley looked as though a freight train was bearing down on her. She sat silently tangling her fingers together as Cavanagh carried on speaking.

"Gambles had been going on about Kyle Quinlan, as you know, and he'd become uncooperative until we looked into this guy. So we did a bit of digging. Turns out he vanished completely back in 2014. Never seen again. We tried last known associates, drew a blank. Nobody has seen him. Seems like he vanished off the face of the Earth…"

Blake shrugged. "Some criminals do that, Matty. This Quinlan could be sunning himself abroad, living on the streets or even shoring up a motorway flyover under ten tons of concrete for all we know. What's it got to do with Laura?"

Laura's whole demeanour had changed; no longer assertive and confident, she pulled her knees up in the chair and hugged them.

"Well, we looked into a few cases involving Quinlan, just a brief pass over them and this Mrs Quinlan pops up. Mrs Laura Quinlan. But we can't find her either. A bit more digging and we come up with a maiden name, Laura Vexley."

Blake glanced at Laura, trying to process what he had just heard. "It's not the most common name in the world but it's possible that it's another Laura Vexley."

"No," Laura said, her voice distant and haunted. "I was Kyle Quinlan's wife. I wish I hadn't been but there you are."

"You never mentioned him before," Blake said. He'd poured his heart out to Laura; about Searchlight, about the death of his little daughter, the loss of his parents. Blake was an open book to Laura but it suddenly struck him how little she had revealed about her own past.

"He was a horrible man, Will, violent and selfish," Laura said. "You once asked me where I learnt how to defend myself. The truth is, I learnt the hard way, from Kyle Quinlan."

"So where is he now?" Cavanagh said, cutting through their conversation and startling Laura.

"I-I don't know," Laura said. "We split up in 2014 and I never saw him again."

Cavanagh frowned. "So, technically, you're still married? What about any property? All your stuff?"

"No. I divorced Kyle. There were no children involved and the house was rented. Kyle wasn't really the domesticated type. When I left, I just took what I needed and shut the door behind me. I wanted to get as far away from him as possible."

"You see, that's what I find hard to believe," Cavanagh said. "We've talked to a few people who knew Quinlan and he was a nasty piece of work. Petty, vindictive and with an ego as big as you like. And you're telling me he just let you go?"

"What are you trying to say, Matty?" Blake said. "That Laura's lying? That she's hiding something?"

"Come on, Will. You know I have to be sceptical. From what I understand, Quinlan wouldn't be happy about Laura wanting a divorce. He'd see it as an insult..."

Laura lifted her head a little. "Kyle was a typical bully; a coward. He came in drunk one night and picked a fight with me again. So this time I fought back. Once I stood up to him, he wanted rid of me."

"And he stayed on at the house?"

"As far as I know, yeah," Laura said. "Honestly, I kept right away from him. I had no reason to go near that house or him. The last time I saw him was when he tried to hit me and I hit him back. Then I left."

"And he was alive when you left?"

"Oh, come on, Cavanagh!" Blake snapped.

"Yeah," Laura said. "He was alive."

Cavanagh raised his hands. "I'm sorry I have to ask these questions, Laura, but it does seem suspicious that Quinlan vanishes and there's not a single person who knows or cares what happened to him."

"Apart from Gambles," Blake said. "Come on, Cavanagh, see this for what it is; it's Gambles trying to muddy the waters for all of us. The last time I saw him, he threatened me; told me I'd pay for handing the case back to you. I wouldn't be surprised if Gambles himself hasn't topped Quinlan and hidden his body sometime in the past..."

"What, in the full knowledge that, one day, Quinlan's ex-missus might get together with his favourite detective? Come on, Will, that's hardly likely. Gambles was pretty focused but nobody could plan that."

"No, but he's smart enough to use a coincidence to create bedlam and derail your investigation. Just scrap the whole interview thing, Matty, build a case against Gambles on the evidence we have. We don't need his confession."

"The only trouble is, Will, I'm not sure I can just leave the Quinlan case without further investigation, at least. And that might have implications for Laura."

When Cavanagh had gone, Blake turned to Laura. "You should have told me," he said.

"It was in the past. How was I to know Gambles would know Kyle and bring all this up? Surely you realise why I want to keep it all buried."

Blake nodded. "I do but, considering my position, doing what I do, didn't you think it might be wise just to say that you used to be married to a criminal?"

"This isn't about you, Will. It's about me. Kyle Quinlan nearly killed me; he beat me to within an inch of my life once. It has taken me years to recover, if I ever have. You tease me about being jealous and I know I can come across as controlling or insecure sometimes, but surely you can see where it comes from now. Years of verbal and physical abuse leaves a mark, Will. If Kyle is lying in a shallow grave somewhere, then good riddance but I didn't have anything to do with it."

"I know," Blake said. "But…"

"No," Laura said, standing up. "You don't know, Will. You can never know what it's like. You either trust me or you don't. It's simple. And it seems like you don't." She left the room and a moment later, he heard the front door slam.

*****

Kinnear stared down at the figure in the hospital bed and puffed out his cheeks in disbelief. Nathan Roscoe, Trevor's boss from the supermarket, lay comatose under the sheets. "It turns out that Trevor Long has been hiding at the caravan all week," Kinnear said. "Once I'd heard that, I guess I assumed the man brought here was Long. The question is, what was Nathan Roscoe doing there?"

"Maybe he figured out what was going on," Vikki Chinn said, folding her arms. "The sooner we can do the same, the better. Any sign of the girlfriend?"

"Zoe Plumb? No, not yet. I sent a car round to her house but she wasn't in. I suspect she is in on it. She 'found' the camcorder with the footage of Long being chased on it."

"That would fit with the two people running from the caravan, a man and a woman," Vikki said. "If Roscoe turned up there for whatever reason, maybe they knocked him out and fled."

"Strange how someone can suddenly change from being a murder victim to a suspect in an assault case."

"It seems that everything to do with Trevor Long turns out strange."

Kinnear scratched the back of his neck. His stomach rumbled, reminding him that it was well past his lunchtime. "The doctors said that Roscoe had been injected with some kind of powerful tranquiliser. Plumb works as a vet's assistant; it's possible that's where she got it from. So where now?"

Vikki stared down at Roscoe. "Well, he isn't going to be answering any questions for a while. I suggest we pay a visit to the vet's. See if they've got anything missing from their stocks. Maybe they can give us an idea of where we might find Zoe."

Merryvale Pet Vets in Clatterbridge was only a short drive along the M53 from Arrowe Park hospital. Kinnear watched the cars flash by. "The thing I don't get is why do this? Why go to all this trouble to fake your death. Why not just leave the area?"

Vikki Chinn shrugged, keeping her eye on the road. "Long has a reputation for being involved in strange phenomena around here. Anywhere else, he'd be a nobody. Maybe he wanted to create an air of mystery around himself. What puzzles me more, though, is that if Long is still alive, where did all that blood come from? Forensics said it was his, but the amount recorded at the scene was huge. Anyone losing that much blood so quickly would have died."

They turned off the Clatterbridge roundabout and found themselves driving down a hedge-lined lane. Merryvale Pet Vets was a large complex built on an old farmyard. A large brick-built barn conversion flanked the customer carpark and beyond that, Kinnear could see a couple of large buildings, one with a tall chimney. "I heard an advertisement for this place on the radio," he said. "It's got its own pet crematorium, too. You can have your pooch baked here if you want."

Vikki pulled a face at him. "Really? I don't think 'baked' is the right word. I think it's quite touching that people want to give their pets a good send off."

"Seems a bit OTT to me," Kinnear said, as they strode across the carpark. "Mind you, I only had a goldfish and we flushed that down the loo when it died."

Vikki rolled her eyes and pushed open the door to the vet's reception. Kinnear almost walked into her. She stood frozen to the spot. Kinnear looked over her shoulder. It was an unremarkable waiting room with two rows of chairs along the walls. Sat in the middle of these was an old lady with a cat in a crate. A few posters clung to the walls, advertising wormer and warning about various terrible pet diseases. Zoe Plumb beamed at them from behind the counter. "Hi, welcome to Merryvale Pet Vets, do you have an appointment?"

CHAPTER 31

Emilio Ogden wasn't really helping Alex in his attempt to climb out of the pit but to be fair, he had been beaten up. So he wasn't in peak condition. Alex looked at him and wondered if those two words had ever applied to Emilio. The young man was stick thin, making his head seem oversized for his body. He reminded Alex of one of those poor souls photographed in Victorian slums.

Alex had tried to get Emilio to give him a bunk up. At first, Emilio had squirmed and sworn whenever their naked flesh touched. "Oh, get off, man. This isn't cool. I'm not gay you know!"

Alex shook his head. "Grow up, Emilio, we're trying to get out of this pit. I'm not really bothered about your sexual orientation, to be honest."

Even when Emilio obliged and allowed Manikas to use him as a stool to climb on, he collapsed under Alex's weight.

"You're lighter than me. Let's try the other way round," Alex suggested. "If I cup my hands, you can climb onto my shoulders. Then try to wedge yourself into the corner and inch your way up."

Manikas grimaced as Emilio put his yellowed, sweaty foot into his interlocked fingers. The young man pushed up and Alex braced himself. The two of them grunted, Alex swore as Emilio's foot landed on his shoulder and dug in. Then Emilio's weight was gone, and he was lying on the floor groaning.

"That fuckin' hurt," he said, doubled up and clutching his stomach.

"Try to keep your balance when you're up there. You can do it, Emilio!" He extended his hands again and bent over.

Emilio looked up at him. "Nah. It's too hard, man. I'm done."

"Look, mate. If we stay here and wait for them to come back, then we will be done. You don't think they're going to let us out of here alive?"

"They might," Emilio said, but he didn't sound convinced.

"Okay, Emilio. Listen, I'm a copper, right? Do you think they're just going to let me go after keeping me down here all night? They'll all go to prison."

Emilio still looked sulky but he was wavering. "Do you think?"

"I know it. They can't let us go. There's too much at stake for them. But if we get away now, we'll be safe. And we *can* get away. I promise."

Ogden's eyes widened. "Okay, then..." Watching Alex warily, Emilio staggered to his feet. This time, he planted his foot squarely in Alex's cupped hands and stepped onto his shoulders. Once more, his weight vanished and Alex saw him pressed against the sides of the pit, soil cascading down from his hands and feet. He pushed and wriggled, his head almost reaching the lip of the pit before he came sliding back down, cursing and spitting out loose soil.

They stood panting for a second. "You almost did that, then," Alex said. "Come on, try again. Third time's the charm, as they say."

Emilio climbed onto Alex's shoulders. This time, Alex got his hands under Emilio's feet and used all his strength to push the lad up. "I'm nearly there!" Emilio whispered. Alex tried to look up but soil tumbled down, making his eyes gritty. He gave a grunt and stood on tiptoes, every muscle burning. Emilio's weight vanished again and more soil tumbled down, but this time, it was a clod of grass, because Emilio had breached the top of the wall and was up. Alex just glimpsed his legs wriggling out of the hole. Then the lad's head popped over. Alex put his thumbs up. "Well done! Now go and get help."

"Yeah, right. I'm in enough trouble as it is," Emilio Ogden said. "You think I'd make things worse for me by helping you escape? I'm gone. See you, loser." He vanished and Alex fell against the wall, sobbing with frustration and exhaustion.

*****

Blake stood in his kitchen, stirring a mug of coffee. He'd only made it to take his mind off Laura's revelation. The fact that she had kept her past so well hidden made him anxious. What if he accepted that she was telling the truth about Kyle Quinlan only to be confronted with some other horror story later on?

Or maybe Jeff was right; maybe Blake was too self-absorbed. Will had been open and honest about his past but then most of it was a matter of public record, given that he was in the public eye while it all played out. And perhaps he was being too needy expecting her to sympathise and prop him up while he anguished about what to do. He should respect her decision to move on from the past and not let it drag her back. Laura was the best thing that had happened to him in a long while. That was the trouble, though. Rejecting the chance of happiness was like a reflex with Blake. He genuinely didn't think he deserved it.

Gwen's tarot reading had been uncannily accurate. Laura was the Queen of Swords; an abandoned woman who tells the truth. Jeff the Five of Swords, representing a person who puts their career first and lets you down. Gambles, the Knave of Swords; someone who spreads gossip and rumour. The only person who came out in a decent light there was Laura. Not that Blake held any truck with such nonsense, but it did clarify his thinking. Who could he trust? Certainly not Jeff. Gambles was malicious to the bone and wanted to hurt Blake; anything he said had to be taken with a whole sack of salt.

"So, stop this messing about and go after her," he said to the coffee mug as he set it down. Grabbing the keys to his Opel Manta, Blake strode across the hall and wrenched the front door open. Gwen stood there with her arm raised and about to knock.

"Oh hi," she said. "Is this a bad time?"

"No," Blake lied. "I – I thought I heard someone on the step… come in."

Gwen glided into the hall. "I don't know why, but I just felt a sudden disturbance. Bad energy, you know? Your name popped into my mind. So I came to see if everything was okay."

Blake nodded. More like she saw Laura driving up the road with tears in her eyes. "I see," he said. "No, everything is fine."

"Really?" Gwen said. She shivered and pulled the wrap she was wearing tighter around her shoulders. "It doesn't feel like it."

"Tell me about the man who lives opposite you," Blake said, trying to steer Gwen away from any talk of Laura. "The old man who seems to clip his hedge constantly."

"Oh, him," Gwen said, her face became a mask of disapproval. "Ian Youde. A nasty piece of work."

"He didn't seem very fond of cats when I spoke to him earlier."

"That man hates the world. Did you notice his garden?"

"Very formal but blooming," Will said.

"Pumped full of chemicals. He clips everything to within an inch of its life. Flowers barely get a chance to bloom before they're cut or pulled up. D'you know, he complained to me about the flowers in my garden once, said they were poisonous weeds."

"What was his problem?"

"He said that they would spread into his garden and he didn't want to spend his life pulling up ragwort and dandelions. Philistine! He can't appreciate nature's beauty."

"Did he ever complain about your cat?"

Gwen shrugged. "He complained about everything. And have you seen those big sheds at the side of his house? I wouldn't put it past him to have them trapped in there."

"Trouble is, I can't just walk up there and demand to look in his sheds. I'd need a warrant even if I suspected far more serious things were going on."

"What could be worse than tormenting defenceless animals?"

"I take your point, but the law doesn't see it like that. Mr Youde's property is protected, too. Otherwise every burglar in town would just say they were rescuing a cat."

"Then what can you do?"

Blake narrowed his eyes. "Leave it with me."

CHAPTER 32

The most private place Zoe Plumb could find to talk with Kinnear and Chinn was a side room where a row of cages lined one wall. Two or three small, nervous dogs yapped and scratched at the bars when they came in.

"I'm sorry but our private rooms are being used at the moment for people saying goodbye to their pets before they're cremated," she said. "I should be over there, actually. I hope this won't take long."

"Can you tell me what time you got into work this morning, Ms Plumb?" Vikki said.

"First thing. Eight thirty, something like that. Why?"

"Is there anyone who can verify that?" Kinnear said.

"Yes. My boss, John Usher. Look, what's going on?"

"I'm afraid we can't discuss that. Can we see Mr Usher, please?"

"He's quite busy, I'm afraid. We get a lot of people in the weekend surgeries. It's more convenient."

"I'm going to have to insist," Vikki said. "We won't take up more of his time than is completely necessary."

Zoe's face darkened. "Fair enough," she said. "Follow me."

She led them out of the back room and across the waiting room where the old lady with the cat looked up hopefully at Zoe. She opened the door on another room and a man in a white coat was holding down a furious looking chihuahua. A thermometer poked out of its rear end. The man looked to be about Blake's age, in his forties, small, with thinning blond hair and a pained expression on his face.

"Zoe, love, I wish you'd knock..." he began but the dog saw its chance and sank its teeth into his wrist. "Ow! You little bastard!" He managed to restore his grip and extract the thermometer.

"Sorry, John but these police officers would like a quick word."

John Usher's face dropped and he looked pale. "Really?" The dog made another bid for freedom and the vet's already bleeding wrist, but he held it firm.

"Sorry to disturb you, Mr Usher but could you just confirm for us the time Zoe got into work today?" Kinnear said.

"Yes," he said, glancing from Kinnear to Zoe to

Vikki and back again.

"And what time was that?"

"She's been here all day. Got in bright and early. We had to operate on a ferret with cataracts, so we decided to do it before the weekend rush, didn't we, Zoe?"

"Yes," Zoe said. "Poor old Rusty the ferret. He's okay now though."

"Is there anything else?" Usher said, regaining his composure. "Only I have the joy of milking this little darling's anal gland now and I'm happy for you to watch if you want but…"

"No!" Vikki said. "Thank you for your time Mr Usher."

Zoe led them to the door. "I hope that's cleared everything up," she said. "Goodbye."

Out in the carpark, Kinnear stood by the car with his hands in his pockets. "Did that feel odd to you, Vikki?"

"Bloody weird," Vikki Chinn said. She peered across the carpark to the large buildings at the back of the surgery. "If Zoe has been here all day, then she can't be involved with the assault at the caravan."

Kinnear nodded. "That vet didn't convince me. Zoe could easily have made it back here from Thurstaston if he's covering for her."

"Yeah. I'd love to have a snoop around," Vikki said, scanning the buildings and outhouses that surrounded the car park. "I wonder what we'd find."

"This whole place looks a bit down at heel," Kinnear said. "I mean, what was all that stuff about the weekend rush? There was one old lady with a cat. The place didn't seem busy to me."

"Well, we can't do much more here," Vikki said. "She's a hard-faced one that Zoe, isn't she? I don't think she'll crack any time soon."

"No," Kinnear muttered, "but Gary Stott will."

*****

Theo, Kath Cryer's boyfriend, sat up in bed, looking so much better than she felt. He still had drips and monitors attached to him but he seemed a hundred percent better than he had the day before. Kath sat at his bedside, struggling to keep her eyes open.

"It's weird," he said. "The doctors can't find anything wrong with me now apart from being a bit dehydrated. My cut isn't infected, blood tests are all clear..."

"It's a curse," Kath said in a small voice. "I walked on a grave and someone cursed me for it."

Theo frowned at Kath. "Are you trying to be funny, Kath? Only that's the daftest thing I've heard in a long time. What are you on about?"

"An old woman cursed me in the graveyard. I keep seeing her everywhere and I've had this water infection and Stanley keeps barking at nothing. There was a bloody crow in our bedroom. It's a curse."

"Are you okay, Kath?" Theo said, peering closely at her. "Only you look terrible."

"I feel terrible. It's the curse."

"Okay," Theo said. "First off, there's no such thing as being cursed. Secondly, if you've got a water infection and you haven't treated it, then you could be hallucinating. Honestly, my nan had one and she thought she could see angels."

"I've got antibiotics," Kath said wearily. "I haven't seen any angels."

"Look Kath, why don't you go home? I can get Baz or Dave to come and pick me up when they finally let me out."

"I don't want to go home," Kath snapped. "It's creepy at home. I feel like I'm being watched all the time. There are noises upstairs. Doors bumping and banging for no reason." She stood up. "I know I sound mad but it's true. I'm gonna get some fresh air."

The air outside was cooler than inside the hospital but it wasn't exactly fresh. Trios of patients huddled by the doors, dragging on cigarettes and ignoring the signs everywhere that said the whole site was a smoking-free area. Kath didn't care. She just wanted to feel better.

"'Scuse me," a voice said next to her. She turned to see a shabby, down-at-heel old man. He wore an old, stained overcoat and Kath could see a frayed collar poking up around his neck. His face looked pinched and sad. "You wouldn't have change for the carpark, would you? Only I've left my wallet at home and..."

"Yeah, sure," Kath said, rummaging in her handbag. "How much do you need?"

"Just enough for the carpark. I think it's £3.20..."

"Here's four," she said, thrusting the cash into the old man's cold hands.

The man touched his finger to his head as though he was tipping his hat to her. "That's very kind of you. Sorry for asking but, are you all right, yourself?"

Kath let out a long sigh. "No. I feel shocking." She hesitated, looking at the old man. "I think I'm going mad. Strange things have been happening. If I didn't know better, I'd think I'd been cursed."

"Oh, now, there's a problem," he said, rubbing his bristly chin. "That's never nice."

Kath looked at him, trying to see if he was

being funny. "Really?"

The old man raised his eyebrows. "My old Mammy was forever cursing people; the neighbours, the milkman, the dog, anyone or anything that didn't go along with her. It was a troubling thing and meant we had to move along more than we should. In the end, all her cursing brought misery on our heads because we had no roof."

"It's horrible," Kath said. "I can't rest or think about anything else. It's doing my head in."

"That's the power of curses. If you know you've been cursed, then you're looking out for it, aren't you? Anything that goes wrong will be the fault of the curse, won't it?"

"You think I'm imagining all this?"

"No. It's just that all this bad stuff would've come along whether you'd been cursed or not. A bit like when they give chalk tablets to people who think they're poorly and they get better."

"Like that guy in Better Call Saul who thought electricity was making him ill?" Kath said.

"Well now, you've lost me a little, I'll admit, but yeah, that sort of thing. If you're thinking electricity is doing you in, then maybe it will."

"So, if I just think it's not real, the curse can't harm me," Kath said, wearily. "That's harder than it sounds."

"You have to do something about it," the old man said. "Settle your thoughts by doing something. A gesture. An act of some kind."

"Right," Kath said. "Thanks. I feel better already. I know just what to do." She straightened up and turned to go back into the hospital.

"Just one thing," the old man called after her. "And it's a bit of a delicate matter but I feel I need to say something."

"Go on."

"It's your skirt," the old man said. "It's tucked into your knickers."

CHAPTER 33

The Aldi in Birkenhead was missing its captain and the stand-in, a Mrs Capstick, wasn't happy with Chinn and Kinnear taking another member of the crew off deck. She looked harassed enough before they had a word with her, as she marched up and down the aisles, hissing orders at shelf-stackers and nudging staff when they coagulated into huddles to share gossip about what had happened to Nathan Roscoe, their boss.

"Gary is one of our hardest workers," Mrs Capstick said, pushing her hair behind her ear. She was a big woman and her matching skirt and jacket wasn't the most comfortable attire for charging around the shop and mucking in where necessary. "Do you have to talk to him now?"

"I'm afraid time is pressing, Mrs Capstick," Vikki said. "Can we use your office?"

Mrs Capstick pursed her lips so hard that it smudged her lipstick. "Very well but please be quick."

Gary was about as pleased to see them as Mrs Capstick had been as they ushered him into the cluttered office at the back of the shop. "What do you want now?"

"Just tell us where Trevor Long is, please, Gary."

Stott looked confused. "What do you mean? I thought you said he'd been murdered."

"We've very good reason to believe that Trevor Long is alive and kicking. So that means he's been wasting police time and so have you. On top of that, it looks like he may be involved in a serious assault on Nathan Roscoe…"

"Bastard!" Stott snapped, jumping up.

"Gary," Vikki said. "Please sit down. I don't know what you're upset about, but I think it's about time you started telling the truth."

Gary slumped back into his seat. "That's the point, isn't it? I have been telling the truth. And I'm the one sitting here being grilled by the police while Trevor's sitting somewhere laughing at me."

"Come on Gary, tell us everything," Kinnear said. "What's been going on?"

"He set me up. He knew I'd be worried. Bastard!"

"What do you mean?"

Gary seemed to shrink and deflate. "He talked about it, but I never thought he'd actually try and do it."

"Please Gary," Vikki said. "Help us out here. We're struggling to keep up."

"Trevor borrowed a load of money off Emilio Ogden, didn't he? And he was struggling to pay it back. Ogden was leaning on him a bit but then this Thor character turns up and ties Trevor to a garage door in broad daylight. Starts throwing axes at him. They all missed, like, but Thor said next time they wouldn't. Can you believe it?"

Kinnear nodded. "Sadly, I can, Gary. Keep going."

"Well Trevor was really scared but something changed in him that day. He became obsessed with Thor and said he had a plan to 'bring him down.'"

"And what was that plan?" Kinnear said.

"He never told me all the details. I didn't think he'd actually do it, though. We posted a couple of videos suggesting that they were up to no good. I know he'd annoyed them by infiltrating one of their parties, but Thor chucked him out."

"So you're telling me that Trevor Long faked his death so that Thor Magnussen would get the blame and then what?"

Gary shrugged. "Then Trevor wouldn't have to pay his debt back, I suppose. Bastard. He didn't even tell me what he was going to do. I thought we were mates."

"But what was he going to do after that? I mean, suppose his plan worked and we believed that Thor Magnussen was somehow involved in his death. What then? He couldn't show his face round here. He'd be in even more trouble with Thor and still owe him the money."

Gary looked crestfallen as he realised the flaw in the whole scheme. "He must have been planning to start a new life somewhere. He was going to leave me owing all the rent on the flat, too. I'd have to move out. Go back to my mum's. Bastard! Selfish, thoughtless bastard!"

"What about this girlfriend, Gary? Zoe Plumb? What was she like?"

"She was a right cow," Gary muttered. "Treated him like shit. Always bossing him around and telling him what to do. Then she tried to break me and Trevor up..."

Kinnear gave Gary a quizzical look. "Tried to break you up? How do you mean?"

"You know, suggesting they went out on the nights me and Trevor did stuff. Like the investigating and recording videos. It was her that encouraged him to do the stupid medium act."

"Sounds like standard girlfriend/boyfriend stuff to me, Gary," Vikki said. "You'd be playing gooseberry. Third wheel. Often the best friend feels excluded."

"Nah. She was cruel. She'd put conditions on Trevor seeing her. Like he couldn't see her on a

Thursday if he'd posted a video the night before. Or if he was going to go out investigating with me the next night. She made stuff up on the spot. It used to drive him up the wall. Best thing that happened was when she dumped him."

"So, what about Nathan Roscoe? How d'you think he ended up unconscious over at Trevor's caravan?"

Gary looked shocked. "Really? I mean, I'd heard something but I didn't realise that…"

"What had you heard, Gary?" Vikki said.

"Just gossip. You'd have to ask Alyssa if it's true…"

*****

When he was at primary school, Alex Manikas had encountered a bully. He was a tall lad with gappy teeth, a big, square head and freckles. He would stare across the class at Alex pointing at him and shaking his fist. At playtime, Alex would hide in the girls' toilets and even skip lunch to avoid this boy. In the end Alex's father had noticed how unhappy he was and forced the truth out of the boy.

"You have to make a choice, Alex," his father had said. "Are you going to let this boy dictate your life or are you going to take control?"

"I don't know papa," Alex had said, looking up at his father's dark, stern face.

"If you don't know your own mind, then someone else will make it up for you. I can complain to the school and they will do what they can, but sooner or later you're going to have to stand up to this boy yourself."

The next day, Alex had stood in the middle of the playground, in plain sight and the bully came. There wasn't any great confrontation or reckoning. The boy hit Alex in the back and Alex punched him hard in the nose. He remembered the look of astonishment on the boy's face; he hadn't expected resistance and didn't like it. Alex also remembered the blood. The boy's nose had exploded in a fountain of red. At first, Alex thought he'd killed the boy. They both got hauled into the headteacher's office and sent home. But that was the end of it.

Now lying at the bottom of the pit, Alex longed to see his father; to hear his voice and feel his arms around him. Most of all, he longed for some words of advice. He didn't have them, so he decided to use the advice he just recalled. Rising to his feet, he looked up at the top of the pit. He wasn't going to just sit here. Just because Ogden had done a runner, didn't mean he was defeated. He was going to try and get out before, when Ogden landed on him, so he could get out now.

It was just as he placed his hands on the wall of the pit that a rope ladder snaked down beside him. Alex looked up to see three heads peering down at him. He climbed up, squinting and slowly letting his eyes become accustomed to the light.

Thor stood, grinning and twitching, stoned and excited. His mates flanked him in their beards and leathers. Bjorn scowled at Alex. The smell of body odour and booze was overpowering, even though Alex had spent the best part of a night and a day underground. In the middle of this unsavoury crowd stood a man dressed in what could only be described as golf club casuals; a pink polo shirt, brown leather belt holding up tan chinos and a pair of brown loafers. His long, white hair was slicked back and held back by a pair of expensive sunglasses. He had a disappointed look on his tanned face and his square jaw was set. Despite long hours of sensory deprivation, Alex was sharp enough to realise that this was Harry Thorpe, Magnussen's father. And he wasn't happy.

"Are you fuckin' mental, Fabian?" He said to his son.

Thor scowled at the use of his old name. "He was poking his nose in where it didn't belong. I thought I'd teach him a lesson, Dad."

Harry Thorpe winced and turned on his son. "You don't teach coppers a lesson, you dozy prick," he said. "You nod, smile and lie to them. Then you go on your sweet way. This is a fuckin' mess."

"What shall we do, boss?" Bjorn said, to Harry, not to Thor.

Harry held up a hand. "Before we do anything, can we get this man some clothes. I can't conduct any kind of business when a fella's John Thomas is swinging free."

Bjorn disappeared for a second and returned with a bundle of crumpled, muddy clothes. Alex snatched them off him and started pulling his trousers on.

"What's your name, son?" he said to Alex.

"Detective Constable Alex Manikas, Merseyside Police, Mr Thorpe. And I'm not happy," Alex said, dragging his fleece on over his head.

Harry Thorpe nodded. "You a good copper, Alex?"

Manikas frowned. He'd never been asked such a blunt question and it seemed even stranger under the circumstances. "Yes. I guess I am."

"Conscientious?"

"Yeah."

"You honest?"

"I try to be."

"So, what if I said there was an envelope stuffed full of fifties in the glove compartment of my car? And what if I said that envelope could be considered a down-payment of compensation for your inconvenience? Do you think you might take it?"

Alex hesitated. He didn't want to take the bribe, but it struck him that Thorpe was offering him a way out. Alex wondered what the alternative was. "Well, I don't know. Your son hasn't exactly been friendly. And bribing an officer is a serious crime..."

"I know what a serious crime is, son, believe me. You know, there was a time when you knew where you stood with coppers. They had a going rate and it was all cushy. It's not like that these days. You can't rely on the police anymore."

Alex scowled at Thorpe. "Look. If you just let me go then I won't say a word. This whole episode doesn't show me in a good light either, I'm not about to go blabbing to my mates back at the station am I? How about we call it quits."

Harry Thorpe tutted. "Really?" he said. "Call it quits?"

Alex nodded.

Harry Thorpe looked at Thor. "Like I said son, you smile, nod and lie. If that doesn't work, you use your money. If that doesn't work, you bury them." Turning suddenly, Thorpe jabbed Alex in the chest. Alex stumbled backwards and fell back into the pit. For a second, he was weightless and then the hard earth stole his breath. He lay gasping staring up at the sky above.

Thorpe's voice drifted down, faint and distant. "Find that other reject and bring him back here. As soon as it's dark, get a bulldozer over here and fill that hole in. And don't ever let me down like that again."

Manikas blinked up at the clouds. Time was running out.

CHAPTER 34

Darkness had fallen hours ago, but Will Blake needed it to be late if his plan was to work. Even now, standing at Ian Youde's front door, he wondered just what the hell he was doing. He should be trying to get in touch with Laura, showing his support for her. But if there was even a slight possibility that Serafina was trapped in that shed, he couldn't ignore it. Leaving Gwen back at her house, Blake had gone home to collect what he needed and formulate some kind of plan. He rapped on the door and waited.

It took Youde a while to come to the door and Blake was about to knock again but the door swung open and Youde stood there, his piggy eyes glittering with anger. "Do you know what time it is? I was about to turn in. What do you think you're playing at?"

"Sorry Mr Youde but I think I saw someone trying to break into your shed as I was passing," Blake said. "I think I scared them off, but do you mind if I check?"

Youde was silent for a moment. "Come on, let's have a look." He pulled a baseball bat that had been leaning against the side of the door.

"I don't think there'll be any need for that,"

Blake said.

"My property," Youde said. "I've a right to protect it."

Blake shook his head but, as he was certain they wouldn't encounter anyone, let Youde lead him to the shed. He pulled a torch from his pocket and shone it into the window. Spades and garden forks hung in size order along the wall. Row upon row of wooden drawers held twine, plant labels or seeds. Another small box held screws in individual boxes. Nothing was out of place. Plant pots stood in regimented rows and in one corner was a pile of magazines, a radio and a chair. Blake felt a stab of guilt. Mr Youde wasn't any kind of catnapper. He was just an old man who liked to keep his garden neat. "Looks undisturbed," Blake said. "I'll notify HQ and alert uniform that there's be a sighting. Do you want to check the lock?"

Youde rattled the lock. "It's fine," he said, looking up at Blake. "You want a cup of tea? Or a beer?"

"Yeah," Blake said, taken by surprise. "A beer would be great. Thanks."

He followed the old man through the garden, cursing himself. He'd been too easily convinced that Youde had something to do with the cats' disappearance. Laura and Gwen had both expressed a dislike for him and he'd let that colour his judgement. Maybe he was only doing this as some kind of weird displacement activity instead of actually going to talk to Laura about the whole Kyle Quinlan business.

Youde led Blake into the house and Blake blinked in amazement. It was a large house like all the others in Rock Park, with tall ceilings and big rooms. It smelt of carbolic and a mechanical, oily undertone. The walls were painted white but almost every inch was covered with a picture of an aircraft or a tank from the Second World War. Blake followed Youde through the hall and into a large kitchen with a scrubbed pine table in the centre. Even here, the shelves were laden with vintage mess kits, tin mugs and water bottles. Everything was clean. Blake wondered how much time Youde spent dusting.

"I'm a collector," Youde said. "World War Two memorabilia. I've got all sorts. Uniforms, gas masks, the lot." He opened a fridge that looked as though it had just been transported from the fifties and pulled out two bottles of brown ale. He popped the lids and handed one to Blake. Brown ale, it seemed was all that was on offer. Fortunately, Blake wasn't fussy.

"No firearms, I trust," Blake said, raising an eyebrow.

"Nah," Youde said. He grinned at Blake. "So, you satisfied I haven't got your cat stuffed in a bag in the shed, then?"

Blake felt himself blushing. "Sorry?" He said.

"All that nonsense about a burglar and calling HQ. Do you think I was born yesterday?"

"I assure you, Mr Youde, I did see someone prowling about the garden and I will notify our patrol cars and ask them to drive by here over the next few nights."

Youde sniffed. "Ah well, won't do any harm to have a few coppers rolling around here, will it. It'll make a change. So you and that Gwen, what's the deal?"

Again Blake felt himself reddening. "Deal? There's no 'deal.' Her cat's gone missing and so has mine."

"It's funny that, isn't it? You looking for a cat with your name."

"I don't follow..."

"William Blake. The poet. He was always writing about cats, wasn't he? Tyger, tyger burning bright..."

Blake tried not to show his disappointment. Ever since he could remember, people had recited that fragment of poetry to him. He couldn't help himself. "Ah, right, yes. Carry on."

Youde looked a little flustered. "Erm, in the forests of the night? What... hand or... eye..." He ground to a halt. "Don't know any more."

"You did better than most people who bring it up," Blake said, raising his bottle in salute.

"Cats, Mr Blake," Youde said, "they come and go. I'll say it again, you wanna watch her. She's batty. Her garden is full of poison. I'm not fooled by all those hippy wind chimes she puts up. I've lived here for forty years. I remember her moving in. Ooh the comings and goings, you wouldn't believe it. All kinds of ne'er do wells hanging around there and not just druggy types. Really scary folks. I was frightened, sometimes and it takes a lot to scare me."

"Well," Blake said, finishing off the drink. "Thanks for the beer. I'd better get off."

"Any time, Mr Blake," Youde said. "Any time. You watch her."

*****

It had taken Alex Manikas some time to get over the shock of being pushed back into the hole. He genuinely thought he'd been on his way off the field and heading back home. Maybe he should have taken the money. He could have used it as evidence against Thorpe. But then there was all the other details surrounding the bribery; Manikas being present at a party where drugs were openly being taken, Blake warning Manikas not to go. Manikas could see that he looked guilty of being stupid at the very least. If he had taken the cash, then Harry Thorpe could have said it was a gift, that Manikas was invited to the party and came along as a friend of Thor Magnussen. Worse, Thorpe could claim it had been stolen. There'd be enough doubt to make Manikas look shady and unreliable.

And now, as darkness grew, Alex was beginning to wonder how he was going to get out of this fix. He had heard the rumble of a diesel engine earlier and knew it was the Sons of Sol bringing the bulldozer across the field. There was no sign of Emilio Ogden who was meant to be sharing this hole with him. Alex assumed they hadn't caught up with him. Maybe they'd dig another hole for him somewhere else once they found him. As soon as the shadows lengthened from the woodland that skirted the field, they'd start filling the hole in.

"The donkey in the well," Alex muttered to himself. It was a story he'd been told in school several times. A farmer has a donkey that falls down a deep well. Try as he might, the farmer can't get the donkey out and he decides to just fill in the well. As the first few shovels of soil land on the donkey's back, it complains loudly. But then, it shakes them off and stands on top of the soil. Slowly, more soil goes in and the donkey steps up. After a while, the level of the soil has risen so high that the donkey can step out and is saved. If only it was so simple. "Maybe it is," he said, craning his neck to try and remember where the pile of earth that came out of the hole was situated.

It was a big mound; Manikas could just see the top of it. He would have to act fast and it was a slim chance. Even then, if he did succeed, he'd have to be prepared to fight his way off the field. If he could get to the woods or the road, he might have a chance. It was a slim one but better than standing still and letting tons of soil bury him alive. He shuddered, trying to put the thought from his mind.

The shadows lengthened and it became pitch black in the hole. Above, he heard shouting. But it wasn't the shouting of men organising themselves, it was an argument. Maybe some of the Sons of Sol weren't that keen on cold-blooded murder. A spark of hope ignited in Alex's chest. Maybe someone would throw a ladder down any minute.

The sound of the engine firing up sent an icy chill through Alex, snuffing out that hope in an instant. He steeled himself as the engine roar grew louder. It laboured as the earth began to move. Alex heard streams of soil sliding into the hole and pressed himself against the far wall, away from where it was being pushed in. More came down and then with a deafening thump, a great pile landed, burying his feet. He heard the bulldozer reversing and balled his fists. The soil would be higher at the far end of the pit and the distance to the top of the wall shorter now. He took a run at the wall and felt his feet sink into the soil, sucking the momentum from him and making his thighs burn as he waded through the loose earth.

Another engine roar brought a rain of dirt down on him and Alex had to stagger back to avoid getting buried. This time. He scrambled forward, clawing at the pile and ignoring the pain in his legs as he pushed forward. He ran higher, gripping a stone that lay there and not letting it go. As he breached the edge of the pit, a burly man stared at him in surprise. Alex didn't even wait, he swung the stone, clipping the man on the temple. He fell to the ground and Alex grabbed the axe that he'd dropped. He was out of the hole and had no intention of going back in.

Alex's sudden appearance, filthy, snarling and gripping a huge battle axe, startled five of the Sons of Sol, and they turned and ran. Bjorn stood his ground.

"Get round him," he said. "Don't let him escape."

Alex crouched, ready as three men edged around him. He swung the axe, making them skitter back. "I'm not going back in the pit, Bjorn," Alex panted. "So you better give up now."

"You can't fight us all," Bjorn said. "We'll overpower you." He gave a yell and the men pounced but Alex whirled the axe, clipping one of the Sons in the head. He fell to the ground and the other two backed away.

Behind them, the bulldozer growled into life again and Alex spun to see the huge yellow monster rumbled towards him. The cab was illuminated and Thor Magnussen grinned, his eyes wide in a berserk mixture of rage and excitement. One of the men screamed as the bulldozer went straight over his foot. Alex used the chance to ram the flat of the blade into the other man's stomach before sprinting towards Bjorn.

Thor yelled something and pushed the throttle down. Bjorn's eyes widened as he realised that Alex was leading the juggernaut towards him, then he too, turned and ran. Alex feinted to the left and then sprinted off to his right, heading for the treeline but two pale faces appeared out of the gloom so he found himself doubling back towards the hole.

The bulldozer rumbled towards him as he stood with his back to the pit. The blood pulsed through his neck and head as if it would burst out. Every muscle ached and his lungs burnt with the effort of running. In a last desperate gambit, he hurled the axe with all his remaining strength at the cab of the bulldozer. It shattered the glass and he heard Thor scream. The vehicle clattered towards him still and Alex had to throw himself to one side or get crushed.

Without pausing to look back, Alex sprinted for the treeline. When he did glance back, he saw the bulldozer nose down in the pit, the cab still illuminated and the remaining Sons of Sol scampering all over it. Thor lay slumped over the controls.

He turned and began stumbling through the wood, uncertain of where he was heading. In some ways, it would be better to be on the road but then if the Sons decided to come after him, they'd find it so much easier.

A bearded face loomed up out of the undergrowth, making Alex yell. Bjorn swung his great axe. Alex threw himself aside and the axe buried itself into a tree trunk. Summoning his last strength, Alex powered forward, head down and butted Bjorn square in the stomach. He felt the zips and studs on Bjorn's jacket dig into his head but the big man fell back, gasping. Not pausing in the onslaught, Alex threw himself on top of Bjorn, punching him hard again and again. He felt the Bjorn's nose crack and a tooth dug into his knuckles but he didn't let up until the man lay still. Spent, Alex slumped over the unconscious man, panting for breath. Finally, he dragged himself to his feet and staggered off into the darkness.

CHAPTER 35

Jeff Blake felt a jolt of anxiety as he sat opposite Josh Gambles. This was his second visit but he knew he would never get used to it. The visiting room was a carpeted barn with rows of strange, upholstered stools flanking small coffee tables. Everything was bolted down but otherwise, Jeff could have been sitting in a local library or the foyer of a busy office. Apart from the fact that uniformed guards stood watching every move.

Gambles hadn't been what Jeff had expected, either. A boyish-looking young man, with dark hair and beard. He sat, one leg up on his knee, dissecting Jeff with his gaze. Gambles had a smug grin that declared who he thought the genius was around here.

"You're still nervous of me," Gambles said. "I can tell. What did you expect? Me all bound up wearing a face mask like Hannibal Lecter?"

"I'll get used to it," Jeff said. "It's just not an environment I'm accustomed to. And, yes, you're right. I do think I'd feel better talking to you through bulletproof glass via a microphone."

"And what do you think I'm likely to do?"

Jeff shrugged. "I don't think you're going to do

anything. It's what you have done in the past that makes me nervous. It's your reputation." Inside, Jeff cringed at such an obvious massaging of Gambles ego but the man seemed to like it.

Gambles grinned and spread his arms wide. A nearby guard shifted his position ever so slightly. "I'm an innocent man until they find me guilty, Jeffrey. I don't think they can shackle me unless I give them cause to."

Jeff pulled out his notebook. "So," he said. "Where do we start?"

"You aren't like him at all, really, are you?"

"Who? My brother? No, I don't suppose I am. Is that a problem?"

Gambles smiled. "No. You're more... ambivalent. Otherwise you wouldn't be here, would you?"

"I'm not sure what you mean. I see an opportunity here and, yes, I could do with the money, I won't deny that but the whole situation fascinates me on an intellectual and emotional level, too."

"The fact that I was arrested by your brother and was the last person to see your mother alive, fascinates you?"

Jeff felt a stab of anger and shame, but he felt excitement, too. "It's more complex than that. The idea of me writing about you, given your background and connection to our family, yes. In some ways, this book is as much about me as you."

"No," Gambles said. "This book is about me."

"True," Jeff said. "But I won't be writing it from a neutral standpoint, will I? I'll try my best, but you have to admit people are going to want to know what I think of you and what you've done."

Gambles smiled but his eyes were cold. "I think you're right. In a sense, you're committing a moral outrage. You should hate me. You shouldn't be cashing in. You're as bad as me."

"Exactly," Jeff said. "But at the same time, I'm not."

For a moment Gambles looked uncomfortable as he grappled with what Jeff might be getting at. "I'm not sure I follow," Gambles said, through clenched teeth.

"In some people's eyes, I could be a saint; all-forgiving and trying my best to understand what it was that drove you to do what you did. There are many layers to this. It will be more than a biography. It'll be a work of literature."

"Art," Gambles said, in a low voice. "I like it. I read your books you know."

"Really? Which ones?"

"All of them. Even Elven Strike. I wasn't too

keen on that one, a tad derivative, but I enjoyed all the others. I'm not surprised they didn't sell well, though. They required a certain type of intellect to fully appreciate them. I bet your big brother hated them."

"I'm not sure he even read them," Jeff said, his shoulders sinking. "Probably too busy. I mean he always made positive noises but how can you really tell if someone likes your work or has even bothered? You can't set them a test, can you?"

"No, I suppose not," Gambles said. "You resent your brother, don't you?"

Jeff nodded. "Of course. He thinks he has a monopoly on grief. He's so sanctimonious and masochistic. Do you know what William Blake the poet said? Shame is pride's cloak. Do you see? Will hides behind his shame. He wears it like a badge of honour. The wounded policeman standing, bloodied but unbowed in the line of duty while we selfish peasants scurry around worrying about our silly little mortgages and schemes..."

"Yes," Gambles said. "I've gone off him, quite a bit, too. Well that quote should certainly appear in the book. Have you told him you're working with me?"

"I have," Jeff said, not wanting to admit that Blake had found him out rather than being told outright.

"And how did he take the news?"

"He tried to throw me out of the house."

Gambles' eyes glowed. "Did you leave?"

"Once I saw what an arse he was going to be about it," Jeff said. "I have property in London. The rent from that covers my costs up here."

"Bravo, Jeffrey," Gambles said, pressing his hands together.

Jeff gave an embarrassed cough. "So, I've started a bit of research. Your family tree, background stuff really…"

"Not my family," Gambles hissed, his face twisting in hatred. "Not that bunch of inbred, ignorant, chavs…"

"But people will want to try and understand…"

"There is no understanding, is there? What is there to understand? Could you ever explain why I plunged those scissors into that girl's eye? I can explain it to you, but few will appreciate the truth. And the truth isn't because my father beat me or my mother abandoned me. I am not a victim."

"No," Jeff said. "Not at all but some background will be necessary, even if it's just a couple of paragraphs; factual stuff, you know, dates of birth, where you were born. I don't need to go near any family at all."

Gambles narrowed his eyes. "Some of my family are all right. It's just knowing which ones you can trust. I was very close to my aunt. You can read that however you like. She'll talk to you. If you need her to."

"Right, we can get into details later," Jeff said. "What I suggest is I knock together a short summary of the project, explaining who is involved, the angle we're taking and what areas it might cover. I'll send it to you for approval. Then I'll send it to my agent. I'm sure we'll sell this. It might be a small publisher; one that's accustomed to taking risks but once it's out there, it'll sell by the million."

"And we'll all be famous together," Gambles said, staring above Jeff's head. "You, me, and Will…"

*****

Alex Manikas stared at himself in the bathroom mirror, thankful to be home. How he had managed to get onto the bus and train looking so filthy, he didn't know. His clothes were torn and muddy from running through the undergrowth. Bruises and cuts covered his body. He had a superb black eye and every muscle ached. He ran the taps and plunged his skinned knuckles under the cold stream. For a moment he forgot everything and just revelled in the feeling of the water on his stinging hands. He was home and safe. That was all that mattered for now. The next thing was to decide what to do about what had happened. He knew his presence at the party had compromised any investigation into Thor Magnussen and the money Trevor had borrowed from him. He should see Blake first thing tomorrow and tell him everything. It would probably mean losing his job but he'd been reckless and possibly let a killer go free.

Apart from anything else, he wasn't sure if Thor Magnussen was even alive. The bulldozer had pitched into the hole and the last thing Alex had seen was Thor slumped in the cabin. If he was dead, then Alex was guilty of manslaughter and he had no doubt that Harry Thorpe would be after his scalp.

If Thor was alive, however, Harry Thorpe might not want any close scrutiny into what happened at the weekend. True Manikas had gone against correct procedure but Thorpe had tried to kill him. God knows if Emilio Ogden was still alive. If he had any sense, he'd keep his head down for a long time. With Emilio gone, there was no witness to verify that Trevor borrowed the money from Thor. In that scenario, it was possible Alex could save his professional skin. He stared at his gaunt reflection and tears prickled his eyes. One moment of stupidity. One bad decision and his whole career was ruined.

Alex knew what the right thing to do was. He'd see Blake tomorrow and face the music.

CHAPTER 36

Blake sat in the Major Incident Room trying to take in everything that Kinnear said but he couldn't concentrate. He hadn't spoken to Laura yesterday; he'd tried to phone her but she didn't answer. He'd considered going round but wasn't sure if she'd have welcomed him or told him to get lost. But there was something else, too. Blake raised his hand.

"Sorry, Andrew, just give us a moment," he said, surveying his team. Kath Cryer looked a shocking grey colour as though she hadn't slept all weekend. Alex Manikas sat on the edge of his desk, his eyes drooping. He had a black eye and his arm was in a sling. He winced every time he shifted his position, which he did a lot. Manikas had asked to see him, first thing but Blake had stalled him. "Kath, Alex, are you two okay?"

"Fine boss," Alex said, feeling the eyes of the team on him. When he confessed, it was to be to Blake only. "I took your advice on Friday and stayed in with a bottle of red. Slipped on a stair carpet and ended up on the bottom step..."

"He's been to his dominatrix again, sir," Kath said, with a sickly smile.

"And how about you Kath? No offence but you

look like shit too," Blake said.

"D'you hear that, people?" Kath said. "Bullying and harassment, that is. No, sir, I'm feeling a lot better. Honestly if you'd seen me yesterday, you'd have thought I was going to die but I'm fine."

"Okay, as long as you're both all right. Just let me know if you need a break or whatever," Blake said. "Carry on Andrew."

"Nathan Roscoe, manager of Aldi in Birkenhead, was found unconscious at Gorse Meadow Caravan Park in Thurstaston. In a caravan belonging to Trevor Long. A witness at the park who knows Trevor claims that Trevor had been there all week. Large as life and as alive as you or me..."

"Half dead then," Kath said, pulling tongues at Blake.

"Right," Kinnear said, disconcerted. "But alive, right? He saw a man in a hoody and a woman flee the caravan. They left in what turns out to be Roscoe's car. Which is missing."

"And Roscoe?" Blake said. "Any news on him?"

"Still out, sir," Vikki Chinn said. "Apparently he was injected with some kind of tranquiliser. We suspect that Zoe Plumb is involved somehow, she works at a vets and we think she would have access to the right drugs to knock Roscoe out."

"But Plumb was at the surgery where she works all day, according to her boss," Kinnear added. "So we're stumped and we don't know where Long has gone."

"So Long's death was a hoax? How did he lose all that blood and walk away unscathed?"

"Don't know, sir," Vikki said. "We've asked forensics to check that the blood is all human and is all Trevor's but that'll take time."

"What about Roscoe? What was he doing down at the caravan?"

"There's a rumour going around the supermarket that he fancied Alyssa Jones and didn't like Long trying to chat her up. Maybe he discovered that Long was alive and went to sort him out?"

Blake frowned. "Why not just tell us? And how did he find out that Trevor was alive?"

"Still a mystery, sir," Kinnear said.

"My money is still on that Plumb girl," Kath said. "She found the camcorder, bone dry. She lied to me about not knowing Long."

"She's as hard as nails," Kinnear said. "And her boss backed her up. Said she was at work on the day Roscoe was knocked out."

"Gary Stott seemed quite put out that Trevor was still alive. Said Trevor hatched a plan months ago to fake his own death and pin the blame on Thor Magnussen. Apparently, Magnussen roughed Long up and threatened to kill him if he didn't pay back the money he owed. According to Emilio Ogden, the money he lent out belonged to Harry Thorpe."

"Any progress on that front, Alex?" Blake said.

Manikas was staring into the wastepaper basket. Kath nudged him. "What? Sorry, guv, erm, no. Didn't really make any progress, I'm afraid, sir. Other than what we knew already that Thor wasn't a fan of Trevor Long."

"Ogden, the witness who told us about the moneylending business in Thor's betting shop has gone missing," Vikki said. "Last seen driving into North Wales."

Blake nodded. "Manikas and Kinnear. Can you focus on Magnussen and Ogden. See if you can track either of them down. I want to know if the story about Magnussen threatening Long is true. See if you can look in on the betting shop, too. Maybe find Ogden's whereabouts."

"Could I have a crack at Zoe Plumb, again, sir? She and I really get on," Kath said, smirking. "She'll be so pleased to see me again."

"I bet she will, Kath. Go on then. See what you and Vikki can dig up." Blake paused and turned to Manikas. "Alex, you wanted a quick word?"

As the others left, Blake sat on the desk next to Alex's chair. "Are you okay?"

"The thing is, sir, I..." Alex began but Blake's phone rang, cutting him off. Blake glanced at the screen, about to cut it dead but then held up a finger. "Sorry Alex, this looks pertinent to the case." He put it on speaker.

"PC Robertson, sir. I've just discovered that Thor Magnussen has been in a scrape over the weekend. He's here in Arrowe Park Hospital. In a bad way but he'll pull through. I thought you'd want to know."

"Thanks," Blake said. "I'll send some people round if he's able to talk. Keep us posted." Blake hung up and turned back to Alex. "Sorry. Looks like our friend the thunder god has been in the wars too, Alex. You sure you're okay?"

A thousand emotions surged through Alex. Relief that Magnussen wasn't dead and hope that, maybe Thorpe would want to hush the whole episode up. These were tinged with shame, too, because Alex knew he couldn't tell Blake. In that moment he had seen a chance to save his career and he knew he was going to take it. "Sure, Boss, honestly. My dad brought me a bottle of Makedonikos. It's my favourite and I hadn't eaten. It went to my head..."

"Makedonikos?"

"It's a red wine, sir. Greek. Like I say, the bottle he brought was a strong one. Knocked me for six but I didn't know until I stood up."

"And you didn't go to Thor's party?"

Alex felt as though Blake could see right through him. Alex looked Blake in the eye. "No, sir. That would have been a crazy thing to do. I took your advice. Stayed in," Alex said.

"Right," Blake said, peering at Manikas. "And this drinking alone. It isn't a habit, is it?"

"No, sir. No more than anyone else."

"Okay. As long as you're all right," Blake said, nodding slowly. "You'd better catch up with Kinnear."

"Thanks, sir," Alex said. He turned and hurried after his colleague, looking skyward and offering a little prayer of thanks. Thorpe could still rock the boat and Alex could only hope that he didn't.

"What was all that about?" Kinnear said, as Alex climbed into the car.

"Blakey just worried that I'm becoming an alcoholic," Alex said.

"And are you?"

Alex looked appalled. "What's that meant to mean?"

"Ooh. Denial. The first sign," Kinnear said, laughing. "I mean, I've had a few beers in my time, but I've never hurt myself because of drinking…"

"To be honest, I went out with some mates on Friday night and got into a bit of a scuffle…"

"Oh my God," Kinnear said, glancing over as he drove out of the carpark. "Did you get the tosser who had a go at you?"

"It was six of one, half a dozen of the other, really. I bumped into him, he spilled my beer. We both got a bit out of control. I sorted it out in the end, though. Don't tell Blake, please."

"No worries," Kinnear said. "As long as it's all sorted, now."

"Yeah," Manikas said, staring out of the window. They went through the tunnel, the faint smell of exhaust fumes filtering into the car. "Did you know, they have two massive fans blasting air through this tunnel? Those towers at the Pier head and over on the other side are air vents."

"Really?" Kinnear replied. "You're beginning to sound like Blakey and his useful factoids about Wirral."

"There's always room for more learning, Kinnear," Manikas said, doing a terrible impression of Blake.

They crawled through the queue at the tunnel barriers and then found themselves on the dual carriageway. "Did you hear about Magnussen?" Kinnear said.

Manikas' mouth felt dry. "Not in detail. What happened to him?"

"Not sure exactly. Some kind of accident with a digger. Anyway, we'll pay him a visit and see if he's able to answer any questions."

Alex didn't say anything but looked out of the window and wondered what he was heading towards.

Arrowe Park hospital was busy and it took Kinnear and Manikas some time to find Thor Magnussen's ward. A nurse told them that he was asleep and couldn't be disturbed at the moment. Manikas looked down on the huge figure curled up in the hospital bed and ground his teeth. To think, this idiot had been trying to kill him.

"You wait here, I'm going to the loo," Kinnear said.

Manikas sat down on a chair next to Thor's bed. He contemplated nudging him awake. Imagine his shock if he saw Manikas at his bedside.

"You've got a nerve," a voice said. Startled from his thoughts, Alex Manikas looked up and saw Harry Thorpe glaring at him.

CHAPTER 37

DI Kath Cryer made a short diversion on their way to see Zoe Plumb. She avoided the motorway and drove through Birkenhead instead, pulling up outside Flaybrick Hill cemetery.

DS Vikki Chinn frowned. "I thought we were heading to the vets, ma'am."

"Couple of things I want to do first," Kath muttered, climbing out of the car. "You wait here. I'll be two minutes." Kath went round to the back of the car and pulled a bunch of flowers out of the boot. Ignoring Vikki's puzzled stare, she strode through the gates and into the graveyard.

It didn't take her long to locate the grave that the old woman had been standing over when Kath first met her. A week had passed but it felt like months. Her head had cleared a little already as the antibiotics did their work. She didn't feel the urge to run to the toilet every ten minutes either. Theo was back home and almost better again. Kath suspected he was stringing it out just to avoid housework. She knelt at the grave and read the name on the stone.

Eric Darlow

Beloved Husband

Kath frowned; She'd assumed that the old woman was the wife of the man in the grave. How was that possible unless she was over a hundred? This was certainly the grave; it was carved in Kath's memory and she'd picked her way along the edge of the other graves to get to this one. With a shrug, she laid the bunch of flowers on Eric's grave.

"So...erm... I'm sorry," she said to the headstone, feeling instantly ridiculous. "I'm sorry I stamped all over this place without thinking. Please forgive me. Okay?" Slowly, Kath stood up, half expecting the old woman to spring out. "So, I hope we're square. I think we are..."

The sound of a foot scraping on gravel made Kath turn and she saw Vikki standing there. "Are you okay?"

Kath felt herself reddening. "Yeah," she said. "Course I am."

"I didn't know you had family round here."

"A distant relative," Kath said. "Come on. Let's go to the seaside."

Vikki looked taken aback. "The seaside, ma'am?"

"You heard me, Vikki. There's a weak link in Zoe Plumb's chainmail that I want to pick at before we go to see her. Let's see if we can unravel this mess."

*****

"Fancy seeing you here, Mr Thorpe," Alex Manikas said, meeting Thorpe's gaze. "Is he going to pull through?"

"He'll be fine. You did a lot of damage the other night, young man," Harry hissed, glancing around at the other beds. "A lot of people are very unhappy with you."

Alex frowned. "Why because I didn't just stand there and let them bury me alive? Can't say as I'm too upset about that."

Harry Thorpe put his hands in his pockets and tilted his head at Manikas, as though he was trying to work out a puzzle. "You haven't said anything about your weekend adventures, have you?"

"I may have. What do you think?"

"Well you wouldn't be here if you'd told your boss, would you? I reckon I'd be sitting in an interview room if you had. You were on your own. I think you're just glad to have got away by the skin of your teeth."

"I can't deny it. I'm happy your son didn't kill me, Mr Thorpe but I'm going to be watching very closely and if you or he puts a foot wrong, I'll have him."

Thorpe's cheeks reddened. "Are you trying to

threaten me? One word to your boss and you'll be out on your ear."

"So, you'd go to Police HQ and tell them that you tried to kill me at the weekend, but you failed and I did a lot of damage? Whatever I did pales into insignificance compared to attempted murder."

Thorpe's mouth flapped but nothing coherent came out.

"You don't even have any proof I was there. It would be my word against yours. And you'd have to explain what your son and his mates were doing on that field. Any search for evidence would probably reveal drug use on the site. Do you want to open that can of worms?" Alex was on his feet, now, his face close to Thorpe's. "Let's leave it at that, eh?"

"You'd do that?"

"It sticks in my throat but I can't see any other way. If I go down, I take you with me. But Emilio Ogden is off limits, too."

"That little toe-rag squealed on me..."

"That's the beauty of this agreement, Harry. Emilio has nothing to squeal about. Anyway, I think you put the wind up him enough. I suspect he's learning to speak Welsh already. It looks like our enquiry is moving away from your son anyway."

"Do you know how much money was in that envelope? You could have been rich."

"Any man who has true friends is rich, Mr Thorpe, didn't you know?"

Thor groaned and squinted from under the covers at his father and then at Manikas. His eyes widened. "Don't wet yourself, Fabian, It's not about the other night. He's just come to ask a few questions about Trevor Long. His mate will be back in a minute and I expect every answer to be 'no comment.'"

*****

Bev Campbell looked startled when she opened the door and Kath flashed her warrant. "I'm afraid I answered all Mr Kinnear's questions, when he came before about the Sons of Sol and Trevor Long. I don't know what else I can help you with," she said as she led them into the living room.

Kath sat down without being invited. "Well for a start, you can explain why you didn't mention knowing Zoe Plumb when you were asked about Trevor Long."

Bev paled. "I did," she said.

Kath pulled out her notebook and flicked through it as though she was reading Kinnear's notes. "Nope. You said something about 'a friend' putting a comment on Long's YouTube page and him following it up. No mention of Zoe."

"Yeah, well that's what happened, sort of..."

"Sort of? We're investigating a murder, Beverley. There's no room for 'sort of' in all this. So imagine our surprise when we talk to Zoe Plumb and she uses you as an alibi for the night Trevor disappeared."

Tears sprang to Bev Campbell's eyes. "I didn't mean to..."

"Cut the tears, Bev. They might work on soppy gets like DC Kinnear but I'm a heartless bitch with a water infection. Now tell me the truth before I frogmarch you down the station and book you for perverting the course of justice..."

"I'm sorry," Bev sobbed. "They just said it would be a bit of fun."

Kath rolled her eyes. "Who said what would be a bit of fun?"

"Trevor and Zoe. They said that all I had to do was say I'd been along to a Sons of Sol meeting and seen all kinds of terrible things. I have met Thor Magnussen but he's a dick and I thought he was from the start. So, when Trevor said they were going to put the frighteners on him by making it look like Thor had killed Trevor, I just went along, really."

"And lied to a police officer. Nice."

"And what was in it for you?" Vikki said, staring coldly at Bev. "Did they pay you?"

Bev's eyes widened. "No. Honest." She looked down at her clasped hands. "To tell you the truth, I was a little bit scared…"

"Of Trevor?" Kath snorted.

"Of Zoe. She's scary when you let her down. Violent scary. It isn't nice. But she trusts me to keep secrets."

"What other secrets have you kept for her, Bev?"

"You don't understand," Bev said, her eyes pleading Kath to let her off the hook. "I can't tell you anything else."

Kath turned to Vikki. "Can you book an interview room, Vikki? I think we may have to do this down at the custody suite."

"No! All right, please. They got married…"

"You what?" Kath said, staring at Bev.

"About eighteen months ago. I was the witness, but they swore me to secrecy…"

Kath shook her head. "This just gets better and better. Who was the other witness?"

"John Usher, the vet bloke. Zoe's boss."

"Did they ever live together? I don't remember anyone saying anything about them being married."

A slight frown creased Bev Campbell's smooth brow. "No. They never did. Zoe persuaded Trev that it would be cool to keep it a secret. She said it would add to his air of mystery. I never knew what she saw in him, to be honest. She could do way better than Trevor. She was ambitious, too. She always told me she wanted to marry a rich man, and Trevor certainly wasn't rich. I never understood why they got married."

"Thank you, Bev," Kath said, jumping up. "Come on, Vikki. I think we need to pay an urgent visit to Ms Plumb." She turned to Bev. "And you. Stay off the phone. If I find out you've tipped off Zoe, I'll be back round here with the handcuffs. Got me?"

CHAPTER 38

Having been expressly forbidden from research-ing Josh Gambles' family background, that's just what Jeffrey Blake went and did. He'd found the interview with Gambles more unsettling than he'd expected. The whole affair had been too convivial to be business-like. Jeff felt as though he'd been groomed in some way; set up and manipulated. Will was right when he said that Gambles messed with your head. Jeff found him likeable and that disturbed him.

It was to set that sense of disturbance at ease, that Jeff was going against Gambles' wishes. He almost wanted Gambles to be angry with him; to fall out with him, so there would be some kind of emotional barrier between them. He half hoped that in his anger the psychopath's mask would slip and Gambles would reveal his true nature.

Sitting in the library, Jeff felt a little of what he thought his brother might feel when he was investigating a crime. An expectant thrill that something juicy might turn up. He'd already done a little preliminary work; the family had been a dysfunctional one, he'd pulled a few newspaper clippings of various local outrages committed by them at one time or another. There were cousins who had been in and out of prison for various minor offences.

Josh Gambles' father had been a labourer; a patchy work record but never in trouble with the law. Mrs Gambles, Josh's mother, was a shop assistant. They had lived in Birkenhead in an ordinary house. On paper, there was nothing to show what horrors the boy had experienced behind closed doors. In the news reports of family members being sentenced for burglary or shoplifting and drugs offences, there was nothing to suggest why Josh Gambles chose the path he did. So all Jeff had was material for a sentence that said something like, 'Josh Gambles lived with his parents in an ordinary terraced house in Birkenhead.'

"Dull," Jeff muttered. He'd hoped that Gambles would give him some more insight but now he suspected that the psychopath would be selective in what he shared. Jeff really wanted to get under the killer's skin. Then something caught his eye. A recent news report. Jeff blinked. "Bloody hell." He picked up his phone and called Will

*****

Superintendent Martin sat at his desk, frowning at DCI Blake and shaking his head. "So, this Trevor Long business, what's going on?"

"Like knitting fog, sir," he said. "It seems as though Long faked his own death but now there's another victim in hospital still in a coma after being injected with some kind of tranquiliser. I'm hoping we can find Long soon."

"Damn well hope so, Will. Wasting Police time like that."

"I hope so, too. I think we're closing in on him."

"At least the investigation has moved away from Harry Thorpe. Thank God for that, eh?"

"I suppose so, sir. It would only have complicated matters and I suspect Harry Thorpe is slippery enough to get his son off the hook."

"There was some kind of trouble over the weekend, apparently. He crashed a digger or something. All on private land, and nobody reported anything, so hard to be sure what went on. Several injuries. Sounds to me like Harry Thorpe has his work cut out trying to control his wayward son."

"Seems so, sir."

"Right. Crack on then, Will. Find Trevor Long and give him a good kick up the arse from me."

"Will do, sir."

Martin looked worried for a second. "Metaphorically speaking, Will," he said.

Outside Martin's office, Blake pulled his phone

from his pocket and muttered a curse. Three missed calls from Jeff. Let him stew. He hoped Gambles was giving Jeff a run for his money. That selfish bastard deserved everything that was coming to him. Blake glanced at the time. He had a pile of paperwork to be done. He'd try and clear some of that before heading off to see Laura.

*****

Thor had proved uncooperative and Harry Thorpe needled Kinnear at every question, reminding his son that he didn't need to answer anything. In the end Kinnear had given up in disgust and decided that checking in on Nathan Roscoe might be the easier option.

"Let's hope Mr Roscoe is more helpful than Thor bloody Magnussen," Kinnear said as they walked up to Roscoe's side room.

"Even unconscious, he'd be more cooperative," Alex said.

Nathan Roscoe looked pale and dazed as he sat up in bed. He looked like he'd been wrestling with a grizzly bear. Manikas felt a fair deal of sympathy with the man, after his experience waking on Saturday morning.

"I don't really remember much," he said, faintly. "I went round there to confront Trevor. I mean of all the things to do. Put everyone through all that worry and inconvenience just to skive off work for a few days..."

"Skive off? You think Long did all that just to pull a sicky?" Kinnear said.

Roscoe looked puzzled. "Yeah, why else would he do it? I'd had words with him about slacking at work and he seemed to have become rather fixated..."

"Fixated?"

"On Alyssa Jones. I mean, I don't blame him; she's a pretty girl but she can do better than him," Roscoe said. "He'd spend all his time hanging around her and talking with her. I had to issue him with a warning. So I thought he might have faked his death to make us all feel bad."

"How did you know he was alive?"

"He messaged Alyssa," Roscoe said, the wonder at such a stupid act clear in his voice. "I mean, he thought it was cryptic. You know, false ID, a photograph of the Dee Estuary and some crap message about missing her but she recognised who it was straight away. He'd been bragging about inheriting his grandad's caravan down in Thurstaston a couple of weeks ago. He'd been trying to get Alyssa to spend the weekend there with him."

"So you went down there. Why didn't you phone us? You knew we were looking for him."

Nathan Roscoe pursed his lips, tears glistening in his eyes. "I'm not a proud man, detective. I know I'm not a great catch or much to look at but… I was jealous."

"Of Trevor Long?" Manikas said.

"I didn't like him trying to seduce Alyssa."

"Seduce?" Kinnear said. "It doesn't sound like much of a seduction."

Roscoe's eyes flashed with sudden anger. "He thinks he's so fucking clever, doesn't he? With his ghost stories and paranormal investigation videos. Well he's not. I may be ten years older than Alyssa but I can offer her security and a home. I pay my mortgage off in fifteen years. Long lives in a flat share."

Kinnear held his hands up. "Whoa. Okay. So, what happened?"

"I don't exactly know. He shit himself when I knocked on the door and asked him why he wasn't in work. He asked me in, said he could explain. I was going to read him the riot act; sack him there and then. That was when I realised he wasn't alone." He touched his neck. "She stabbed me with something. I was floating…"

"Can you remember who she was? Did you recognise her at all?"

Roscoe shook his head. "It's a complete blank, I'm afraid. All I can remember is a silhouette, lots of dark hair. And Trevor said something really odd, it was my last thought before passing out. I thought 'what a weird thing to say.'"

"Take your time," Kinnear said, allowing Roscoe to collect his thoughts.

"He said, 'where did that come from?' What did he mean by that?"

Kinnear shrugged. "I'm not sure, Mr Roscoe. Was he looking at you or somewhere else?"

"He was looking behind me. Yes. He was looking at the woman," Roscoe said. His eyes widened. "He was scared…"

"You had just turned up on his doorstep unexpected."

"No. It wasn't me he was scared of. It was the woman. Thinking about it now, he looked terrified the moment he opened the door. I thought it was me he was afraid of, but it wasn't. It was her."

Kinnear's phone buzzed. "Kath," he said. "We're at the hospital. Nathan Roscoe has just been talking to us."

"Anything?"

"Only that Trevor was frightened witless by whoever was with him in the caravan."

"Interesting. We've just spoken with the lovely Beverley Campbell again. She was witness at Trevor Long and Zoe Plumb's wedding, would you believe. About eighteen months ago."

"What?"

"Not only that, but the other witness was John Usher, the vet. Vikki's just done a simple google search of Merryvale Pet Vets and, after all the adverts and the very out of date website, there are some reports about it almost going bankrupt and not complying with health and safety regulations. Around the same time that wedding bells were ringing for Trevor."

"You think the two are linked, somehow?"

"I think if we do enough digging, we'll find a life insurance policy with Trevor's name on it. We've fannied around with this long enough. We're heading over to the vet's to pick Zoe up. We've got enough to charge her with obstruction and I'm sick of her pulling the wool over our eyes. Meet us at Merryvale."

CHAPTER 39

The surgery was eerily quiet as Kath and Vikki pulled up in the empty carpark. "Doesn't look very busy," Kath Cryer said as she climbed out of the car.

"Looking at some of the comments below the line on the news reports, I don't think it was very popular," Vikki said. "There's an ongoing investigation into the place by the Royal College of Veterinary Surgeons."

"That would explain why they had to advertise," Kath said. "I mean most vets just have local trade, usually."

"They offer a crematorium service," Vikki said. "It seems like a big place. Maybe they just got overambitious."

"What's John Usher like?"

"Dunno, really, Ma'am. The only time I met him he was wrestling with a chihuahua. He barely said anything other than to confirm that Zoe had been at the vets all day Saturday when Roscoe was assaulted. Some of the chatter on social media that I can see suggests he's a bit hapless and the clients aren't always happy."

"In what way?"

Vikki pulled out her phone. "I found a private Facebook group after my last visit here. It seems to be for disgruntled customers so obviously, they're going to have a bit of bias but comments such as 'panicked when Duke started barking at him,' 'stabbed himself with the needle instead of the cat' that sort of thing. He sounds like he doesn't have a natural affinity for the profession he chose."

"Let's have a word." They tried the surgery door, but it was locked. Kath frowned at Vikki. "Seems like they're shut."

Vikki peered in through the window. "Looks deserted."

"Better see if we can find them, come on." Kath led Vikki across the carpark and round the back of the building where a number of barns and out-houses stood. A couple of cars sat out of view from the main surgery and next to them stood a car wrapped in tarpaulin. Kath pulled at it and revealed green metal. "I bet if we pulled this tarp off, it'd be Nathan Roscoe's car underneath."

"If the wind just happened to blow the tarp up and expose the registration number, Ma'am, I can check it," Vikki said, pulling out her phone.

Kath smirked and dragged up the tarp a little higher to reveal the number plate and Vikki nod-ded. "Ooh, look. We've got one of them for car theft, then."

The building next to it had a tall chimney poking out of its roof. "D'you think that's the crem?"

Although the building had been covered in cladding to look like a log cabin, it was clearly a small steel barn. At its side two large doors would allow a forklift or dumper to carry the carcass of a large animal inside, whilst at the front was a smaller doorway for owners to enter. Kath went to the mourners' entrance and rattled the handle. Locked.

"Listen," Vikki said. "Can you hear something?"

Kath pressed her ear to the door. The noise from inside sounded muffled and scared. A wordless screaming as though someone was trying to cry for help through a gag. "Come on, let's try the side."

They ran round the building to the large doors which were also locked. "The front will be easier to get in."

The screaming grew louder and Kath hammered on the door. "Police. Open this door!"

"What are you doing?" A male voice yelled. "You can't! No!"

Kath rammed her shoulder against the door and Vikki joined her. The shouting continued and suddenly, the wood gave way. Kath and Vikki tumbled inside, falling on top of each other.

The room was a place where bereaved pet owners would normally sit as they said goodbye to their beloved furry friends. But the armchairs and rugs had been pushed to one side to accommodate an operating table. A naked man lay gagged and bound to it. Another small table held a syringe, surgical equipment and bottles. Kath glimpsed a wicked looking hacksaw.

Zoe Plumb was in the process of trying to drag the table towards what looked like a giant green metal chest freezer with its lid open. Except Kath knew this wasn't a chest freezer; it was an incinerator and Zoe was trying to throw the man in there alive.

A red-faced John Usher clung onto the table, his heels dug into the ground. "What's the difference?" Zoe Plumb yelled. "He's going to be dead either way!"

Kath clambered to her feet, straightening her jacket. "Will everybody just stop!" Kath shouted. Silence fell and Zoe Plumb stared in shock at her.

"Zoe Plumb, I'm arresting you on suspicion of attempted murder you do not..."

Screaming with rage, Zoe charged towards Kath, aiming to barge past her. Kath rolled her eyes and gave her a shove as she passed, sending her sprawling onto the floor. Vikki pounced with the cuffs and dragged Zoe to her feet. "It

314

was all *his* idea!" Zoe screeched, nodding her head at the startled vet. "He made me do it."

Kath shook her head. "Oh dear. That's disappointing. Letting the side down there, luv, blaming the nasty man." She turned to John Usher. "Come on criminal mastermind, show us your wrists."

Vikki sat Zoe down on the edge of one of the armchairs and hurried over to the man on the table. She undid the straps holding him and pulled the tape covering his mouth.

"Ow!" he snapped. "That hurt!"

"You're welcome," Vikki said. "Trevor Long, I presume."

*****

Blake's phone had been buzzing all day. Jeff didn't seem to want to give up. A part of Blake wanted to answer and tear his brother off a strip. But that's what he wanted, wasn't it? To continue the battle. To wind Blake up a little bit more. He was just doing Gambles' bidding, by behaving like this. How could he be so shortsighted by playing into that psycho's hands? Blake was having none of it. Angry thoughts chased each other around Blake's head all day. When the news of Zoe Plumb and John Usher's arrest came through, he was glad of the distraction.

"We're bringing them in, sir," Kath said on the phone. "Caught bang to rights. It looks as though they were about to knock Long out and cremate him. Another minute or two and we'd have lost Trevor Long for good."

"Well done, Kath, that's great work," Blake said. "Are you taking them to Birkenhead?"

"Yeah, once the RSPCA are here…"

"There are animals there? Can't you phone their owners?"

"It's just that we also opened up one of the other sheds and there were loads of cats."

"Cats?"

"Yeah. All in cages. Usher admitted they were stolen, ready to sell on."

"I'm coming over."

CHAPTER 40

The phone rang again and this time, Blake answered it as he headed out of the door. "Jeff, I don't know what you want but as long as you're working with Gambles, we've got nothing to talk about."

"Will, you've got to listen..."

"No, Jeff, I don't have to listen to you. I always tried to cut you a bit of slack but this time you've excelled yourself. Gambles is playing you for a fool and I won't be any part of it. Ring me back when you've decided not to write that book."

"But I've found out..." Blake ended the call and hurried over to his car.

It was too much to hope. Could Serafina be in that vet's shed? Blake tried not to get his hopes up. All the same, he couldn't help thinking how pleased Laura would be if he could share some good news. He needed to talk to her soon. He needed to apologise.

Blake drove through the tunnel and across the Wirral as though he was on an emergency call. Cars flashed by and the fast lane of the motorway was his. Soon, he was turning into the carpark of the surgery. Crime Scene Investigators were pulling up and a number of uniformed officers were ensuring the cordon was secure. Blake flashed his warrant card and climbed out of his car.

Kinnear was there to greet him. "Sir, I thought you'd be interviewing over in Birkenhead..."

"Cats, Andrew. Where are the cats?"

"Cats, sir?"

"The stolen ones," Blake snapped.

"Oh in that shed over there, sir."

"Right," Blake said.

"Sir," Kinnear said, stopping Blake in his tracks. "It's a crime scene. You need to suit up."

"Okay," Blake said, stamping back to his car to get his suit. He dragged it on muttering under his breath but knew that Kinnear was right.

The smell from the shed as he opened the door made him gag. It was a narrow building with a concrete floor. One wall was lined with cages each with a cat in it. There was food and water in each cage but they hadn't been cleaned out recently. Covering his face with the crook of his arm, he scanned the cages hoping to see Serafina glaring back at him. At one point his heart leapt as he saw a blue/grey Persian in one of the end cages but it wasn't her. She wasn't there. Blake let out a sigh of frustration.

"Are you okay, sir?" Kinnear said, appearing at his shoulder.

"Yeah," Blake said. "Sorry, mate. I was hoping my cat might be here but she's not. She's gone missing."

"Sorry to hear that, sir," Kinnear said, awkwardly. "Have you tried the neighbours?"

"Done all that," he said. "The neighbour's cats have gone missing too. That's why I think they've been stolen. What kind of sick bastard steals a family pet, Kinnear?"

"Dunno, sir. Maybe you should ask John Usher, that."

"Bloody good idea."

*****

John Usher looked as though he'd hadn't slept in a week. At first glance, he didn't seem to be the Mr Big of cat smuggling and abduction. A solicitor sat next to him, smart in her pinstripe suit and pointy glasses. She didn't seem too impressed with the vet either as she leafed through the papers in front of her.

Blake leaned forward. "Before we get onto the issue of attempted murder, let's talk about cats."

The solicitor looked confused and Usher's face crumpled. "I was desperate. You don't know how much it costs to keep that place going." The solicitor gave Usher a disgusted sidelong glance.

"No, I don't and I don't really care, either," Blake said. He noticed DS Vikki Chinn shift uncomfortably in her seat next to him, but Blake had to know. "So tell me, John, do you get many Persian cats through your smuggling business?"

John Usher looked confused. The solicitor mirrored his expression.

"Have you had one recently? Within the last week or so. A blue Persian about so big?" Blake said, holding his hands wide.

"What's this got to do with anything?" Usher said, glancing at his solicitor.

"Just answer the question."

"Possibly. Persians are popular. Expensive, too. I had a big one through the cages at the start of last week, I think."

Blake tried not to leap over the table and grab the vet by his lapels. "And where did it go?"

"God. I don't know," Usher said. "Cats like that usually go to a good home, where people will pay. There's falsified paperwork in my office. I'm sure you can find out easily enough."

"Right," Blake said, breathing out a sigh. Sifting through all Usher's paperwork could take weeks if it was even deemed a priority or pertinent to the case."

Usher picked at his fingernails. "Aren't you going to ask me about how Zoe Plumb framed me and tricked me into this whole sordid business?"

"We're coming to that, Mr Usher," Blake said. "If you'll allow us to steer the interview. So, how long have you known Zoe Plumb and Trevor Long?"

"Zoe came to work for me three years ago. I didn't know her before that. I was just coming out of a messy divorce and was struggling to cope with the business. She was a… great help at that time."

"And was she seeing Trevor Long then?"

Usher reddened. "No. She knew him from school or something and they frequented the same pubs but nothing else."

Vikki Chinn leaned forward. "When you say Zoe was a great help after your divorce, in what way?"

"She kept the business running and… yes… we were lovers, too. I didn't mean for it to happen, but we fell in love. I didn't realise what a monster she was then."

"So, when she started seeing Trevor Long, you must have been upset about that," Blake said. "You were in love, after all."

Usher looked down at his chewed fingernails. "It was all part of Zoe's plan. Although we'd kept the veterinary business going, we'd cut corners.

There were complaints. Plus we'd tried to expand our way out of trouble, offering the cremation service too..."

"We?"

"Zoe suggested the cremation service early on in our relationship. She said there would be a massive demand. So we forked out for a huge equine incinerator." Usher looked haunted. "Thinking about it now, I think she planned all this way before she met me."

"Really? That's a bit far-fetched, isn't it?"

"At her interview, Zoe knew everything about the business. She'd really done her research. I remember at the time, thinking it was as if she'd selected me. I was quite flattered then but now..."

"When did she start seeing Trevor Long?" Blake said, keeping the interview on track.

"About two years ago. She'd spent a year helping me with the business and propping me up. To be honest, I was probably getting to be a bit of a drag to be around. At first, I thought she just wanted some freedom but then she came to me with this strange idea he'd suggested to her."

"This was the idea to fake his death."

"Yeah. It all sounded so wild. Like something out of a film. Apparently, he was in some kind of fix and needed help to make it seem like he was dead. He wanted to start a new life, apparently."

"And how did he do that?"

"You saw, didn't you?" Usher said. "The coat, the blood? We took some blood over a period of a few weeks. Kept it in cold storage. Zoe said you couldn't ignore that amount being spilled. Zoe and Trevor added all the touches. There was meant to be a video of him being chased. Some link to a gang or something."

"So how come Zoe ended up marrying Trevor?"

Usher looked as though Blake had just slapped him. Clearly, he hadn't reckoned with how much they knew. "That was Zoe's idea. I wasn't in favour of it..."

"What was the plan? Life insurance, something like that?"

"You have to believe me," Usher pleaded. "I didn't want any part of this but we were desperate. The business was going down the tubes. I had an investigation by the Royal College of Veterinary Surgeons hanging over my head. When Zoe told me that she'd taken out life insurance on Trevor, I told her that we couldn't actually harm him..."

"It wasn't just Trevor who need to start his life over again, was it, Mr Usher?" Blake said. "It was you."

"What? That's insane. I just needed a cash injection..."

"You'd like us to believe that you were an innocent victim in all of this. A poor dupe who was dragged along by the wiles of some femme fatale. Yeah, you could go bankrupt and sell up the business. You could be struck off but you'd still need money. What was the plan? Live abroad off the proceeds of Trevor Long's murder?"

"No. I don't know. None of it was my idea."

"Oh come off it. I think you knew exactly what you were doing."

"It wasn't me."

"Then who knew how much tranquiliser to administer to knock Trevor out? Zoe? She doesn't have any medical training. She isn't a nurse. You'd have to have advised her about that."

"She forced me to. She said she'd leave me and then I'd be ruined."

"Was the plan that you'd pick up Trevor's unconscious body from the caravan and dispose of it quietly in your incinerator?"

John Usher sighed. "Zoe had arranged to meet Trevor at the caravan. I dropped her off and then waited nearby. She was going to give him the tranquiliser and then... you know..."

"No, Mr Usher," Blake said, relishing the man's discomfort. "Can you tell us?"

"She was going to make it look like he'd killed himself. She said that, by the time the body was discovered, the cause of his death would be inconclusive. But then that Nathan Roscoe from Trevor's workplace turned up and she panicked. Trevor jumped in Roscoe's car and I had to chase after them. We all ended up back at the surgery, but Zoe wanted to carry on with the plan. Please. All I ever wanted was to be a good vet. I didn't want to harm anyone…"

"I think you wanted so much more, Mr Usher. I'm pretty sure that Zoe and Trevor will confirm my suspicions."

CHAPTER 41

Zoe Plumb deserved an Oscar, as far as DI Kath Cryer was concerned. Tears stained the girl's face and she sobbed between every word as she told them her story. A mountain of crumpled tissues sat at her elbow already. Her solicitor had come prepared with a large box and sat, her head cocked sympathetically as she listened and scribbled notes.

"You don't know what it's been like," Zoe said, shuddering. "Being torn between two controlling men. Trevor was constantly going on at me about his plan to start a new life. He wanted me to steal blood bags and IV tubes from John's surgery so he could collect blood. I was worn down by it all."

"I see," Kath said, thinking she could tell this slip of a girl a few things about feeling worn down. "And what about John Usher."

"He tricked me." Zoe began to sob into yet another tissue and it was all Kath could do to stop from rolling her eyes. "I left a perfectly good clerical job at the university to join his surgery. He said they were expanding and needed more admin. I love animals." She smiled over at the solicitor. "I used to keep rabbits as a little girl."

"Sweet," Kath muttered. "So things weren't quite as they seemed once you joined Usher at Merryvale Pets, then."

"No. The place was a shambles. John just kept going on about his divorce and how much money he owed. I felt sorry for him at first," she lowered her gaze, demurely. "And, yes, we were lovers for a short time but then he changed. He became obsessed with keeping the business going at whatever cost. I said that he should let it go; that we'd be happy together whatever we did. But he wouldn't stop."

"So where does Trevor fit in with all this?"

"I've known Trevor since we were little. We went to school together, but our lives took us along different paths, I suppose. We'd see each other down the pub and catch each other's eye but we were like ships in the night."

Kath did roll her eyes this time. "It's just the bare facts we need, Zoe, I don't want a Mills and Boon masterclass."

"All right," Zoe said, a flash of irritation marring the soft image she had come so close to pulling off. "I saw one of his films on YouTube and really liked it. So I told him next time I saw him down the pub..."

"Gary Stott told me that Trevor didn't drink."

"He didn't when Gary was around," Zoe said.

"Trevor had this thing about keeping a 'professional' image in front of Gary because Gary hero-worshipped him. But Trev let his hair down with me. Gary didn't like that. Bit jealous, I think."

"So you started seeing Trevor..."

"Yeah. Maybe I just attract the wrong sort of guy, I don't know, but Trevor seemed so funny and mysterious at first. He was full of spooky stories and anecdotes. But he was just interested in being a local celebrity a cross between Tom Slemen and Derek Acorah..."

The solicitor looked up and frowned.

"Tom Slemen writes books about spooky happenings in Merseyside," Kath said, helping her out. "You should try one, they're good. Derek Acorah? TV medium? Was on that TV programme, Most Haunted or something like that. No? You more dinner parties and radio four? Derek passed away a few months back. Hasn't been in touch since..."

"I finished with John. Told him our relationship had to be strictly business."

"And he was okay with that?"

"I thought so. At that point. He didn't know Trevor, so hadn't been wound up by him or anything. Trevor has a knack of rubbing people up the wrong way."

"Trevor's obsession with fame. You weren't happy with that?"

"No. He went and borrowed loads of cash from some shady character, bought a load of professional equipment, hoping it would help him make better films, but he couldn't change the raw material could he? Then things started getting really difficult for him."

"In what way?"

"Well, he couldn't pay his debt, his rent and all the other bills, could he? He kept going on about ending it all; saying he was a failure, and nobody cared whether he lived or died. That's where he got the idea to fake his death from. I remember it well. We were watching 'It's a Wonderful Life,' you know the Christmas film where that bloke, George Bailey, gets a chance to see what life would be like if he'd never been born. Trevor said he could do the same. Just vanish and start again."

"And you agreed to help him?"

"No. He was stuck on the idea though. He even wanted to know if I could get John to cut off some fingers so he could make it look really dramatic. I told him that, if he was going to do it, blood would be less of a sacrifice. I'd read somewhere about a case where someone had been murdered but they never found a body, only lots of blood. I didn't mean to put the idea into his head. But I was afraid he was going to hurt himself badly. Then he started going on about it all the time. I had to do something."

"You're a martyr, Zoe," Kath said, leaning back in her chair and folding her arms. "So how did John Usher become involved?"

"I told John about what Trevor wanted to do and he pounced on the idea of insuring Trevor. He said that Trevor didn't have to actually die but if we made it convincing enough, then we could be rich."

"And was Trevor party to all this?"

"Yeah," Zoe said. "He was totally up for it. It was his idea to get married to make it seem more legit. We were going to split the money three ways. But I think John was a bit jealous of this arrangement."

"In what way?"

"He didn't like sharing me with Trevor..."

"But I thought you'd finished any romantic entanglements with John Usher."

"I think John still loved me. I think he saw this as a chance to get rid of Trevor and win me back."

"So throughout all of this, you were just a rag doll caught in a tug of war? You were being a good girl and doing as you were told?"

"I didn't have much choice, did I?"

"Oh, behave. You don't strike me as the kind of woman who just does as they are told. I don't suppose you were aware of John Usher's trade in stolen cats, either."

"No," Zoe said. "I swear."

"And I suppose Trevor forced you to inject Nathan Roscoe with tranquiliser at the caravan, too."

"No, that was John's idea. He'd sent me to sedate Trevor so we could bring him to the surgery. I was going to warn Trevor that John was up to no good, but that man appeared and I panicked."

"The dose you gave Mr Roscoe almost killed him. He was a bigger man than Trevor. I'm wondering if you meant to kill Trevor in the caravan and leave him there to be found some time later."

"No. I'd never hurt Trevor."

"So, how come, when DS Chinn and I entered the crematorium, your first words were," Kath looked at her notebook, "'he's got to die?'"

Zoe pursed her lips for a brief second. "I never said that. I said, 'he can't die.'"

"Whilst dragging the trolley that Trevor was on towards the incinerator. It looked very much to me like you were all for throwing him in alive and turning the heat up."

"That isn't what I was doing. I was trying to stop John."

"I find that hard to believe, given that you've consistently lied to me and my colleagues throughout this investigation."

"I had to. I was scared. Ask Trevor. He'll tell you."

Kath stared deep into Zoe's eyes. "Don't worry. I will."

CHAPTER 42

The coffee in the drinks dispenser at the custody suite made everyone wince except Blake. As far as he was concerned, it was wet and warm and meant to give you a kick. If it tasted like boiled camel droppings, that added to the jolt and suited him fine. Now Vikki, Kath, Andrew Kinnear and Alex Manikas huddled around the coffee machine, staring down into their mugs in disbelief.

"Whoever makes these machines needs arresting," Kinnear muttered. "Is there any sugar anywhere?"

"Not sure that would help, love," Kath said. "Maybe if you put some different coffee in it... and different water... in a different mug..."

"So, what do we think?" Blake said, taking a long, slow sip of his coffee to everyone's disgust.

"Zoe is pulling up the drawbridge and leaving John Usher high and dry," Kath said. "But I think she's the mastermind behind all of this. Honestly, boss, if you'd seen her face when she was trying to drag Trevor towards the incinerator, you'd know it was her."

Blake nodded. "I don't think Usher is the hapless fall guy he makes out, either. I think they're in it together. I think they planned it carefully together and Trevor was their victim."

"Let's be honest, sir," Kinnear said. "You wouldn't find a better victim. With the exception of Gary Stott, I couldn't find a single person with a good word to say about Trevor. Even he's seen Trevor in a different light, now. His own mum doesn't like him."

Blake gulped down the last of the brown sludge in his cup. "Let's go and find out for ourselves what's so off putting about the fella. Bring one of those coffees; maybe we can threaten him with it."

For all the trouble he had caused, Trevor Long struck Blake as an innocuous-looking young man. He was slight with lank black hair that was already thinning and thick, horn-rimmed glasses. Kath had managed to procure some ill-fitting clothes, but they swamped him. He sat, one leg twitching and his fingers drumming the table. A purple bruise blossomed on his forehead.

Blake sat down opposite, and Kath Cryer settled next to him. He introduced himself and checked once again that Trevor had decided not to have a solicitor present. "That's a nasty bruise you've got on your head, there, Trevor."

Trevor Long touched the wound, self-consciously. "Yeah. It turns out I don't like the sight of blood. I fainted at the graveyard when they splashed it all over my coat..."

"That was when you faked your death."

"It was just a prank, really. An illusion."

"A prank?" Blake muttered.

"I'd decided to fake my own death and then make a miraculous return. It would have made a big splash if some other people hadn't messed things up." Long rolled his eyes.

"Messed things up? I think it was a bit more serious than that, don't you?"

Long's eyes tracked around the room as if he was looking for the answer to Blake's question on the walls. "I don't know what you mean."

Kath Cryer snorted. "When I broke into the crematorium at Merryvale, Trevor, you were tied to a trolley, surrounded by surgical equipment. I suspect they were going to kill you. You were screaming or at least you would have been if they hadn't taped your mouth shut."

Long shrugged. "Things just got out of hand, that's all."

"Too right it did. To kick off, you're guilty of wasting police time, assault on Mr Roscoe, conspiracy to defraud an insurance company, not to mention desecration of a grave and general littering. There's probably something we could look up to do with creating a biological hazard and endangering public health, the amount of blood you left splattered all over Flaybrick Hill."

"Fraud?" Trevor said, his eyes widening. "What do you mean, 'fraud?'"

Kath leaned forward towards Long, making him flinch. "Zoe and John took out an insurance policy on you. They say they were going to split the proceeds with you."

"That isn't true," Trevor said. "It was just a trick, that's all."

"You knew it had all gone wrong when Zoe came for you at the caravan, didn't you, Trevor?" Blake said. "Nathan Roscoe told us that you sounded genuinely scared when she produced the syringe."

"I thought she was going to stab me with it."

"She was until Roscoe turned up," Kath snapped.

Blake frowned. "What was your exit strategy from all of this, Trevor? What were you going to do when it was all over?"

Trevor blinked at Blake as he thought. "I was going to live in the caravan for a while. Lie low and then come back. I was writing a script for a new video to upload onto YouTube. I wasn't sure whether to go the full supernatural path or the David Blaine stunt type thing. You know, 'ha ha! tricked you all. I wasn't dead really."

"But you'd still owe money and the people you borrowed from would be pissed off. They'd come for you."

Trevor wagged a finger. "Yeah but I could make a fortune selling my story and monetising my YouTube channel. I was thinking of doing magic tricks on TikTok..."

Blake looked at Kath. "I think I got about half of that, Kath. You?"

"Dunno, boss," Kath said, staring at Long. "All Greek to me. So, Trevor, you reckoned you could make enough money out of the publicity to pay off your debts and make a living. Is that what you're saying?"

"It was going to be like a launch. A way to raise my platform. I didn't know anything about any insurance," Long said. He stopped as the realisation sank in. "God. They really were going to kill me weren't they?"

Blake hissed through his teeth. "Well, what do you think, Trevor? Of course they were. If DI Cryer and DS Chinn hadn't arrived when they did, they'd have put you down like a dog and burnt your body. There would have been no evidence."

"Why didn't you involve Gary Stott in any of this? He was your best friend, after all," Kath said.

"He'd have told me not to do it," Trevor said, then he smiled. "Anyway, he was the perfect person to carry the news. He believed all that crap about the Sons of Sol. There's no better witness than one who thinks they're telling the truth."

"He was really upset and worried," Blake said. "He's also pretty hacked off about being used and manipulated by you."

Trevor shrugged. "He'll get over it. If I'd made my comeback like I planned, he'd have been made up."

Blake terminated the interview and left the room to find solace in the coffee machine once more. Kath joined him, declining his offer of another drink. "He's a dupe," Blake said. "I don't think he's on the same planet as Zoe Plumb or Usher, let alone the same page."

"Seems so, sir," Kath said.

"Let's you and me have one more go at Zoe," Blake said.

Kath gave a wicked grin. "With pleasure."

*****

Someone had cleared the pile of shredded tissues at Zoe Plumb's elbow but she was dutifully working on a new one. Blake let out a long sigh and stared at Zoe.

"You're not an unintelligent woman, Zoe," Blake said at last.

Zoe frowned. "No. So what?"

"So how come you ended up mixed up in all of this? Fraud, conspiracy to murder, attempted murder, assault, kidnapping..."

Zoe's face crumpled. "I don't know." She gave a shuddering sob.

"And why would you throw yourself at John Usher. A total loser. Hopeless at his job, a poor vet and an even worse businessman. What were you thinking?"

"I didn't know he was all those things, did I? I thought he was successful."

Blake gave a conspiratorial smile. "Yeah but that's not true is it, Zoe? Usher was amazed at the amount of detailed information you had about his business when he interviewed you. You'd done your homework. I bet that once our team in the lab have pulled apart your computer and analysed your browsing history, we'll find out all kinds of things. Research into Merryvale Vets and equine incinerators, blood transfusion techniques. I think we'll find that you planned this all from day one."

"I didn't!" Zoe snapped. Then her face changed. "You can't do that. Can you?"

"It'll take a while but once those tech people

get going, it's amazing what they can find. Now, I don't think you did this alone. I think John Usher helped you. He doesn't have the wit to concoct a plot like this but he isn't a dupe, either. Your poor manipulated bimbo impression won't float then and, frankly, it does you a disservice. We can build a case that focuses on you as the prime mover or you can help us out and get to the truth."

"Why are we wasting time, boss?" Kath said. "Zoe's the one who planned it all. You can tell. We can get the evidence from her computer. We've got her bang to rights. Trevor is blinking like a rabbit in the headlights and Usher will testify against her."

Blake suppressed a smile. Kath's sense of timing was perfect. "It's the truth we want, Kath. The truth. I don't want a jury being misled by the testimony of two men ganging up on poor Zoe, here."

Zoe looked from Kath to Blake; emotions battling within her. "Okay," she said at last. "John and I planned it together. I knew Trevor from school. I never really liked him. He was a bit weird and nobody likes him. Nobody would ever miss him. When I saw his YouTube videos, I knew he'd be the perfect fall guy; someone who believes that alligators live under Bidston rubbish tip will believe anything. But I didn't know how to go about it."

"That was where John Usher came in," Blake said.

Zoe nodded. "He came up with the blood idea. Trevor dramatised it and bought the axe to frame the Sons of Sol or at least throw up the suggestion. The idea was that, in the end there'd be no actual evidence pointing to anyone but a strong presumption of murder. That way Trevor would be declared dead more quickly."

"So you could cash in the insurance. The poor grieving widow," Kath said. "But Trevor didn't know about that side of things did he?"

Zoe shook her head. "No. He didn't."

"But why take it further? Why actually try to murder Trevor?" Kath said.

Blake thought about his missing mother, the house, Jeff. "Because these things take time, don't they, Zoe? And Trevor Long is an egotistical loose cannon. You couldn't have him popping up from the grave before you'd processed the insurance claim, could you? And even if he reappeared long after you'd cashed the cheque, it might cause you problems. Better to just get rid of him, right?"

Zoe's shoulder sank and she nodded. Her tears were genuine this time.

*****

Back at the coffee machine, Blake downed another cup of the bitter, brown sludge Apart from never getting used to how cruel human beings could be to each other, Zoe's admission had brought up thoughts of his mother and the house. He needed to sort that out and soon.

Kath had risked another cup of coffee. "Well, we got there in the end, sir," she said. "I'm pretty sure Usher will fold when he hears that Zoe is telling us everything."

Blake nodded and pulled his ringing mobile from his pocket.

It was Laura. "Will, it's Cavanagh. He wants to talk to me again. Can you come over? Now."

CHAPTER 43

Blake arrived outside Laura's flat at the same time as Cavanagh. The young detective climbed out of his car and frowned at Blake. "What're you doing here, Will?"

Blake shrugged. "Laura asked me to be here while you questioned her," he said. "Any objections?"

"I dunno. Seems a bit like a conflict of interests, if you ask me."

"I'm just here as a friend. You aren't going to charge her with anything are you?"

"No. Should I?"

Blake shook his head. "You're incredible."

They stood awkwardly at the front door of the flats, waiting for Laura to buzz them in. When they got up to her flat, Blake felt awful. She greeted them, tear stained, eyes swollen, her nose red. Without a word, she walked back into the living room of the flat. Cavanagh frowned but said nothing.

"You okay, Laura?" Blake said, his words sounding ridiculous and trite.

"Yeah, just fine, Will. I love being dragged back

to memories of my failed marriage and all the abuse that went with it."

Cavanagh cleared his throat. "Look, I'm sorry about this," he said, "but Gambles has opened a can of worms and, as much as I'd love to walk away and forget the whole thing, I can't."

"It's always Josh bloody Gambles," Blake hissed. "Why are we dancing to his tune?"

"He gave us a lead. We have to follow it. So, Laura. Last time we spoke, you said that Kyle Quinlan assaulted you and you hit him back. When was this?"

Laura sat down in her armchair. "Early 2014, February, maybe or early March. I'd been working out a lot. When he came home drunk one night and decided to try it on yet again, I snapped and made the decision there and then to leave him."

"You snapped?"

"I fought back. I'd had enough. I decked him."

"You mean knocked him out?"

"Yeah. He went down," Laura said. The implication of what he was saying dawned on her. "Oh no. Not like that. I didn't kill him. He was drunk, he fell onto the sofa. It wasn't like he cracked his head or anything."

"But you didn't see him again, so how would you know?"

"He signed the bloody divorce papers, numb-skull," Laura snapped. "He couldn't do that if he was dead, could he?"

"Jeez, Cavanagh. Is there any logic to this? You asked her this before and she answered honestly. I mean, who was Quinlan working for before he went missing? Have you looked into that? He was a crook. Bad things happen to bad people."

"Of course I have, Will. He was working for Harry Thorpe."

Blake rolled his eyes. "Him again? You mean the notorious, property developer, betting shop owner, loan shark and all-round pillar of the community? Come on! Quinlan could be up to his eye sockets in concrete anywhere from here to London if he crossed someone like Thorpe."

Cavanagh rubbed his temples. "Yeah, I know, Will. I know and we're looking into that possi-bility. But Thorpe had a number of properties; one of them was rented out to Mr and Mrs Quin-lan."

"So? That would suit Thorpe down to the ground. Payment in kind, off the record sort of stuff. What's so amazing about that?"

Cavanagh turned to Laura. "Maybe nothing, really. Just one of those itches that you can't scratch. A nagging feeling that something isn't all it seems. You said you just wanted to get away from Quinlan, right?"

Laura reddened. "Yeah," she said.

"And so you moved here?"

"That's right but..."

"If you were so desperate to get away from Quinlan and the memory of abuse. How come you moved into a flat that directly overlooks your old home?" DCI Matty Cavanagh pulled back the living room curtain slightly to make the view of the back garden clear. "You can see right into the back of it from here Laura. Why would you do that? Why risk being spotted by Quinlan?"

Blake stared at Laura and stepped over to the window. He could see the overgrown rear garden of the block of flats and then beyond that, the back of the other house, with neatly trimmed bushes and a large patio. "Is that true, Laura?"

"I can live where I want, can't I?" she said. "Why do I have to justify it to you, Cavanagh?"

"Because I've got a suspicious mind, Laura. Could it be because you want to keep an eye on what's happening in that property?"

"Why would I want to do that?"

Cavanagh shrugged. "I dunno? You tell me. What's hidden over there?"

"Did you come all the way over here just to make groundless accusations, Matty, or do you have any kind of hard evidence? There could be a hundred and one reasons why Laura chose this flat." He looked over to Laura but could see the haunted look in her eyes. Clearly, the reason for staying so close wasn't a rational one.

"Okay," Laura said, her voice trembling. "Haven't you ever heard of the saying, 'hidden in plain sight?' I thought being this close would make me less easy to find. And, yes, I could keep an eye on things, too. I wasn't sure whether or not Kyle would carry on living there and I wanted to know where he was and what he was doing. But if you think I've been watching the garden all these years just in case somebody digs up the patio and finds a body, then you're mistaken."

Cavanagh flinched at the mention of a body. Obviously, that was exactly what he suspected and he didn't like it being said out loud.

"I hope you're going to give Harry Thorpe the same careful attention, Matty," Blake said. "Any other pet conspiracy theories you want to check with Laura?"

"There's no need to be like that, Will," Matty said. "You know you'd do the same if you had this case."

"All I know is I never saw Kyle in the back of the house after I left," Laura said. "I'd tell you if I had. If someone has buried him, I'd shake their hand but he was fine when I left him."

Cavanagh raised an eyebrow. "Did you ever meet Harry Thorpe?"

"He came round once or twice to talk to Kyle. That's all. He played the perfect gent but I wasn't fooled; I knew he was a reptile."

"And did Kyle ever talk about anything he was involved in that might have led to his disappearance?"

"Kyle didn't really share much with me. We weren't soul mates. The less I knew the better as far as Kyle was concerned. As long as I played the good little housewife, he was happy. No, I'll rephrase that, he was never happy. Kyle's main problem was his overinflated opinion of himself. If he did get into trouble, it'll have been his own doing. I wouldn't be surprised if he crossed Thorpe, stole from him or tried to undermine him in some way."

"You don't have a very high opinion of your ex-husband," Cavanagh said. "Makes me wonder why you married him in the first place."

"My word, you must be a mind reader," Laura said, archly. "I was young when we first got together. I didn't know any better. He was cool and tough and full of swagger but that only gets you so far in life. The gloss fell off pretty quickly. I think the second time he landed himself in prison, I started to wonder what I was thinking of marrying him."

"Did he ever talk about Josh Gambles?"

"You think I wouldn't have recognised the name when Will was investigating the case? No. Kyle never talked about his jail time. Ever. If Gambles has brought this up then, as Will said last time we met, you should be talking to him."

Cavanagh left with a surly apology for wasting Laura's time but Blake could tell he wasn't satisfied. When he'd gone, Blake stood by the window, staring out at the garden below. "I'm sorry I didn't trust you," he said. "I was out of order."

"It's all right, Will," Laura said. "Thanks for coming to support me."

"What else would I do?" He moved towards her but she shrank away. "No," she said. "This has churned up too many bad memories. Maybe we should just ease up a little. Have some time apart. You know? If there is fall out from this, I don't want Gambles to drag you down..."

"Screw Gambles," Blake said. "This is exactly what he wants. For us to be miserable. Don't let him win, Laura. Please. I don't care about your past; I care about you and who you are right now."

Laura gave a brittle smile. "I'm sorry, Will. I can't, right now. Give me some time. We won't let Gambles win, I promise. Just let me get my head together."

"Well," Blake said, at a loss what to do. He solved problems; that was his job and here he was standing like a spare part. "Maybe I should get off..."

"Any news on Serafina?"

"No. I thought I was onto something. A vet in Clatterbridge was selling stolen cats. Serafina wasn't in the lot we rescued, though. I even had a beer with Youde, too..."

Laura pulled a face. "How did you manage that?"

"I don't really know. I don't think he's a catnapper, though."

"What about that mad Gwen woman? Has she done any more tarot readings for you?"

Blake smiled briefly. "Jealous."

Laura looked at the floor. "Anyway."

"Yeah," Blake said. "See you, soon." He gave her a brief peck on the forehead and hurried out of the flat.

Laura returned to the window and stared down on the garden and the patio.

CHAPTER 44

All the way home, thoughts of Josh Gambles and his plotting bounced around Blake's head. The man wasn't as clever as he liked to think he was, but he had a knack of throwing well-aimed spanners into the works. He'd warned Blake. Told him he was going to lose his girlfriend, his brother... and the cat. He'd said something about the cat at their second interview last week. "The cat," he muttered to himself. Other pieces of a jigsaw tumbled into place and he phoned Laura.

"Will I just need..." Laura began.

"What was it you said to me about Gwen and her cat?"

"I said she's weird, Will and I'm not jealous."

"No, something about the cat's name."

"Yeah. She hasn't told you the cat's name, has she? Mrs Inchley asked us if we'd seen Merlin. We didn't know if it was her pet dog, cat or macaw. Pets are people to their owners, right? They have names. I just thought it odd that she never actually named her cat when she talked to you."

"You're right," Blake said. "Something doesn't add up. I'm going to have a word with her."

"Will what is it?"

"I dunno, Laura. Something I need to check. I'll call you later if I learn anything, okay?"

"Right."

Blake hung up and headed home.

*****

Laura frowned as she put the phone down. Something wasn't right. She could tell by Will's voice. He had that same haunted tone as when he talked about Gambles. Her phone rang again. It was Jeff.

"Laura. I've been trying to get hold of Will all day but he either ignores my calls or kills them dead. I need to tell him something."

"He's heading home, Jeff. He said something about checking up on Gwen…"

"Shit. I'm coming round to pick you up."

*****

It was going dark as Blake pulled up outside Gwen's house. He couldn't go home until he'd put the crazy notion in his head to rest. He climbed out. It was a still autumn night and a thin mist had drifted in from the river, a bell rang somewhere in the hazy darkness. Blake shivered. The pointed outlines of the rooftops loomed over him. He pushed the front gate open and it squealed in protest. The tangle of bushes in the front garden deepened the darkness as he approached the front door and knocked on it. The door swung open; it had not been shut properly.

"Hello? Gwen?"

Blake took a tentative step into the house. The only light came from a door further down the hall. A long plaintive meowing drifted through the house. The whole place smelt of incense and cigarette smoke underscored with a sweet note of cannabis. "Anybody here?"

He came to the door and looked down a flight of steps, feebly illuminated by a flickering bulb. The meowing was louder here and came from what Blake assumed to be a cellar. He put a foot on the first step and then pain exploded in the back of his head. Legs buckling under him, Blake tumbled down the steps. The ceiling became the ground and the stairs were above him as he rolled and bounced to the bottom. At one point, he glimpsed Gwen, her face twisted with hatred and a walking stick in her fist. The last step clipped his temple and Blake sprawled onto hard, concrete. The dim light faded into blackness.

*****

Blake couldn't move. The funny thing was, he didn't mind; he felt warm and fuzzy. It struck him that maybe he should be in some kind of pain because Gwen had hit him with a big stick. He grinned. Her face looked quite funny all twisted up with anger. What was she angry about? Maybe she was jealous like Laura. A thin rope bit tight into his arms and legs. It felt kind of strange, like it was going to cut him into pieces. For a second, he wondered if he was made of plasticine. He imagined the rope cutting right through him, cutting him into segments and chuckled. Then Gwen could roll him into a ball and make him into someone else. It would be quite nice to be someone else. He shook his head and blinked a few times, trying to make sense of his surroundings. The air was heavy with the smoke from incense mingled with marijuana but there was another stink fighting against them; decay, musty and dank. He giggled. "Jeez, I'm stoned," he muttered to nobody. "Unless it's just this smoky air."

He sat with his back against the wall of a large cellar. Above him, the plaster had crumbled in places to reveal the floorboards above. The walls were in a similar state; cracked plaster showing damp brick beneath. All around, someone had draped black material to cover the cracks and damp stains. Candles stood everywhere, on the floor, on makeshift shelves on old packing cases. Shadows danced as the flames flickered. The place was like a set from a horror movie.

"A Hammer House of Horror," Blake muttered

and chuckled again. Two black candles guttered on a stone dais that stood to his left. A large goat's skull stood between the candles. In front of him was a big kitchen table. Blake's brow knitted in confusion as he saw that a coffin lay on top of the table. Why would Gwen have a coffin down in this dusty old cellar?

Another wall was lined with small cages. Chickens sat clucking miserably in a few of these, magpies and crows hopped around in a few more. Two burning orange eyes stared out at him. Serafina gave another plaintive meow.

"Serafina," Blake said, "Hello puss. What are you doing here?" The thick atmosphere filled his head, slowing his thoughts and movements. He was forgetting something. Something that had occurred to him on his way over here. It was something to do with names. Not telling names, not naming things. Jeff had told him he'd found something. It all fitted together when he was driving. Now his mind felt like molten wax, like the candles on the dais, dripping and pooling into another shape. Changing. There it was again. He'd like to be a different person. Then he wouldn't have to worry about Jeff or Gambles. Or Laura. No. He wanted to worry about Laura. Not worry. Care. He wanted to care about Laura. Maybe he could be a cat. A silver tabby. What would his name be? Blake blinked. "The silver tabby didn't have a name," he said, thinking back to when Ian Youde had said he didn't know Gwen had a cat. "It didn't exist"

His mind began to crank up now. Maybe whatever he'd been drugged with was wearing off; that would explain the growing ache in his legs and back, not to mention his pulsing head. But why would Gwen pretend she had a cat?

"To ensnare me," he muttered, "and she'd only be able to do that if she knew Serafina was missing." But why would she do that? Jeff had been so eager to get in touch after he'd met with Gambles and started his work. He said he'd found something, but Blake had cut him off.

The door at the top of the stairs creaked open. Blake peered through the smoky gloom. Someone was coming slowly down the steps, taking each step one at a time, as though relishing the moment. His phone buzzed in his pocket. Like an angry bumble bee. Blake grinned again. It would be Jeffrey. Jeffrey the angry bumble bee. Jeff had been trying to ring him all day. Trying to tell him. The realisation sobered Blake quickly.

Jeff would have done some basic research first, for his book. Early life. Family. Jeff was trying to warn him. Blake blinked. Jeff had realised who Gwen was long before he had. And now...

Gwen stood before him, shrouded in smoke and incense. She wore a long black robe and a strange crown made of horns, some so long they scraped the ceiling. She held a knife with a long, curved blade.

"So, is it Gwen Gambles?" Blake said, his voice slurring. "What are you, his sister?"

"I'm Aunty Gwen. Joshy and I have kept in touch since he was a little boy. His father, my brother, treated him so badly. Joshy is a free spirit. It runs in the family. And what are the odds that you'd come to live so close to me?"

"I suppose that's how he knew where I lived." Blake said. His head was clearing rapidly, but a growing pain slowly replaced the lifting fog.

"He was overjoyed when I told him," Gwen said, she ran a finger along the top of the coffin. "Of course, being local proved to have other benefits."

Tears prickled Blake's eyes. "My mother's in there? She's been here all along?"

"When Joshy brought her to me, she was barely conscious. We could have called an ambulance but what good would it have done? Joshy insisted we keep her here. So near and yet so far away."

"You must have seen me searching for her. How could you just sit here, knowing the pain we were going through?"

Gwen pulled a face. "Joshy didn't want me to tell you and what Joshy wants, Joshy gets."

"You need to stop this, now. Cut me free and call the police. You're in enough trouble as it is."

Serafina gave a long, sad wail.

"Cats are interesting, aren't they, Will? They kill for fun; toy with their prey. They're unlucky for some, but lucky to others. The Egyptians worshipped cats. These days, most of them are just pampered house pets." Gwen squatted down and traced the knife along Blake's cheek. "But I believe that some cats are special, Will. I think that some have transformative powers."

"Just stop and think, Gwen. Whatever you're planning on doing, it will only make things worse. My friends know I'm here. If I go missing..."

"Serafina was here when your mother arrived. Oh, yes, she often pops in for a chat and an extra bowl of chicken. You've been starving the poor girl, Will Blake. Serafina has magical powers. She brought you to me. When I was thinking of how to get you down here with a blade to your throat, it was Serafina who suggested the plan. I made up the silver tabby to make some common ground between us. Serafina is a goddess. She can give and she can take away."

"What are you talking about?" Blake felt wide awake now. His head pounded and his body ached, but he strained at the ropes that cut into him.

"Think about it! She took your mother from you but gave you Laura Vexley. She's a clever cat. Knows just what's good for you. Unfortunately, you don't know what's good for yourself. You've upset my poor Joshy. He thinks another chapter needs to be added to his story." Gwen's eyes flashed as she waved the blade under Blake's nose. "The cards agree and I get to be in it."

"You'll go to prison," Blake said. "Whatever happens to me, you won't be able to hush it up. My friends know I'm here. People will search."

Gwen laughed. "I know. And imagine what the papers will make of it. You alongside your mother in a cellar full of candles and witchcraft! Joshy will be famous and so will I!"

CHAPTER 45

Blake's panicked reaction to the blade coming close to his face had devastating results. Trying to get away from the knife, Blake, bunched his feet beneath him and hurled himself upward from the floor. His head came into contact with Gwen's chin sending her staggering backwards across the cellar. The knife whirled through the mist of incense, clattering on the floor. Gwen continued to fall and crashed into the stone dais.

The candles wobbled and then toppled over, hot wax spilling across the cheap black cloth that shrouded the dais. A bright yellow flame leapt from the cloth and the wooden structure beneath it was ablaze. Gwen screamed and tried to bat the fire down but her gown was made of a similar material. Straining at the ropes binding him, Blake stared helplessly as flames wrapped her body, shrivelling her hair. She beat at herself, screaming shrilly, stumbling around the cellar. At one point she bumped against the coffin in the centre of the room, sending it crashing to the ground. The lid shifted and Blake looked away.

Smoke filled the cellar as the drapes on the walls caught fire. Blake struggled to breathe and, still bound, half crawled, half rolled to the cages on the other side of the cellar. Serafina crouched at the back of her cage, ears back growling in fear. Dragging himself to his knees, he tried to focus on the cage latch. It was a simple pin and hole arrangement. He pressed his head against the mesh. Serafina rewarded him with a hiss and batted her paws at his face. Blake ignored the claws raking his cheek through the mesh and, hands still tied, bit the top of the pin and pulled it out. He spat the pin out and the door of the cage swung open. Serafina hissed again and leapt onto his shoulder.

Merlin meowed pitifully in the next cage, but the smoke was thick now. Blake's head was swirling with the poisoned air and smoke coated his mouth and throat. He had to leave now. Using his shoulder as a launching platform, Serafina leapt away and scurried up the stairs. Merlin stared at Blake with yellow eyes. He couldn't just abandon him. Leaning forward again, he bit down on the pin and dragged it out. The door opened and Merlin gave a last meow and scampered over Blake's back.

"You're welcome," Blake croaked, falling to his knees. He wanted to save the chickens and crows that screeched and bounced around the other cages but didn't have the strength. His vision started to darken but the discarded knife glinted close by. Falling onto his side, he wriggled towards it. The coffin lay on one side, a block of darkness in the grey mist. Blake didn't want to see in there. His mother had been in this cellar for two years. He was going to die and he didn't want his mother's decayed body to be the last thing he saw. Gwen lay whimpering somewhere on the other side of the table, but Blake couldn't help her. The knife was so close now but even though he could see it clearly, he couldn't free his hands to use it. The smoke choked him. The knife was useless and anyway, there was a boot standing on it. Blake frowned. A boot. Fancy that. He looked up and saw the round, glass eyes of a gas mask staring down at him. Then all went blank.

*****

Something rough scraped away at Blake's cheek. It felt like somebody was sandpapering his face. With a groan, he brought a hand up and found thick fur. Slowly opening his eyes, Blake saw Serafina and nothing but Serafina. She filled his vision. Raising himself to a seated position, he realised he was at home on his sofa. Ian Youde stood in one corner, talking to a uniformed police officer who was taking notes. Blake noticed that Youde clutched a World War Two gas mask in his hand.

Laura sat on the arm of the sofa. "Are you okay?" she said. Her face was lined with worry. "What is it with you and fire?"

"What happened?" Blake croaked, running his fingers through his hair. His throat felt thick and smoky. His head thumped.

"Mr Youde," Laura said. "He spotted you going into Gwen's and got suspicious. But then he saw smoke and hurried over. He has an extensive collection of old gas masks." Laura gave Blake a look that said, "I told you he was weird but he went back in for the birds and got them out, so he can't be all bad."

Blake smiled, then his thoughts clouded again. "What about Gwen?"

Laura shook her head. "Doesn't look good. She's been taken to hospital. She was badly burnt. The house went up like a bonfire; firemen are trying to get it under control, now."

"She had my mum in a coffin. Did they get the coffin out? Did they get mum?"

"Your mum was down there? In a coffin? I don't think they... Oh God Will, what happened down there?"

Blake shook his head. "Gwen was going to kill me. I... I don't know what else she had planned. I don't want to think about it." Blake frowned. "Anyway. How did you know to come here?"

"Jeff," Laura said. "He'd been researching Gambles' family tree and found out that Gwen Gambles lived just up the road from here. Apparently, he found a fair few news cuttings outlining her antisocial and violent behaviour in the past. He's got as suspicious a mind as you. We came over as soon as he let me know. Apparently, he'd been trying to tell you."

"I know," Blake said, shame faced. "I thought he was going to try to justify writing Gambles' life story again. Is he here?"

Laura looked up and Jeff stepped into view, ashen faced. He stood not sure quite what to do.

"Thank God you're okay, Will. I'm so sorry, I tried to ring you but..."

Blake waved away Jeff's attempted apology. "No, Jeff, I'm the one who's sorry. I thought the worst of you and didn't answer your calls. If I had, we could have sent a car round and rescued the cats at the very least. Anyway, now you've seen what a headworker Gambles is. Imagine him doing this to us, to plan all this, knowing it was going on while he sat in front of you. I hope this has shown you what kind of monster he is."

Jeff looked pained. "Will I..."

"No. Just listen. I can't pretend I'm happy that you're writing that book and I won't help you with it at all but I'm damned if Gambles is going to break up our family. You do what you see as best. If you have to write it, fair enough. I've finished with Gambles. He has no relevance to my life anymore. I'd just ask one favour."

CHAPTER 46

Josh Gambles looked surprised to see Will Blake. He'd obviously been expecting Jeff but Will had taken his place.

"I have to say, Will Blake, I didn't expect to see you sitting here today."

"No. Sorry about your aunty Gwen, by the way. If I could have saved her I would but my hands were tied."

The muscles in Gambles' jaw undulated and Blake thought he heard a tooth creak. "I know. That's what DCI Will Blake is meant to do, isn't it? Save people. Save the day. Sometimes." Gambles muttered. He gave a fleeting smile. "So, you've come to gloat?"

"No," Blake said. "Just to thank you."

"Thank me?"

"Yes. You said when we first met that you wanted to help me. That I was a shadow of my former self. And you were right. But it wasn't fame I needed to put me right. I just needed to make a decision."

Gambles watched Blake warily, waiting for the trap or the insult. He couldn't fathom this new person sitting before him. "What kind of decision?"

"Drive your cart and your plough over the bones of the dead," Blake said.

"What?"

"It's a quotation from William Blake? I thought you were familiar with his work. Maybe you should have paid more attention to my namesake. It sounds like a horrible thing to do. But it's good advice. Move forward, leave the past behind. I can't help the dead. But I can live a little and that's what I intend to do."

"I'm pleased to have been of some help," Gambles said, narrowing his eyes. "But we aren't done."

"We are," Blake said. "You've got nothing left. I've got my mother's body back and, quite frankly, I don't want to hear about the details surrounding her death. Even if there is some cute stunt yet to come regarding Kyle Quinlan, I don't care. Someone else can deal with that. So, this is goodbye, Mr Gambles. Enjoy your notoriety for what it's worth. I think the shine will wear off quite quickly."

Gambles shrugged. "Jeffrey is still writing my book. You wait and see, Will Blake. I've not finished with you."

"No. But I've finished with you. You're not important, anymore, Gambles." Will Blake stood up and walked out of the meeting room.

EPILOGUE

She stretched, letting the late autumn sun warm her back. It was early and the birds sang loudly in the trees surrounding her house. She knew instinctively that today was a good day to kill. She'd find a victim; of that she was certain. She always did. After eating breakfast and having a quick wash, she ran out, letting the new day explode on her senses.

The garden path felt rough beneath her paws as she crept along it. Then, tail in the air, Serafina bounded across the lawn; today, she was a hunter.

ABOUT THE AUTHOR

J. E. Mayhew

Jon Mayhew lives on the Wirral with his family and has done all his life. A teacher for many years, he enjoys traditional music and plays regularly in ceilidh bands and sessions. Jon is also an award-winning author. His dark children's books are published by Bloomsbury.

Find out more at www.jemayhew.blogspot.com

Find JE Mayhew on Facebook and twitter.

BOOKS BY THIS AUTHOR

A Poison Tree

The murder of a young girl found barefoot in a country park and the re-emergence of shoes from the victims of a serial killer from over forty years ago. A coincidence or a connection?

Will Blake is determined to find out, but as he unearths the past, questions are raised about the original investigations and it becomes clear that The Wirral has a killer on the loose once again.

Victor Hunt, the father of the last dead girl from the original case, lies in a hospice with weeks to live. The truth lies hidden in Hunt's tangled family tree, and the actions of his wayward daughter. Time is against Blake and his fractious team. If they don't get to the root of past crimes, then innocent blood will flow again.

A Poison Tree is the first thrilling mystery in the Will Blake crime series. A great read for fans of Luca Veste's DI Murphy and JD Kirk's Jack Logan series. The first DCI Will Blake novel A Poison

Tree is available now.

Fearful Symmetry

Hilbre Grove is a quiet cul-de-sac like many others on the Wirral. But when a couple return from their holidays to find a mutilated, decomposing body in their bungalow, The Scissor Man's reign of terror begins. With another woman missing, DCI Will Blake is determined to stop the psychopath from killing again.

And this case is personal. As bodies pile up it becomes clear that the killer is fascinated by Blake's past appearances on Searchlight, a true-crime TV programme. To hunt down The Scissor Man, Blake must face up to his painful past, and put his career on the line. But every home has its own dark secrets, nowhere is safe and time is running out for Blake and all he holds dear.

Fearful Symmetry is the second exciting Merseyside Murder Mystery thriller in the DCI Will Blake crime series.

Made in the USA
Monee, IL
26 September 2020

43373880R00225